What happens when a Norwegian crab fisherman decides to become a bootlegger?

What happens when he falls in love with an elegant young woman who has fallen on hard times?

What happens when one of her relatives tries to run him off?

This is what happens....

And Wasn't It Grand

Love and Prohibition on Puget Sound

By Ross Kane

© 2011 Ross Kane

And Wasn't It Grand is a work of fiction. Life re-imagined. Embroidery, carefully interwoven through and over events that actually happened, used here for fictional purposes, and totally inventing things that never did, but might have, could have, been true.

A Ross Kane Enterprises Book

Copyright © 2011 by Ross Kane
All Rights Reserved.

www.rosskane.com
www.createspace.com

ISBN 978-1461182993
Manufactured in the United States of America

To my family.

Especially Helen and Cameron.

Prologue

When we met them, we were children. They were old. Or at least, they seemed so very old. They were the parents of our parents. They were "old" friends of the family. "Good, old…" so and so. It seemed like they had always been old. Certainly, we would meet them on a Sunday, at Church, standing on the steps after the service, or, at weddings, funerals, family events. Our parents used the opportunities at these events to try and teach us polite manners. How to shake hands was the basic skill for boys.

Sometimes, we had no recollection of ever not knowing these old people. They were just there, part of life, the furniture. Just like our parents, or the house we lived in, the bed we slept in, the houses and the trees in the neighborhood.

My father's parents, my grandparents, were that way. Just always there. Other adults called him Hank. Or Dad. We kids called him Papa. She was always called Florence. Nothing else, and no one, no one, ever, called her 'Grandma'. She wouldn't allow it. She would not answer to it. Everyone called her Florence.

They lived in this big, old house out in the very north end of Everett. Thinking back, it was a house filled with sun light, with beautiful woodwork and antique furniture. More often than not, you got a slice of blackberry pie for breakfast, along with your bacon and eggs. Waxed wood floors were covered with oriental carpets collected from their travels. Interesting paintings, framed photographs, and, oddest of all, there were two grand pianos.

We were always at their house for Christmas Eve. Dinner was always roast duck. Bread sauce. Champagne, even a taste for all of us kids, before dinner, and red wine with the duck. Florence gave really neat Christmas presents, in these dark green Frederick and Nelson's boxes. Uncle Freddie's, as everyone in our family called the store, had a really cool toy department. Although sometimes I thought Papa was willing to take us up to the toy department on the fourth floor so he could look at the imported English and Italian shotguns that were nearby.

The huge collection of framed photographs documented my grandparent's extensive travels to Europe, the Middle East, Hong Kong. I remember a picture of them both sitting on camels, with pyramids in the background. They seemed to visit Paris quite often.

Occasionally, during an illness at my home, or when my parents went on a trip without us kids, I got to go and to stay with my grandparents for a few days, or a week. They had a neat yard to play in, it was really big, although there wasn't much to do in the evenings except read or listen to music. They never owned a television.

They did have those pianos. The one in the living room, downstairs, the Chickering, was smaller. You could goof around on that one. Either one of them would help you pick out a tune. Florence taught me how to read music. But you weren't allowed to play the big Steinway upstairs. You weren't even supposed to go into the so-called piano room, unless invited, although we did.

It was odd. I'd stay over night, and when I woke up in the morning, I always knew where I would find them. Up, dressed, sitting on the piano bench, side by side, not playing, just quietly talking and drinking coffee. I mentioned this once to my father, after an over night.

"I don't know," he said. "They were doing that most mornings when I was your age. Go figure."

When I got older, I tried to do just that: go figure. Over the years, I kept asking questions. Occasionally, I would try to splice the answers into a story. Slowly, I was able to fit the pieces together.

And Wasn't It Grand

Love and Prohibition on Puget Sound

By Ross Kane

Everett, 1916

It was a late afternoon in November. Overcast and cold. It had snowed the night before, just enough to cover the ground and make everything white and soggy for a few hours. There was no wind, or sunshine, just a tarnished, silvery gray, overcast. The waters of Puget Sound are never still. The tides go up and down twice a day and the currents follow the tide changes. But today the surface of the water seemed unmoving. Scarcely a ripple appeared to disturb the slate colored gray-blue. A small passenger ship, the *Chinook*, less than a hundred feet long, and built from wood, cut through this monochrome. Her wake rolled in white undulating ripples in a V from her stern, adding touches of contrast to the gray-blue. Powered by a steam engine turning an underwater propeller, she made a swishing sound as she went on her way.

Every day, Sundays included, and this was a Sunday, the *Chinook* made four scheduled round trips between Everett and Coleman Dock in Seattle. In a few more minutes, she would dock at Pier 1 in Everett, completing her third round trip for the day. The last trip of the day would be made in total darkness, though in the summer, on a sunny day, the last trip was the prettiest with the sun setting over the Olympic Mountains to the west and casting a red-hued glow over the Cascade Mountains far off to the east.

Today, the mountains couldn't be seen through the low clouds and no one was outside on the upper promenade deck to stroll in the salt-washed air or to enjoy the view. It was too cold. It could snow again tonight. The center deck, the passenger deck, was all undercover and enclosed with large glass windows. The many windows offered a view almost as good as the promenade deck. There was also heat, provided by hot water radiators linked to the steam boiler.

There were a few single men seated here and there. One was reading a newspaper, another a book. People stared out at the passing scene from time to time, checking their progress against the shoreline landmarks - the houses at Richmond Beach, the City of Edmonds, the big dock at Brown's Point, another dock and the lighthouse at Mukilteo, wondering how long until they would be at home. More noisily, there were family parties coming home from church, visiting or other amusements in Seattle. The parties mixed and mingled, for in Everett most people knew everyone else. Or, if not, knew someone you knew or were related to, or attended church with.

Three small boys played a game of tag that involved much jumping and screaming. Occasionally one of the women shushed them, which had an effect for a minute or two. A very small infant slept in its mothers arms.

Several of the gentlemen also slept. Everett was a dry town, by a vote of the people under a "Local Option" State Law. As the nearest big city, Seattle was a bit more tolerant. Even on Sunday you could legally purchase a medicinal shot, or four, at a pharmacy. A man with a taste for a lot of medicine who had overmedicated himself might fall into sleep on the way home. One of the little boys crawled up on a bench seat and jumped off. He landed with a loud thud and a giggle. No one paid much attention.

On the lower deck, the freight deck, Florence wasn't sleeping. Although it would have been nice, because she had been up since dawn and was tired, she was too tense. She sat, her posture erect and perfect, on her steamer trunk, the balance of her luggage and boxes spread out around her. Beside her was a wide open door, just a few feet above the level of the water sliding past. When she had changed ships in Seattle, the crew had used this door to unload and load freight. A blast of warm air from the engine room kept her warm, although even wearing gloves her hands were cold. She could have joined the other passengers, but she felt too tired, not inclined to be social, and it was comforting, being able to sit surrounded by all of her own things.

She was not accustomed to riding on ships. Even though she had been raised by two maiden aunts who lived on Vancouver Island, on the west coast of Canada. She had been born there, in the City of Victoria, the capital city of the Province of British Columbia. This was the first time in her life that she had ever been farther than five miles from home. Not in all her nineteen years. Until today. And already, this was her second ride on a ship. Or boat. She wasn't certain which term applied. This ship – or was it a boat – that she was on now was large, but it was nothing like the steel hulled steamship, the *Princess Victoria,* almost an ocean liner, that had carried her this morning from the crowded and bustling Inner Harbor of Victoria, first to Seattle, where she had to disembark, before boarding the *Chinook* and traveling on to Everett.

"Watch out for German submarines," her Aunt Margaret had teased her, half joking and half serious, as she climbed the gangplank in Victoria in the early morning light. As they cleared the breakwater in Victoria and headed for the open sea, she had kept a vigilant watch, and had been frightened – who could forget the sinking of the *Lusitania* – but no one else seemed worried as people crowded the elegant dining room with its white linen cloths and gleaming glassware to enjoy a lavish breakfast buffet. She decided her Aunt had been joking. Still, she skipped the breakfast and lunch. Which did explain why she presently felt so hungry. On the trip from Victoria to Seattle, she sat near a lifeboat and made a point of locating where the life vests were stored. After all, joke or not, there was a war on. People were dying. You had to be careful. She was leaving the British Empire and sailing to another country, a neutral country, the United States, that was, at present, not at war with Germany.

She was being sent away, to live in a town she had never visited – and barely knew existed before yesterday. "Everett, Washington, USA," had been only a postal address, used when she sent a card or a thank you note to her Aunt Mary, her mother's oldest sister. An Aunt she remembered meeting only twice. Both times at funerals. Her Aunt who had married an American businessman. Her rich Aunt, who lived in Everett, almost directly east of Victoria, and not that far away in miles, really, except that there was a lot of water, and Whidbey Island in the way.

"It is in another country," her Aunt Francis kept repeating. "A neutral country. You'll be safer there." Aunt Francis had not been joking. Aunt Francis never joked. Aunt Francis sniffed and frowned when other people told jokes.

Florence suspected that money, not safety, was the real reason she was being sent away. She hadn't been allowed to continue her ballet or piano lessons this fall, and she knew her school fees for the fall term had not been paid. She had casually mentioned that perhaps she could work, and earn money, but both her Aunts had been horrified. There was no point in arguing. She didn't have any money of her own. Her parents were dead. She had to do what she was told.

The *Chinook* passed a raft of logs, and then a small green hulled tugboat towing the logs. She could read the name in bright white letters across the stern, the *Maggie B*. She had to laugh. There were dozens of seagulls, all lined up in a row with their heads tucked down and their double-chins standing out, looking as serious as a bunch of old ladies sitting in a pew at church. She watched a man carrying a lantern hop, skip and nimbly skitter his way from one log to the next, until he came to the rear end of the tow where he hung a paraffin oil lantern on some sort of pole, giving the log tow a stern light. Florence wondered how he got off, and back on, his boat, but the *Chinook* was moving much faster than the *Maggie B.* and she was soon too far away to be able to watch. Ahead, she could see the shapes of buildings and the lights of a small town emerging from the dusk.

Probably Everett. She'd been told twenty thousand people lived there, but it looked smaller. Certainly not as impressive as Victoria, or Seattle, where tall buildings seemingly climbed into the sky. She stood up, and went to lean in the doorway. There was more breeze, and she wished her coat were warmer.

There seemed to be so very many long, low wooden buildings built right beside, or out over the water, on pilings. Rafts of logs lined the shoreline. Small boats were anchored off shore. Docks on shore were covered with pallets of cut lumber, the bright tan stacks of freshly cut wood a contrasting color to the faded charcoal gray of the surrounding warehouses. There were so many smokestacks, the smoke rising straight up in the cold, quiet air, then drifting away over the city. It wasn't full dark, but the brighter lights on shore were beginning to shimmer and stray out over the water, with the buildings along the shore fading into darkness and shadows. The thumping vibration from the steam engine eased and Florence could feel the *Chinook* slow and settle deeper in the water. She wondered if her Aunt Mary would be at the dock waiting for her. Almost dead in the water, almost stopped, they were standing off the dock, drifting. The *Chinook* didn't appear to be in any hurry. Florence wondered why. She strained to get a closer look.

"Oh," she finally said to herself. "There." "There" was another ship, in their path, blocking access to the dock. She could only see the other ship's stern, but she wasn't close enough to make out the other ship's name. The other ship was also in the process of docking, hardly moving. The *Chinook* slid closer. The stern and upper promenade deck of the *Verona* – she could read the name now – seemed dark, and heavy, for the *Verona* was listing, tipping rather alarmingly, she thought, in towards the pier. Was a ship supposed to be able to do that? She didn't know. As the *Chinook* came even closer, she became aware of the shouting, and the dark mass resolved into movement, and people, dozens and dozens, it would have to be hundreds, of people, standing outside on the decks of the *Verona*, crowded against the rail, massed all on the side of the *Verona* that would first meet the dock, shouting, shouting, shouting. It was like a play. A massed crowd in a pageant. For a huge crowd had come to meet the docking *Verona*. A huge mob that spilled out across the dock, with everyone seemingly shouting and waving their arms. It was like, just like, the opening lines of Romeo and Juliet, the fair city of *Verona*, some ancient grudge. Would there be civil blood spilled to make civil hands unclean?

Then the *Verona* was stopped, in position alongside the dock, ready to tie up. The *Chinook* had drifted past, so Florence's view was of the dock, the side of the *Verona*, and the end of the dock. What was going on? What was this spectacle? Some sort of social outing? A local celebration? Some part of the American Thanksgiving? Wasn't that soon?

The captain of the *Chinook* gave two sharp whistle blasts. Florence, on edge already, nearly jumped out of her skin. But she interpreted the signal correctly: Move. You're in my way. I have a schedule to keep. As the whistle blasts echoed away she could finally make out individual words distinctly across the water. Men. Men shouting at each other in a rage. Words of hate. Profanity. Fists shaking. Two groups of shouting men. On the ship. On the dock.

The *Verona* was almost within arm's length of the dock, and the gestures and out flung arms of the men lined up on the dock made them look like they were trying to reach out to the *Verona* and draw her in close, into a deadly and hateful embrace. The narrow patch of sky and water that was all that kept the two groups apart kept getting narrower and narrower. And the screams grew louder. And louder. It was impossible now to hear individual voices, single words. There was just a thunderous cacophony of hate, hate, hate that built towards a crescendo, like some mad, dark symphony of bleating brass and pounding tympani.

Then above the noise a gunshot rang out. Then another and another until the staccato of gun fire was sustained and became one continual sound of its own. The captain of the *Chinook* blew three short whistle blasts and reversed his engines. Full reverse. But as Florence watched, she saw a man, or at least someone wearing trousers, pitch forward and fall from the promenade deck of the *Verona*, fall ever so slowly, his body turning over slightly, landing awkwardly on his side, arms flailing, with a huge splash between the *Verona* and the dock.

Suddenly the *Verona* began to back away from the dock. Her Captain gave five sharp blasts on his whistle. Then he did it again. Danger! DANGER!! Now the shooting was sporadic. Men who fell off the dock, or the boat, were swimming in the widening gap. Men on the pier shot down at the swimmers. Then the shouting died out. In the relative silence, she heard someone, who sounded desperate, yelling , "For the Love of Christ…." It might have been someone on the *Verona*, or even the *Chinook*. Impossible to tell.

She could hear, on the deck above her on the *Chinook*, a woman screaming. It seemed like a very appropriate response. A crewman surprised her.

With his large hands, very white against the pale green of her coat, he gently took her by the shoulders and led her away from the freight door and back to sit on her trunk.

"Here, Missy," he said to her, "you stay here." He emphasized this last point with a firm but gentle shake, before racing away up the stairs towards the sound of the screaming.

Suddenly, Florence felt very faint; she gulped down some air, eased her head back against the ship's bulkhead and closed her eyes. All that summer and fall she had followed reports from Europe, reported in the Victoria *Daily Colonist*, as the Battle of the Somme, a huge offensive against the German lines by the British and the French and her fellow Canadians that had gone on and on, month after month. She read the local casualty lists of the dead and wounded. No one said so, but it was easy to surmise that thousands of other boys had also died. Were dying. But it was all abstract. Far away, almost like history in a book.

She tried to block the thoughts and images, but she kept seeing that man pitch forward and fall. He hadn't waved his arms or done anything to break his fall. He just crashed into the water. Crashed. You knew he was dead. She had seen dead people, seen them in their coffins, seen a dead body once where it had washed ashore on the beach at Oak Bay. But she had never seen a man die because some other man had shot him.

It was like a war. Was Everett somehow like France? No, that was foolish. The U. S. was a neutral country, and she had never read in the Colonist that there was any kind of local conflict. The U. S. Civil War had ended fifty years ago, hadn't it?

And there had never really been Indian Wars on this coast. Yet what she had seen was some sort of a war, still going on. She shuddered. She had almost landed in the middle of it, between the belligerents. She could have died. Thank God for the Captain of their ship!

And then she saw, and heard her Aunt Margaret, who with a lifted eyebrow and her voice dripping sarcasm, said, "Dying might be better than living with your Aunt Mary." She laughed to herself at this joke, but she hoped it wasn't true.

Miles away to the east, unaware of what was happening at Bayside, wearing hip boots up to his crotch, Hank sloshed through river water up to his knees. He was hurrying to pick up his duck decoys before it was completely dark. He was hunting a flooded cornfield, since he preferred the taste of corn-fed ducks to ducks that dined on eelgrass in saltwater. He pulled his flat bottomed skiff behind him, packing the decoys into two big gunny sacks settled in the stern. He stopped to count. Counted again. He had them all.

It took some effort to step into his boat because of the hip waders. He picked up the oars and made for the low spot in the dike. This part of Spencer Island was below sea level at high tide and flooded almost daily on a high tide, or in winter with the rains. He was out in the current, but this wasn't the main stem of the river. This was Union Slough, one of the smaller ribbons of the bigger river, the Snohomish, part of a huge delta where freshwater met tidewater. Hank had several miles to row upriver, before he could turn and float with the current. He hoped the exercise would warm him up. He was cold. Should have worn another sweater, he thought.

The evening was now full dark. There was only the thunk of his oars, the swish of canvas on canvas as he moved in his coat. Once he startled a small animal and heard it rustle away. Probably a beaver. Not good eating, unless you were real hungry. Otherwise it was quiet.

The current became stronger as he pulled closer to the main stem, but then he turned the corner, swept sideways and faster, going with the current downstream. He pivoted his boat, pointing the bow upriver, and stern first, resting on the oars, he drifted downriver. The Snohomish River runs in a huge upside down, backwards, J along the east and north end of the peninsula on which the city of Everett is built.

A single light in the night watchman's shack at Two Brothers Iron Works announced the onset of civilization. Lights on the hill stretching up from the riverbank showed off the small community of Lowell. Hank worked at Two Brothers as a machinist. Having started as an apprentice at fourteen, he was now a journeyman. Most of his family worked there. His brothers, some of them younger than he was, were all married, had children, their own homes. Hank was still living at home with his parents.

The building and sheds of Two Brothers, the long low stretch of dock, and a barge he knew was full of sand for the foundry, were dark, then darker shapes as they slid out of his vision. Then there were more lights, for many people lived here in the area of Everett known as Riverside. Occasionally there was the shrill note of a whistle and the crash of metal as a steam engine shuttled freight cars in the Delta yard.

He was nearing his destination, a gently sloping stretch of riverbank just downstream from Swallwell's Wharf at the east end of Hewitt. Hewitt itself ran uphill for two miles from Riverside, peaked at the corner of Hewitt and Colby, then went downhill for another mile all the way to Bayside and Pier 1. Where the steamboats from Seattle docked.

Swallwell's Wharf was the center for people and freight moving upriver to the cities of Snohomish and Monroe, although the new electric trolley, making the roundtrip across twenty thousand acres of cow pasture and river bottom land to Snohomish, six times a day, was killing passenger business on the river.

But Hank could make out the silhouette of the small sternwheeler, the Gleaner, tied to the wharf, ready for its early trip in the morning. Hank turned his boat, aimed the bow for a spot on the bank he couldn't see, but knew was there, and pulled hard for the shore. He was startled when a match flared on the bank, then the flame disappeared. Someone was waiting for him . A pipe smoker. The bow of his boat scrunched on the beach. A man stood up to meet him. He was short, wearing a shapeless hat pulled low over his eyes, an overcoat, a pipe stem clenched in his teeth below a long droopy mustache, carrying something like a blanket in his left hand.

"Older Father," said Hank, laughing and speaking Norwegian, calling his father 'grandfather', "did your woman push you out of the house? It must be that cheap tobacco you smoke." His father suffered somewhat from arthritis. It was uncharacteristic of him to be out on such a cold, damp night.

"Speak quietly, and speak English," Carl Eide said quietly, but his tone was intense. "Your mother sent me to fetch you home safely."

"Safely?' Hank said quietly in English. "I'm no longer ten years old."

"I know," said Carl, "but she is worried. So am I," he added. "People have been shooting each other today. Hand me your shotgun." Hank took a long canvas roll from the boat. Carl folded the blanket he was carrying over and around the canvas roll obscuring the shape completely.

"There," Carl said, "now some drunk can't mistake you for an armed Wobbly." Which was a union man, a member of the International Workers of the World.

"Carrying two sacks of decoys and six dead ducks? What is going on?"

"Six ducks? Very nice. But how many shells? Eh?"

"Six," said Hank. "I had a good teacher."

"Thank you," said his father. "Good decoys, a good call, bring them in close. Any fool who can breathe can shoot ducks."

"Who is shooting people?" asked Hank, getting back to the point.

"Some other fools. Unload your boat and I'll tell you."

Hank set his two sacks of decoys and six ducks, tied into a string, on the bank. He tucked the oars beneath the center seat and with his fathers help dragged the boat twenty feet up the bank, above the high tide line, where they turned the boat over so it wouldn't fill with rainwater, or small children looking for a place to play. Hank picked up the decoys and the ducks. Carl carried the gun in a blanket. It was ten blocks through a quiet residential neighborhood to home. The homes were modest, most owned by immigrants.

"Remember that business the other day, when the police arrested those men and ran them out of town?" The six men were Wobblies, members of the I.W.W. They came to Everett to support the shingle weavers who were on strike for higher wages. Although he didn't have a family to feed, Hank didn't think there was any amount of money that could get him to saw shingles six days a week. You could pick a shingle weaver out of a crowd. He was the man with the mising fingers. Or hand.

"Yes," said Hank. "I remember."

"You heard they were taken out to Beverly Park and then beaten with ax handles?"

"I heard that."

"Well, the Wobblies came back this afternoon," Carl told him, "with a boatload of their friends from Seattle." His father stopped to relight his pipe and stood smoking in silence for a moment.

"What happened?" prompted Hank.

"After church we saw these important businessmen, rich men who own automobiles, were racing back and forth across town. They all had a bottle. They were all drinking. Then we bumped into our neighbor, Ramstead. He said he heard that someone in Seattle telegraphed the County Sheriff these Wobblies were coming up to Everett today, on a ship. Then the Sheriff deputized all these drunks. Ramstead was going to walk up Rucker Hill and watch the show."

"Can these rich men just shoot people, like they were dogs?" Hank interjected.

Carl shrugged and turned up the steps of his own front porch. "Ramstead came by about two hours ago. He saw the whole thing. The ship came in. Both sides had guns. People got shot. Killed. Ramstead is talking about moving away."

"What's he going to do? Move back to North Dakota to starve again?"

"No," said his father, standing on the porch of his two story house with bright blue trim. "I don't think he will. I know I won't." He knocked his pipe out on the railing. "You're probably too young to remember, but sod houses are cold and wet. And I'm no farmer. I learned that the hard way." Carl and his wife had left Norway together to try homesteading in North Dakota. Then Alberta,

Canada before giving up and coming to Everett when Hank was ten.

"I came here for the chance to work for wages," said Carl. "We have a nice home and a good life. I'm not leaving. Even if I went, your mother wouldn't go with me. She prefers indoor plumbing. She likes the electric. So go clean those ducks. Then come and play us something on the piano." He stepped through his own front door and closed it behind him.

Hank had started piano when he became an apprentice, at age fourteen, and could afford the lessons - and the piano. He enjoyed ragtime, but his parents preferred the hymns from church. He carried his gear around back. There wasn't an inside door to the basement. Down the half-stairs, he set his decoys aside, and using a dim electric light bulb hanging from a wire, plucked and cleaned his ducks.

Northern France, 1918

It was April, 1918. For the first time U.S. troops of the Second and Third Division, primarily National Guard units mustered in January, were moved forward into the line of battle. The French and British were holding the line against a furious and desperate last attempt by the Germans to break through, drive the British back on the seacoast and collapse the French. Important parts of the battle would come down to history and be known as the Battle for the Belleau Woods. The British called it the Second Battle of the Marne.

As U. S. troops moved up in support, certain French units, battered and worn out by four years of trench warfare, fell back in retreat. "You should retreat, too," one French commander suggested to a company of Marines. "Retreat? Hell, we just got here," was the American response. General Pershing, leader of the American Forces, had concisely set out the task for U. S. Troops before they landed in France: Heaven, Hell, or Hoboken, by Christmas, 1918. Hoboken, New Jersey was where most of the troops had disembarked for Europe, and where they would return – if they survived.

Hank was a machinist and a mechanic. His job was to fix things- artillery field pieces and the trucks that pulled them - when they broke, which was often. He was assigned to an artillery brigade. But what Hank was trying to do on this particular June evening at twilight was not very mechanical. Face down in the mud, he was simply trying to stay alive. It wasn't easy.

He crawled forward. Lieutenant Hadley was in front of him, and occasionally Hank tapped Hadley on his left side, steering the other man towards a slight rise in the terrain ahead of them and a small clump of trees and brush. Cover. The Lieutenant was wounded, and disoriented, his left eye and vision obscured by caked blood from a three inch gash above his left ear, clotted now, but not before blood covered his face to the chin, smeared and streaked by the rain and mud.

The only weapon they had was the Lieutenant's sidearm, which Hadley carried now in his right hand, squished into the mud with every movement forward. Hank was certain the barrel was packed with mud. The gun was useless, unlikely to fire, likely to jam. But it apparently made the Lieutenant feel safer to carry it in his hand, so Hank kept his mouth shut.

They crawled - it was almost too slow to be called a crawl - another hundred yards. They oozed forward in the mud, like slugs, Hank steering into the brush, under the trees, up to the base of a waist high boulder. With a groan Lieutenant Hadley put his head down and collapsed.

"Sir…Sir..," Hank hissed at him, but there was no reply. The Lieutenant had obviously passed out. Probably for the best. Cautiously, Hank loosened the Lieutenants grip on the Colt. He set the gun to his right, within reach, but with the muzzle pointed away from them both. He noted the hammer was cocked, the safety on. He suspected there was a round in the firing chamber.

Hank had the two waterproofs rolled together like sausages and slung over his back. The waterproofs and the contents of his pockets was all he had. The Lieutenant didn't even have an overcoat, only what the officers wore, a light cotton thing, called a trench coat. Very dashing, but not very useful for crawling around in the mud. Hank checked the Lieutenant's pockets. Nothing in the coat. Both pockets in his pants were empty. Nothing in his uniform jacket. Nothing, nothing and nothing. But wait, tucked inside his uniform coat, in the front of his starched shirt, was a handkerchief. It was the only useful thing Lieutenant Hadley carried, besides the gun, but it might be enough.

He unbundled the waterproofs and spread the first one, doubled-up, over the Lieutenant. Keep him warm. Let him sleep. He took off his tin helmet and set it on the ground in front of him. Then he arranged the second waterproof over his back and head, stretching out in front of him. The result was a small, covered tent space maybe the size of a dinner plate, with his helmet in the center. Hank produced his first two contributions, a stump of candle, not even two inches long, and a small box of wooden matches. Carefully, Hank lit the candle. He dripped wax into the center of his helmet, shaped like a shallow soup bowl with a wide brim, and set his candle in the center of the bowl. He wasn't going to have a lot of time. They couldn't stay where they were and the only safe way to move was under the cover of darkness.

Hank produced his final contribution, his jackknife. It wasn't real fancy. About four inches long. Working at his mother's kitchen table back home, with a set of watchmakers tools he'd borrowed from a man he knew from church, Hank had stripped out the two blades and four different tools the knife had been sold with, and only added two blades back to the case. The first was a thicker than normal knife blade, made from an old chisel he'd tempered and re-ground. In some ways it resembled a straight razor, and it was just as sharp. The second blade, as long as the first, was a file, a slice from a #8 bastard metal cutting file to be exact. The tip was shaped to be a flat head screwdriver. You could do your nails, sharpen a fish hook, or clean a magneto with that little file. Hank opened both blades and picked up the Colt. A 1911 Colt .45 Service Pistol.

Miracle of miracles. With some gentle coaxing the clip holding the bullets slid out of the handle. It was dripping, but not too full of mud. Hank set the clip in his helmet. He cut the Lieutenant's handkerchief into quarters. Using the piece with the monogrammed 'H' he worked over the exterior, trying to remove the mud from every nook and cranny. He cleaned the inside of the pistol grip where the clip slotted in. Then he unloaded the clip. He polished each bullet - there were seven - and polished the clip. He thumbed off the safety and cautiously tried to work the slide. He was hoping to eject the one bullet remaining from the firing chamber. No go. He re-set the safety. Tried to release the hammer. No go. He considered his options and the time and tools he had available. All his choices were foolish, stupid and un-safe. Shit. He began to recite the Lord's Prayer. "Our Father, who art in Heaven…." as he gently probed the muzzle with the file blade, scraping out packed mud and grass. "Hallowed be thy name…." And please don't shoot off my hand, he thought.

"Thy Kingdom come, Thy will be done…" He'd worked his way about three inches up the five inch barrel. Then four. He used a piece of the handkerchief as a swab to try and clean more mud out of the barrel. When he was finished, it was still dirty, but there was no longer caked mud. "On Earth as it is in Heaven." He was little more than four inches up the barrel. On the other hand, the gun hadn't fired, and Hank decided he'd gone as far as luck, safety and God's will would allow. He sat up a bit straighter to ease the pain in his back. The urgent pain in his bladder decided him. He didn't have any light machine oil, so he used the only lubricant available. He unbuttoned.

"Give us this day our daily bread…." He pissed into the end of the barrel.

"and forgive us our trespasses…." And please don't shoot my balls off. "As we forgive those who trespass against us." He'd filled up the barrel. He emptied it. The hand holding himself shook. Finally he was empty.

The gun wasn't. He put his matches back in a dry pocket. Blew out the candle. Pushed the waterproof to one side and took off his overcoat. Taking the gun in his left hand, he wrapped the waterproof around both his hand and the gun and tried to smother the muzzle. He pointed the muzzle towards the ground, then stopped and listened.

There was the sound of rain. Far off, the sound of artillery. He could hear his own breathing and the pounding of his heart, and the raspy, crooked breathing of the Lieutenant. Nothing else. No voices. No mechanical noise.

"Deliver us from evil." He pulled the trigger. Nothing. The safety was on. He thumbed it off. "For Thine is the Kingdom and the power and the glory forever…." He pulled the trigger again. The gun fired. "…and ever." The sound was muted, but it still seemed terribly loud. "Amen." Couldn't be helped. We don't have all night, thought Hank. He re-established his shelter and lit the candle again. The explosion of the bullet had done what he hoped it would do: move the slide. With a strong grip and sustained pressure, the slide released. The rest was easy and quick. Clean and polish. File. Particularly on the inside of the slide. If he had oil, this was where he would have used it. He used a dab of candle wax. He went for clean and smooth.

His candle was disappearing fast. He loaded the bullets back into the clip, loaded the clip into the handle of the gun. Worked the slide. The action was considerably smoother. The gun was now re-loaded, cocked and ready to fire. Better yet, it would do so reliably. He thumbed on the safety. Tucked the gun inside his tunic. Warm, semi-dry, but no mud.

All that remained of the candle was a puddle of wax and a flickering wick. He picked up his tools, then blew out the flame and poured the wax on the ground. He changed position, sitting up cross-legged Indian-fashion, and started in on the job of waking the Lieutenant. After a few minutes of being nudged and poked, the Lieutenant actually sat up and looked around. "What time is it?"

"Sir?" asked Hank.

"What - time - is -it?"

"No idea, Sir," Hank answered. "Maybe midnight."

'Where are we?"

"Under some trees, about half a mile from where we got shot up."

Lieutenant Hadley took a deep breath. "I don't have a map or a compass," he admitted. "Do you?"

"No, Sir."

"Great," he snorted. Hank could see he was smiling. "Suggestions?"

"I think I can find our way back to the car." Hank paused, then went on. "After that we follow the road."

"Help me up." Hank helped him to his feet.

"You lead, Hank. I can't see much."

"Yes, Sir."

"Oh." Lieutenant Hadley stopped and scanned the ground. "You've got the gun?"

"Yes, Sir. I cleaned it. Here."

"No - you keep it. I was never very good with it when I could see out of both eyes - God knows what I might shoot now."

Hank couldn't think of anything else to say except, "Sir, yes, Sir."

They stumbled out of the trees, Lieutenant Hadley going down once, and Hank nearly twice, with Hank stopping every 50 yards or so to make sure Lieutenant Hadley didn't drift back, out of touch. After what Hank judged to be half an hour, Hank called a halt and they sat down, each huddled under a waterproof.

Lieutenant Hadley didn't make any conversation, but sat with his eyes closed taking deep breaths. Then his breathing slowed and Hank was certain he was asleep, but then he said a single word, "Better," and struggled to his feet.

Now Hank stopped not just to wait, but to take bearings. They were in an area of small woodlots and open pasture. The trees behind him, rising to the top of a ridge, had disappeared into the mist, and it took real effort not to walk in circles. Hank used the fact the Lieutenant Hadley trailed behind to take a sort of back bearing and kept moving forward. Staring backwards while walking forward, Hank missed the sudden change in slope. Suddenly he was sliding forward, then falling, then with a thud, sprawling to a stop. More cautiously, Lieutenant Hadley slid down the slope behind him.

"I see you found the road," said the Lieutenant. He was laughing. He helped Hank to his feet. "Not much of a road ," he added, stomping his feet. "About all you can say is the mud is a little harder." Hank laughed.

"That way?" Hank said, pointing.

"I agree."

For maybe fifteen minutes they made good time, then Lieutenant Hadley slowed.

"Hank, I'm about done," the Lieutenant said, in a normal voice.

"Sir, that farmhouse," Hank whispered back. Hank wanted him to be quieter.

"Oh," the Lieutenant whispered back. "Yes."

Earlier that day Hank had volunteered to drive when Lieutenant Hadley was told to take a French artillery Major and his Adjutant forward towards the line of battle to reconnoiter the country in front of their position. To map a route to a piece of high ground, where the Americans would move and sight in a dozen big guns. Since the French were loaning the U.S. most of the artillery field guns the U.S. had in place at this time, every effort was made to maintain good relations. Lieutenant Hadley was something of a gentleman, and spoke French that he had learned in college. He practiced law back home, and in the normal course of things was a man Hank would probably never have met.

Hank volunteered to drive for the chance to actually see the front. So far his war was just a smudge on the horizon. He was amused to see that the French had arrived driving an American made 1915 Packard Limousine. The driver sat in front, with a windscreen in front of him, and a roof overhead, but otherwise out in the weather, while the passengers rode in enclosed, upholstered luxury in the rear.

Lieutenant Hadley and the French Major sat in the back of the staff car and babbled away in French. The French Adjutant sat in the jump seat in back and occasionally rapped on the glass partition, barked directions and pointed the direction he wished Hank to drive. The country was empty. No people. The houses they passed were burned ruins. A few outbuildings still stood, but there were no signs of life or livestock. There were no other vehicles on the road. Hank was disappointed. There was nothing to see.

The road was rutted and full of holes, but the surface was reasonably firm and drivable. They came around a corner and the road dipped slightly into a gully that opened out to their right. Concealed in this fold was a small house, not much more than a hut really, invisible and unseen until you came around and down the turn.

The glass windscreen exploded. Glass and bullets rained down on them. Then finally the noise caught up to the bullets. Machine gun!! Probably hidden beside - or even inside - that hut. Hank jammed on the brakes, and the big Packard slewed to a halt. He slammed the gear shift into reverse, grinding the gears, popped the clutch, jammed down the accelerator and away they roared, backwards.

The machine gunner hadn't anticipated this reversal of direction and bullets were tearing up the road thirty-five yards in front of them. Hank went faster. He could see the rounds start to traverse back in his direction. The hut was still in sight when rounds hammered into the engine cowling. Then the hut was gone, hidden behind the fold of the earth. They were safe. A thought that immediately evaporated when the engine stalled out and died. Hank coasted as far as he could, then set the handbrake before they might roll forward, back into the field of fire.

Hank turned to Lieutenant Hadley, expecting orders, but the glass partition was shattered and Lieutenant Hadley sat with his head thrown back, eyes closed, the left side of his face crimson with blood. The French Major was dead, his head blown away, spattered all over the leather upholstery and the back window, the stump of his neck all that was left. The Adjutant in the jump seat still had his head, but he was slumped over, with a large part of his skull above the hairline missing.

Panicked, Hank rubbed down his own head, but his hands remained clean. Then he noticed the pattern of holes in the windscreen. Bullets had visibly bracketed his head, but missed. Hank scrambled out of the wreck. There were two waterproofs and not much else in the boot. He rolled them into a tube and tied the ends with a length of twine. Feeling like a Wobbly bindle-stiff, he went to salvage the Lieutenant's gun.

Lieutenant Hadley was still breathing. There was no time to consider what he could or could not do. He hauled Lieutenant Hadley out and over his back in a fireman's carry and set out across country, slightly uphill, away from the car, into the twilight. He ran a distance he estimated was about the length of Bagshaw Field back home, telling himself that he ought to be able to do it twice. He was gasping for air when he went for three lengths, and he went a bit farther before his left knee buckled and down they went.

Now, hours later, having almost come full circle, Hank gave the Lieutenant some support and they limped forward together. There it was. The hut was a darker shadow before them. Hank slowed, and they inched forward. Maybe fifty yards away, down a slight incline, a window seemed to be outlined, lit from within. Hank turned his head from side to side. He wasn't at all sure what he was seeing. The Lieutenant was beginning to stumble. Off to the far side of the road, screened by some brush, Hank lowered the Lieutenant to the ground.

"Sir, wait here, Sir", he whispered in his ear.

"What?"

"Wait. Here."

"Oh." Or maybe it was a sigh. Hank wasn't sure the Lieutenant understood, but it seemed unlikely that he would - or could - move.

Pace by pace, with frequent pauses, Hank slid forward. He fished the Colt out of his tunic and carried it in his right hand but with the safety on. If he stumbled and fell he didn't want to wake the neighbors. A dog - a dog that barked - would also bring this adventure to a speedy and unhappy end. He prayed for no dogs. He was within ten feet of the building. Now he was certain he saw a window. He could also smell wood smoke. He thumbed off the safety. He decided that whatever happened he would move towards it, not run away. The Lieutenant couldn't run. That meant he couldn't either.

There was something like a blanket hanging over the window, a crude attempt at a black out curtain. Most of the glass was missing. One edge of the curtain thing was ragged and allowed him to peer inside. He could hear the snap of the fire, small sounds of movement and subdued conversation. As his eyes adjusted to the light the first thing he saw was the barrel of the machine gun. This was the crew that had shot them up! Movement in front of the fire attracted his attention. Two men sat there talking.

Hank didn't understand German, but there were some similarities between the language the men were speaking, and Norwegian, and Hank was pretty certain they were talking about food. A third man came and knelt before the fire, taking up a small burning stick which he used to light a cigarette. He tossed the cigarette box on the table. Hank could almost imagine he could smell the smoke. Hank dropped into a crouch and crawled around the hut, but there were no additional windows, and he thought he was almost back where he had started, when he came upon a door made from a piece of canvas. Gingerly, Hank took hold of the canvas and pulled it aside until he had a peephole.

The three men were still in front of the fire, but now Hank noticed two more, asleep on the floor. He had almost missed them. Five. Shit. Five was too many. He couldn't successfully take five men captive. Hold them at gunpoint. Tie them up with - something - he wasn't sure what. The Lieutenant wasn't going to be able to help.

The Colt could fire five shots at five different targets in less than a minute, provided you had a steady hand and steady nerves. More importantly, if you shot someone at close range with a .45 caliber bullet, they were going to go down and stay down. The gun was up to the job. Am I? There was only one way to really know. He thumbed off the safety.

Hank brought the Colt up to his peephole and took careful aim at the man who had earlier lit the cigarette. He took a deep breath, and as he let it out, he squeezed the trigger. One of the figures on the floor rolled to his feet and Hank shot him at close range in the torso as he pushed through the canvas at the door. He fired twice at the two remaining men in front of the fire. The other man on the floor had pulled himself into a sitting position and was reaching for his rifle when Hank shot him in the head. Gun pointed, he twirled in a circle to cover all the corners, but there was no one else hiding or waiting to try and kill him. His ears rang. They hurt. They ached. They stung. He could hear nothing. It had all happened very fast, in less than a minute. He set the safety on the Colt, set the gun on the table beside the cigarettes, and dragged the last man he had shot outside. He came back for another. One blanket was a bloody mess, but a second had escaped harm and he set it aside. Several of the uniforms were very elaborate with piping, braid, and multiple medals. Did all German soldiers go to war this well dressed? Hank didn't know. These were his first Germans. He had heard the Germans did go in for a great deal of spit and polish.

One of the men at the fire, sitting next to a table, had been cleaning a bird. There was a pile of feathers on the floor. Hank examined the carcass. Glory be, it was some sort of duck. Although he had no idea where it had come from. Some poor farmer, Hank decided. He put the bird on the table and went to fetch the Lieutenant.

"Hank? I heard shooting."

"Yes, Sir. Come on, Sir. We can get warm."

The Lieutenant made no more comment, even when they stepped past the pile of bodies to the right of the door. Hank sat the Lieutenant down in one of the chairs and dropped the blanket over his shoulders. Hank sat down as well.

"Cigarette?"

"You're joking."

"Nope." Hank lit a cigarette, handed it to the Lieutenant, lit one for himself.

"Hank?" The Lieutenant stretched his legs towards the fire .

"Sir?"

"Am I alive? Or is this Heaven? Or Hell?"

"I think it's a bit of both, Sir." The Lieutenant laughed.

"You a praying man, Hank?"

"I go to Central Lutheran."

"I go to Trinity Episcopal." He and Hank were both members of a National Guard unit, and from the same town. "But I never prayed much outside church. Until tonight."

"I know what you mean, Sir," said Hank, thinking about cleaning the Colt.

There were two small tin pots on the floor in front of the fire . One held water. The other was empty - except for two small onions, not much bigger than eggs, and one large misshapen potato. Using his pocket knife, Hank finished cleaning the duck. He boned out the two breasts, keeping the skin. He cut the two legs and thighs away, then cut the meat off the bones and into pieces about the size of a walnut. He cut the breasts into similar pieces. He rubbed the onions and the potato with water to clean them. He left the skins on, and cut up both into cubes.

Everything went into the one empty pot, including the duck liver, and he added water to cover. There was a third chair in the room and Hank broke it up and added the wood to the fire. Quicker than Lieutenant Hadley could believe, the fire was burning brighter and hotter and the duck was bubbling away on the fire, giving off incredibly delicious smells.

"Hank?"

"Sir?"

"Where'd you learn to do this?"

"With seven children, five of them boys, my mother has one hard and fast rule: If you shoot it, you clean it, and then you cook it."

"Good rule," said the Lieutenant with a grin.

Hank nodded. "We live over on Riverside and we're always bringing stuff home. Fish. Crabs, clams. Rabbits, ducks, wild geese. Even a raccoon every once in a while, though I don't care for them myself."

"No deer?"

"No deer rifles. Just shotguns."

"One of the few things I've hunted, besides fish," said Hadley, "is deer. You can ride that little train out of Arlington, up-river along the Stillaguamish."

"I've done that." Hank had ridden in a boxcar. He assumed Hadley had gone as a paying passenger.

"But if you manage to shoot a deer," continued Hadley, "you end up with almost more meat than you can eat before it spoils. I've seen men take just the choice cuts and leave the rest for the scavengers, but that seems like such a waste."

"I agree," said Hank. They fell silent again. In a few more minutes Hank set the pot on the table. They passed Hanks knife back and forth, spearing pieces of the stew, slurping the broth, burning their tongues, sharing out the water remaining in the other pot. Hank suggested leaving about a cup of water in the pot, which they did. He put three of the cleaner handkerchief quarters in the pot and set the pot on the fire to heat.

He felt Lieutenant Hadley watching him.

"I'm sorry, Sir. I borrowed your handkerchief earlier."

"I wondered how you cleaned that Colt. But how did you see?"

"I had a bit of candle stub, Sir."

"Oh?"

"If a motor stops you can't fix it in the dark," said Hank, as if that explained everything.

Lieutenant Hadley burped. "Hank, I think that was the best meal I've ever eaten in my life. Thank you."

"I enjoyed it myself, Sir." They both grinned like fools. "Let's clean up your eye."

The Lieutenant nodded agreement. Hank handed him a hot, wet quarter of the handkerchief and the Lieutenant gingerly at first, then more vigorously worked at removing the caked blood from his eyelid and socket. Soon, he had the eye open.

"I can see," he announced. He sounded very relieved. "I've been trying not to worry. I'm alive, and I hate to tempt fate by being too greedy."

"I know what you mean. I felt the same way about the duck and the fire."

"Yeah."

Hank handed Lieutenant Hadley one of the two remaining squares, and the Lieutenant began to clean his face. "Under your chin," Hank suggested.

"Very good. You use the last one, Hank." Hank did. It felt heavenly.

"So Hank," the Lieutenant said at last. "Is someone coming to pick us up?"

"No, one, Sir," Hank said puzzled.

"Then I think we should go, don't you?"

"I need your chair, Sir."

"Oh?" The Lieutenant stood up. Hank broke up the chairs they had been sitting on and added them to the fire. He pulled the ammunition belt out of the machine gun, and made sure the breech was clear. Then he tossed the gun and its tripod onto the fire.

"Think it will melt?" asked the Lieutenant.

"No, no chance, but I think it will warp. And its all I can think of." The Lieutenant nodded.

Outside, both men emptied their bladders, then they set out on their early morning walk. It had stopped raining. Dawn was a few hours away. Stronger, determined, and with a good surface to tramp, they made progress. Sunrise found them approaching an Allied camp, a sentry challenged them, then started them up the chain of command and soon they were face to face with a British major who asked them innumerable questions, sat them down and fed them tea and a biscuit and sent them on their way with his car and driver.

"Good show," the major told them, and "never trust a Frenchman for directions. To anything. Or with your wife." This came out so full of bitterness and sorrow that it sounded like the voice of experience talking, and Hank and Lieutenant Hadley chuckled about that all the way back to their own headquarters.

Where Lieutenant Hadley promptly dragged him into the Officers Mess to sit at a table with white linen, and where Hank felt very out of place. As Hank ate his way through three eggs, a heap of fried potatoes, four strips of bacon and two cups of hot chocolate, Lieutenant Hadley ate his own meal and told their tale to anyone who chanced to pass.

Finally, Colonel Anderson said, "Both of you. Get some sleep. Now." The Colonel looked Hank in the eye. "Corporal Eide, well done." That's what he said, but Hank felt the Colonel knew they'd been damn foolish to get ambushed and damn lucky to get back alive.

"Thank you, Sir," said Hank, rising. He saluted and he left. Back in his own tent, he barely managed his boots before stretching out on his field cot and falling instantly asleep.

Two days later Hank was turning replacement parts on a turret lathe when Hadley stepped inside the three sided shed that functioned as his machine shop. Hank powered the lathe by blocking up the rear wheels of a small truck, removing the rear tire and running a belt from the rim of the rear tire to the lathe. With the truck in first gear, you had plenty of power, and more than enough noise. Seeing the Lieutenant, Hank disengaged the lathe, took the truck out of gear, and stopped the engine.

"The Colonel sent me to find you." Lieutenant Hadley was positively bouncing up and down. He was dressed in a clean, pressed uniform. Every button gleamed, like his boots. Hank was wearing a dirty shop coat. His hands, nails especially, were stained and dirty.

"You and I have five days leave," announced the Lieutenant.

"Leave?" Hank hadn't requested any leave. Ever. It was impossible to get unless someone in your immediate family died - and that exception probably no longer applied, since they were in France. They weren't going to let you go home for the weekend to attend a funeral.

"Leave. Darn right," exclaimed Hadley. "We're going to Paris."

Hank shook his head. No. "Why?"

"Those men you shot?" Hank had been trying to not remember those men. He made no response. "That British Major," continued Hadley, "sent a patrol to investigate right after he sent us on our way. One of those men was a Von something or other, and an officer. He was carrying some very important papers - letters and a map, apparently." Hadley came and stood beside him, speaking quietly now. "The Brits and the French think this is the best thing since Bell invented the telephone. You're a hero because you did the deed and saved me, and I'm sort of a hero because I was your commanding officer, on the scene, when you did all this hero stuff." Here Hadley stopped.

Then continued. "You, Sir, have been promoted. You are now Sergeant Eide. And we've got five days leave in Paris - I'm paying for everything - no arguments, and when we get back the French are going to pin on some medals and kiss us on both cheeks."

"Oh, shit," said Hank, his first cogent response.

"Merde," said Hadley. "Exactly. But I'm still hopeful that we can get kissed by French women, in Paris, so come on Sergeant, get your gear. Our car and driver isn't going to wait all day."

Hadley held out his hand to shake. Hank took it. "You coming?"

"Oh, shit," said Hank. It was all he could think of to say. He shrugged off the shop coat and ran for his duffel.

Stiff and sore from a long day spent bouncing over bad roads, they arrived in Paris just before eight in the evening. Good as his word, Hadley checked them in to their hotel. They each had their own room, which Hank thought unnecessary, but he was impressed with the Turkish carpets, gold and green brocaded black-out curtains, private bath and huge double bed.

"What's the name of this place again?"

"This, my son, is the Ritz." Hadley went off to his own room.

He was still inspecting all this splendor when Hadley knocked and came back in.

"I've ordered you a meal - they'll bring it up. Leave your duffel in the hall along with your dirty clothes and everything will come back clean and pressed in the morning. I'm going to run a bath and go to bed." He smiled and left.

Hank was too excited to immediately fall asleep. After soaking in more hot water than he had seen in months, he turned off all his lights, opened the blackout curtains and two glass paned doors, genuine French doors, he thought with amusement, and sat down on his balcony. He remained there to eat his steak, drink red wine and thoroughly enjoy himself and the warm evening. Then he slid between the clean crisp sheets and wasn't aware of anything until someone knocked on his door in the morning.

There was a young girl, about twelve, with a tray holding a pot of hot chocolate, bread, and what he figured was more oleo, but turned out to be real butter and jam. She curtsied and left. Hank sat down to eat, again on his balcony, when someone else knocked. For a private room, thought Hank, going to open the door, there certainly was a great deal of traffic. This time it was an old man with a small cart. He smiled at Hank, then proceeded to unload shirts, washed, starched, pressed and on hangers, which he hung in the closet. Then stacks of folded clean underclothes, no longer gray, that he put in a drawer. Shiny boots. Even his duffel had been washed. The man bowed and left. He went back to his breakfast, but something nagged at him. He went to check his shirts. There on the sleeves, where last night he wore Corporal's stripes, this morning he was a Sergeant. Hadley, thought Hank, disbelieving. It was all so hard to believe. He returned to his breakfast.

Dressed, Hank set out to find Hadley's room. He didn't have to look far. Hadley was right next door. Hank knocked. Hadley pulled the door open and returned to knotting his tie.

"Morning. How'd you sleep?"

"Like a baby."

"Me, too. Ready. Let's go, Sergeant."

"Thanks. Also for dinner. Especially the wine."

"You're welcome." Hadley knew what Hank meant. Back home, their city, Everett, their county, Snohomish, and their state, Washington, were all dry. Alcohol was illegal and had been for years. To order a meal like Hank had eaten, you had to break the law.

"I was here before the War, in 1910," said Hadley. "After I graduated from law school. One summer. This way," he pointed, "or at least I think this way." They set off, Hank wondering about how many years of school it took to graduate from law school. He didn't even have a guess, except to say, more years than his own eighth grade education.

They toured a huge museum, the Louvre. Saw Napoleon's Tomb. Took lunch, with wine, at a small café in the shadow of Notre Dame, which they toured, and better yet, another smaller church nearby, called St. Chappelle. A string quartet was playing a piece by Handel from the Messiah as they came up the narrow winding stairs into the main chapel, and the music and the stunning stained glass windows, the height, the beauty of the colors, left both men speechless. They sat for over an hour, until the quartet packed up and went home. Hank and Hadley followed them out.

They reversed field, walking back in the direction they had started, then strolling up the Champs Elysee, where they climbed the steps to the top of the Arch de Triumph. The view was magnificent. Back at their hotel, they agreed to meet in the dining room for dinner. Rested and pink from another long soak in the tub, Hank browsed down a long hall lined with small shops selling incredible and incredibly expensive merchandise. One shop in particular sold jewelry the like of which he'd never seen or imagined. He was sitting at a table in the dining room, trying to puzzle out the French bill of fare, when Hadley came in with two gorgeous, and beautifully groomed and dressed, young women, each in their early twenties.

Hank stood up and was introduced to Marie. And Claire. Hadley ordered champagne, which appeared to be a very popular choice with Marie and Claire. Claire was very taken with Hank. It was distracting and embarrassing. Hank was trying to concentrate on turning French words into English, when Hadley said, "On the menu, the "Maigret du Canard", that's breast of duck." They discussed other possibilities, but both ordered the duck. Also more champagne, and two bottles of a red wine by somebody Rothschild that Hadley said was supposed to be very special. The girls and Hadley drank glass after glass, and even Hank drank more than he ever had in his life.

The duck was rare, tender, and flavored with a sauce that included mustard, and just a bit of rhubarb. The vegetables were crisp, and a potato dish, thin, crisp, flavored with cheese and cream - Hank had never had a meal like that in his life.

"Well," said Hadley, finishing his wine. "That's the second best duck I've ever eaten." Hank joined in his laughter.

When Marie and Claire accompanied them upstairs, Hank felt uncertain, but by the time Marie and Hadley disappeared into Hadley's room, Hank had it figured out.

He was surprised at how rapidly Claire took off all her clothes, and naked, slipped into bed. He wasn't at all surprised at how quickly he joined her. They kissed, and she took hold of him, and his erection filled her hand. He was surprised when she dove beneath the sheets and took him in her mouth. He had heard of such things, but not to anyone he knew. This was a first. But when Claire scooted around and beckoned with her arms and open legs to him, he was astounded. Then he quit thinking, and followed his tongue.

And in that instant was lost and gone forever, as possible husband material, to the prim and proper girls of Central Lutheran Church, back home.

Victoria, June 1908

Yesterday had been sunny and warm. The morning in particular had been beautiful. Today, the storm that had been building for days out in the Pacific, a huge ridge of low barometric pressure that had slipped a thousand miles south out of the Gulf of Alaska, creating misery for ships at sea but otherwise doing no harm, today that storm moved east, pushing its way ashore along the length of the Straits of Juan de Fuca, bringing charcoal gray clouds, low visibility, high winds and heavy rain.

Housewives in Victoria bowed to the inevitable and took their laundry indoors. Children stared out the window at the rain soaked lawn and wondered if summer would ever come back. The new Empress Hotel was being built by the Canadian Pacific Railway, to attract tourists to Victoria. The masons working on the facade downed tools, declared an afternoon holiday and directed their steps indoors. Rum and a warm fire at one of the many taverns that ringed the inner harbor could be an effective antidote to snotty weather.

At the Ross Bay Cemetery, where the headstones cling like limpets to a finger of rock and gravel that points south into the Straits, the blue and black rolling waves slammed onto those rocks and smooth pounded stones, then splintered into a million diamonds of white, joining the rain which showered down upon the small party of mourners gathered around two graves.

Miss Francis Harcus ground her teeth, and tried not to flinch as another soaking sheet of wind-driven spray and rain washed over her back. She had picked the date. She had made the arrangements. She had paid for everything in advance. She intended to proceed regardless of the weather. She would not bow to inconvenient circumstances. Never, ever. Never!

"Almighty God," began Tommy Crawford, a member of the congregation whom Francis had asked to conduct the committal service, "we pray that you will send the Holy Ghost to dwell among us, and comfort us, as we commit two of your Saints to the earth." All heads were bowed, nearly all eyes were closed.

Another wave crashed behind Francis, and her first instinct was to duck. She was drenched, wet to the skin, water dripped from her nose and she was starting to shiver. Her umbrella was a twisted mess of wire and shredded fabric. She ground her teeth harder and pressed her eyelids even more firmly shut. She stood ramrod straight. At the same time she tried to hover over little Florence and protect her from the weather.

Miss Margaret Harcus, sister to Francis, stood on the other side of Florence. Margaret was so angry she could spit. Not that anyone would notice a bit more moisture, but it might make her feel better. She had discreetly mentioned, and more than once, she thought, more than once, that perhaps-maybe - there was really no hurry, no need, you see? To hold another service at the cemetery today? Today? That was the point she was trying to make. Also "another service", didn't that say it all?

Months ago, before Christmas, soon after they received the telegram bringing them the terrible news, they had held a proper memorial service at the church, with a reception after. True, they held the service without the two bodies, but at that time they had not known when, or even if, the bodies could be recovered and sent home. What was the point of today's service ? Francis kept saying it was a committal service. Committal of what? This was a charade. Did Francis actually expect her to believe there were two dead bodies in these two very plain caskets that had been made in China and shipped to Victoria from Hong Kong? Did Francis really believe that the mortal remains of Jean, their sister-in-law, and their brother, James, had been transported halfway across China during a civil war in that country, then loaded aboard a ship and sent half a world away to the West Coast of Canada? Margaret started to laugh, then turned the laugh into a choking sob, hand in front of her face.

Fine. She would play her part. But she would bet two nickels and a box of hatpins that those two caskets were filled with rocks, shells and sand, and that Francis had paid for everything, including the rocks, shells and sand. Anything to keep up appearances. Although why that was important she didn't know. Besides the undertaker, and his staff, there was only old Willie, their Chinese house boy, Mr. Robinson from the bank, their immediate neighbors the Denbigh's and the Harshman's, and Frederick, who had wisely urged his elderly parents to stay home.

She stifled her laughter, but enjoyed watching her sister as the heavy starch of her black mourning ensemble leached away, reshaping itself revealingly over her sisters ample torso. Another wave crashed and was spun into spindrift and it was like being hit with a full bucket of cold water. This time Francis did flinch and Margaret did laugh, out loud. Margaret thought in straight lines. Unfortunately, Victorian society and the proprieties of the day insisted she speak in circles. But each bucket of cold water was a little speech, all by itself. She laughed again.

Mr. Doniger, the Senior Partner of Doniger and Sons, Undertakers and Morticians, was determined to say as little as possible to all concerned. Miss Francis Harcus hadn't asked him a direct question and Doniger wasn't volunteering to answer any question not asked. His staff had been told to say nothing - absolutely nothing - and refer all questions to him. He had simply reported to Miss Francis Harcus that he was in receipt of the two caskets she had ordered and paid for. He said no more, no less. She asked about dates. She asked twice. He said, it's your choice. She selected a date. He said fine. She asked the price - she asked! - and paid for a full committal service. Including embalming. And here they were. "In Jesus' name we pray, Amen," finished Crawford.

Amen indeed. Doniger kept his eyes closed and his head bowed because he didn't want to watch as his best dark green awning was flogged to pieces as the frame holding it up collapsed. He didn't want to see the two shallow graves scraped out of the gravel that was literally the burial ground in this poor excuse for a cemetery. He didn't want to see the two coffins that he had personally nailed shut with his own hands. His own hands. Because then he would remember the telegram he had received nearly a month ago. Sent from Hong Kong. By the shipping agent for Canadian Pacific Steamships, Ltd.

"Am in receipt last remains M/Mrs J. Harcus Stop Authorities here insist immediate cremation Stop Cannot ship please advise Stop CPS Ltd."

Doniger knew that death occurred many months ago. He didn't know that Jean and James had been hacked to death by an angry mob of anti-Christian belligerents determined to drive away the white faced Christian missionaries, but he had been a mortician for over 35 years. He could well imagine the state of the bodies. He had wired back immediately: "Family advises immediate cremation. Bill me c/o Victoria." He supposed he would get stuck for the expense. Miss Francis Harcus was unlikely to part with even one more penny. And if any of this got out, he would have no choice but to move somewhere else. Maybe Chile.

"Precious," said Crawford in his soft Scots burr, "precious in the sight of the Lord is the death of his Saints." He was speaking without notes or a text, although he did have a small Bible in a dry pocket under his arm and close to his heart. "I'm not a minister with a college degree, I'm not a priest with fancy vestments and a church decorated with golden images. I'm just a man who has listened and heard the Lord." And here God added his own pounding, howling crescendo of agreement, and Crawford had to stop and wait for it to subside. "What He tells us," he finally went on, "is that He loves us so much that he sent His only Son who died on the cross so that we might live and have eternal life. Which is why the Lord celebrates and welcomes home His children." Florence liked this part. And as she was wearing a waterproof fisherman's jacket complete with hood that Margaret had cut down to her size, she hardly noticed the bad weather.

"James and Jean are not here with us," Crawford continued. Doniger shuddered, and prepared to run for his life. Did Crawford know?

Margaret's thought was, "Amen!"

"To be absent from the body is what?" Crawford asked. "Anybody?"

No one spoke, but then Margaret realized how few people were present, so she blurted out , "To be present with the Lord." What a bunch of ninnies, thought Margaret. Stand here and freeze for want of a bit of scripture.

"To be absent from the body is to be present with the Lord, that's right. Jean and James are in Heaven, right now, at peace and at rest, their journey over, for ever and ever. Amen." For the rest of her life, that's how Florence saw her parents, living in Heaven, with God, in one of those many mansions. She hoped they had a nice garden.

"A bit more butter, if you please," said Frederick Wentworth III, leaning over the tea table. He would avoid the seed cake at all costs, but the hot tea scones smelled divine.

They had all walked back to the Harcus home in Oak Bay. Margaret had changed out of her black mourning, and wore pink and white. Francis had gone upstairs and Margaret suspected she would not be back. Besides Florence, the Denbigh's and the Harshman's were the only persons present. Willie had built up the fire, and with Francis absent, Margaret had discreetly offered sherry to one and all. She herself was on her second glass.

"So good of you to come," she murmured to Frederick.

"Nonsense. My best friend," Frederick murmured back. He and James had been at school together. Frederick had been his best man at his wedding to Jean. Carrying his butter drenched scones on a flowered bone china plate, Haviland, he was certain of it, Frederick returned to standing in front of the fire. It warmed his wet legs. Nice home. Worth quite a bit. Damn good looking woman, too, thought Frederick. Good figure. Not at all like her sister. Francis was such a prig. That part worried him. You'd hate to find out later that Margaret was just like her sister.

Wonder how much of their father's money they've got left? Frederick smiled at Florence who had come to stand beside him at the fire. Pretty child. Frederick had tried to sound out Robinson from the bank after the service, but the poor man had been soaking wet, his teeth chattering so hard he was unable to speak. Frederick put him in a cab and sent him on his way. Maybe try again over a good dinner? He wasn't sure. He'd have to think on it.

In due course, the neighbors left and Frederick knew it was time for him to leave as well. He said his thanks, patted Florence on the head, shook hands with Margaret – damn, she was a pretty girl - and left. Outdoors, he stopped in the shelter of the brick porch to light a cigar. Normally, he would be out to the club this time of day, after playing a quick nine holes, and would be enjoying a late dinner in the bar.

Considering the weather, and the service, the golf had been out of the question. But the bar wasn't. He went to find a cab.

Victoria, August 1909

Stroke. Stroke. Stroke. Stroke. Stroke. Glide. The boat surged forward. Check your direction. Smile. Repeat. Stroke, stroke, stroke, stroke, stroke, glide. Smile. Frederick felt the beginnings of confidence. This wasn't so hard. Indeed, it felt good to use your muscles to propel yourself in such an elegant way.

It was a spectacular summer day. A day when the weather actually matched the August date. Not a cloud in the sky. A very light breeze, just enough wind to keep the mosquitoes at a distance. The surface of the water reflected back four figures seated in a long, narrow lapstrake rowboat. Florence sat wedged in the bow. Margaret had draped herself all over the stern. She carried a cream-colored parasol. Frederick was in the rowing seat, wearing double-breasted blue and a hat with more gold braid than Admiral Lord Nelson had ever worn in his entire career. Francis was perched on the third seat forward from the stern, in-between Frederick and Florence in the bow. She held on with both hands to each side of the boat with white-knuckle courage. She disliked boats. More to the point, she hated Frederick. He reminded her of that totally no good son of Queen Victoria's. The Prince of Wales. Now the King of England.

Margaret shimmered in lacy folds of sheerest muslin, all white, white, white, relieved only by yellow roses, perfect stems, twined artfully about the wide lacy brim of her hat. She smiled. She and Frederick enjoyed a flirtation of sideways glances, nodded heads and dipped shoulders, smiles and laughter, with hardly a word spoken. It had been over a year since her sister Jean was buried. It was time for romance.

This went on for nearly an hour, as Frederick moved their boat through the Gorge, a long ribbon of salt-water lagoon, bordered on both sides by substantial and stately homes, with striped sun awnings, porch swings, perfect green lawns, ordered rows of rose bushes. Occasionally, they passed a lapstrake boat like their own rocking gently against the shoreline, seats empty, the occupants spread out on shore like laundry drying in the sun, enjoying a picnic, or replete and resting after their meal.

Frederick had set himself some goals for today. There were a few things he needed to know before he and Margaret could have a really serious conversation.

"Margaret," he said as he leaned towards her, and spoke quietly, "has your sister always worn black?"

Margaret had been waiting and hoping for questions like this. She recognized the serious nature of this preliminary question. "Always? Oh, no," she said with resolution, shaking her head, no, as well.

"But I always see her in black," persisted Frederick.

"Lately? Oh, yes." She nodded yes as well, and her eyes met his and didn't flit away.

"And she's wearing black today." It was not a question. Francis was wearing black.

"Yes," Margaret agreed.

"Why?"

"It's difficult to understand, Frederick." On such an intimate topic, Margaret thought she could use his first name. "Think of her as in mourning. For Queen Victoria."

Frederick did not understand. "Victoria died six years ago."

"I believe that is correct. And Francis still wears black in her memory."

"But…"

Margaret put her hand on Frederick's arm. "It's a little bit like playing dress up. If it makes her happy, who does it hurt?" Frederick picked up his sweeps and began to row again.

Very well, thought Frederick, very well. If she does no harm…. He stole a glance at Francis over his shoulder. She was, indeed, dressed all in black. If only that had been all. Her dress was long sleeved, high necked, ankle length, unrelieved black. A black sun hat. Frederick didn't know such a garment was available. She was also wearing another garment which Frederick guessed was designed to be a life vest. It reminded Frederick of two dozen long, black bolognas, tied together into a cape, or coat. Heavy, bulky, absurd. He took another glance to be certain. She sat with her eyes closed. Sweat dripped from her chin. It was like a rehearsal for a disaster at sea.

Oh, well, thought Frederick. No harm. Even if she lives with us, we'll have a big house. I won't see her except for the occasional dinner. No harm. He flexed his shoulders and pulled on his sweeps, nodded that he understood, and smiled his acceptance of eccentricity. Margaret was proud of him. It was a lot for a man to swallow. They were going to be very happy.

They passed a small boatyard, and the sound of caulking mallets came to them across the water, and the smell of paint and turpentine. A small workboat with a gasoline engine towing a single huge boomstick passed them going the other direction. The boatman tipped his hat to Frederick. There was an old Indian man squatting on his haunches at the tide line. Florence waved, he waved back. No one else seemed to see this man.

"You know," said Frederick, "last Sunday there must have been a hundred boats out on the Waters."

"Then isn't this more pleasant," cooed Margaret.

"Very beautiful," Frederick said, catching Margaret's glance and staring straight into her eyes. Margaret held the glance, then blushed and looked away.

"How far?" croaked Francis. She sounded like a raven croaking.

"What?" said Frederick.

"What did she say?" insisted Margaret..

"How far?" repeated Florence, in a quiet voice from the bow.

"Florence says ...", began Frederick, but Margaret cut him off.

"Yes. Thank you Florence. Now Francis," she went on much more sharply, "you know we talked of going as far as the Esquimalt Bridge." Francis remembered no such conversation. Neither did Frederick. But if that was where Margaret wanted to go, so be it.

"Your wish," he said gallantly to Margaret....

"Nonsense", interrupted Francis. "That will take us another hour and I am not going to sit here for another hour." Another hour and it was a certainty, she would vomit.

"Ah, see there, the Chestertons," said Frederick, tapping Margaret on the knee and indicating another passing boat. He gave some hard pulls on the oars, trying to keep pace. But the Chestertons had two men rowing, and pulled away. Frederick and Margaret both waved, and Mrs. Chesterton, seated in the stern, waved back.

"That must be her brother rowing in front of Bob," speculated Margaret.

"Yes, I think you're right", said Frederick. "Had lunch with Bob yesterday at the Club. Told me an awful story about that Reverend Doctor Smith."

"Oh, dear, is Doctor Smith unwell?"

"No, no his health is fine, at least so far."

"Such a nice man. We had him to dinner last week. Lamb with mint sauce. He ate with good appetite. Said they seldom see lamb. Such courageous work." The Reverend was raising funds for his missionary church in West Africa.

"Certainly worth doing, as long as you do what you say." Frederick stopped. He had a terrible thought. "I hope, that is to say…I hate to ask…but you didn't give him any money?" It wasn't exactly scandal, but you didn't want to end up the laughingstock of Victoria.

"Oh, no, no, no", began Margaret. Frederick felt so relieved. He had almost given the man money himself. But he was short on funds. "I never do that sort of thing, " Margaret went on to assure him.

"Why?' cut in Francis. No one except Florence heard her. "WHY?" Francis asked much more loudly.

Because of the preemptory tone, Frederick answered without thinking. "Because he was arrested. Seems he doesn't actually have a missionary church in Africa."

"NONSENSE," retorted Francis. "NONSENSE."

"Miss Harcus," Frederick began.

"I have seen the photographs!"

Frederick tried to reason with her, which was always a mistake. He twisted around on his seat, so he could face her. "The photographs are real," he tried to explain patiently, "but unfortunately there is no relationship between the good doctor, the Church or the photographs, and the authorities have taken him into custody and charged him with fraud."

"I don't believe it," said Francis "I - DO - NOT - BELIEVE -IT." She had secretly and quietly given the good Doctor $600.00. Cash. Money she could ill afford to spend. There had to be a Church . "He is a man of God."

Frederick didn't like being yelled at. "Perhaps," said Frederick with irritation, before Margaret could stop him, "but he is apparently neither a Doctor of Divinity nor an ordained minister."

"LIES!" shouted Francis, rising to her feet.

"Miss Harcus…", began Frederick.

"Francis, sit down at once," said Margaret. The boat was rocking from side to side.

Francis knew she was going to vomit, and standing, she tried to lean out over the side of the boat. The boat tipped a few inches and she lost her balance. Frederick, forgetting where he was, jumped up to save her, dragged her back from the precipice. Unfortunately, they were both leaning the other way over the precipice on the other side of the boat. Now the boat tipped dangerously in this new direction. Directly they both lost their balance. Francis fell first, onto her back, pulling Frederick in, nearly on top of her. He missed only by converting his fall into a sort of head first dive, that swept away his gilded hat and left him floundering upside down, underwater. The boat rocked back to level. Overwhelmed by the romance and the sense of play in this tableaux, Margaret triumphantly rose to her feet, and swooned backwards, in a perfectly choreographed fall, over the stern, into the water. She nearly laughed as she did it. A swoon dive. Suddenly, in less time than it takes to count five, Florence found herself alone in the boat.

Francis, the cold water soaking into her black finery, could not remember another occasion when the water had felt more cooling, more restorative. She closed her eyes, and gave a sound somewhere between a sigh and a moan.

Surreptitiously, as if she was attempting to tread water, Margaret spread her skirts over the water. The sunlight was dazzling. She waited for rescue. This was the moment she and Frederick would re-create for their children and grandchildren over the years. Sitting companionably before the fire in their old age. Sipping tea. How they were swept together by fate.

Frederick was in a total panic. Frederick Wentworth III didn't know how to swim. Had never learned. Could sometimes be heard at the Members Only bar telling his fellows, "I couldn't swim four feet to save my own life." He'd never had to put this to the test. Until today. He was proving himself right.

He thrashed. He flailed. He kicked. He clawed. But there was nothing to claw or grab, except water. Worst, there was no air. He had to breathe. His chest was heaving. Oh please God don't let me drown save me save me save me save me save me save me save me save…. His head found the surface. He gulped a mouthful, half air, half water. He choked. He spit. He screamed, "Help." What he thought was a mighty bellow, was really a very small chirp. But Margaret heard him.

Love was still alive as she waded to his side. Love was dying as she tapped him on the shoulder. He grabbed at her. Twisted his legs around her in a frenzy. Climbed her like a ladder to the pure sweet air of August.

"Frederick," she attempted, but he was too far gone. "Frederick," she said, and she slapped him hard across the face. "STAND UP YOU NINNY ITS

ONLY FOUR FEET DEEP." Frederick unwrapped and extended his legs. He feet touched the bottom. He stood up, and looked on the face of his beloved. All he saw there was contempt. Taking him by the arm, Margaret led him ashore, where he sank down on his knees, kissed the ground, and sobbed hysterically.

Florence, for reasons she could never explain, had taken the oars and rowed ashore, but to the opposite bank. She sat, beached, safe, but a hundred yards away. Margaret had reached her limit. She was through pretending. She ripped off her soggy white sun hat and slammed it to the ground, scattering wet yellow rose petals all over someone's green lawn. Then she sat down and pulled off her shoes and stockings.

"But Francis", implored Frederick, "Save…"

"Francis could swim from here to Japan," Margaret said with asperity. She, Francis and Florence had all learned to swim at the Crystal Palace Pool. "She could have rescued you, me and the boat, if she wanted to."

"But her life vest," protested Frederick.

"She was just being silly," Margaret said, as she ripped through thirty tiny pearl buttons, and added the shredded blouse to her growing pile of wet clothes stacked on shore.

"That seems damned odd," opined Frederick, pushing himself up into a sitting position. He felt he might eventually regain the upper hand. "Damned odd."

"No, Frederick," said Margaret, standing up to step out of her long skirt. She ripped a piece of lace off her hat and tied her long hair in a knot at the back of her head. "Odd, damned odd, is when a man rents a boat to take three ladies out for the day, but doesn't know how to swim. Or wade," she added, driving home the last nail. "Excuse me." Dressed in a short cotton chemise, her shoulders bare and the sun glistening on her wet skin, Margaret dove into the water and proceeded to swim across to Florence and the boat.

Lunch, December 1918

Tuesday, Florence had the big brick house at the top of Rucker Hill all to herself. She could wander from room to room, gaze at her leisure at the panoramic view of both the Cascade and the Olympic Mountains, at the bustle of the activity on the waterfront down below. She could sit wherever she liked, do what she wanted. She liked the empty silence. There was no one to tell her she had to do this, or do that.

Susie had Tuesday as her day off. Susie was the housekeeper. Monday was washday. Susie, who was seventy, and barely five feet tall, washed and ironed and did the work of several people all day. There was noise from carrying in extra firewood and filling tubs with hot water. Clothing, sheets and table linens were carried upstairs and down. There was what seemed like confusion to Florence all day, although Susie had a routine that was designed to get all the work done.

Part of the routine was that on Monday, Florence prepared dinner. Without fail on Sunday, Susie would serve a huge standing rib roast after Church. Oven browned potatoes and carrots. Brussels sprouts. Fresh rolls. Fruit pie, chocolate cake and cookies. On Monday, it was up to Florence to slice and serve the cold beef. She peeled and boiled some potatoes, all under Susie's watchful eye, reheated the vegetables in some melted butter. Warmed up the leftover gravy. All easy. Nothing Susie couldn't supervise while ironing shirts and sheets from wet to dry.

Florence cut herself the first time she tried to use the carving knife, bleeding all over the rare roast beef. Susie shushed her, wrapped the cut fingers in a dish towel, rinsed the meat in the sink and taught Florence how to sharpen a knife and carve without getting her fingers in the way.

On her day off, Susie always went to visit her sister and brother-in-law at their farm "near Snohomish". Florence had no idea where that was. Mr. and Mrs. Waters ate at the Golf Club. The children were at boarding school in Seattle, but would soon be home for Christmas.

Wearing an old floor length dress of Mrs. Waters that Susie had helped her alter, particularly the bodice, which had to be made much smaller, Florence was in the kitchen making Spritz, a Norwegian butter cookie Susie had taught her to make. In a big, brown bowl she let one pound of butter soften. Then she added one cup of sugar, salt, a little vanilla, an egg, and she creamed this mixture together.

Next she worked in a cup of sifted flour. Then more flour. She worked quickly, careful not to let the dough get too warm. You want a stiff dough, Susie explained. Now fill a hand cranked dough press. Put the rest of your dough on the ice. On the bread board, crank your dough out into ribbons. Hurry, said Susie. You don't want your dough to get too warm. Using a small knife, cut a length of dough long enough to go around your thumb, then gently press the dough together to form a circle. Put the cookie on a baking sheet. Repeat. Bake two dozen at a time, eight to ten minutes. Watch them carefully.

They'll burn if you don't pay attention. Hurry. Do it again. Again. Again. You should end up with about a dozen, dozen. Pack in tins. Hide from Mrs. Waters. This last instruction said very quietly.

Florence took her last batch out of the oven. Her cookies weren't all a nice uniform size, but she hadn't burned any. And she was certain the taste was the same. Susie was probably the only one who could tell the difference. She felt very pleased.

Someone knocked on the front door. Florence washed her hands, took off her apron, ran for the door. She was reaching for the knob, when the door burst open, smashing into her right foot, which saved her from a broken nose. But her foot hurt so badly she almost fell down.

"Florence," Mrs. Waters gushed. "Darling." And she captured Florence in an enfolding embrace. Florence was lost in the folds of her Aunt's fancy brown silk, ample bosom, and the overwhelming reek of cigarettes and liquor mixed with the cloying floral scent of her perfume. There were shrieks of delight as other women crowded past through the front door.

"Florence", Mrs. Waters said again, standing up straight and actually managing to walk a few steps. "They're painting at the Club for another Victory party." Mrs. Waters added her coat to the heap in the middle of the entry way floor. The Armistice ending the War had been signed a month ago. "The Club positively reeks of paint thinner, so we came here." There were shrieks from the dining room, the clink of glasses, and Florence realized they were all very drunk. "Be a good girl," Mrs. Water cooed, patting her on the cheek. "Make us lunch." Florence felt frozen in place. "Now," Mrs. Waters barked. "And hang up these coats." Then she stomped off in the direction of the dining room, and the party got even louder.

Nine pair of beady glass eyes stared back at her from the hall floor. Nine dead foxes now had the pleasure of adorning nine wool coats. Florence picked up this menagerie and hung it in the hall closet. Lunch for nine. She didn't think the ladies were going to be happy with the grilled cheese sandwich she had been planning on fixing for herself. Florence went to the kitchen and sat down, her head in her hands. What was she going to do? She had never made lunch from scratch for nine people in her life. Plus, there was no food in the house. It was impossible. Surely Mrs. Waters knew it was impossible. Florence would remind her. Patiently explain: There is no food. Up, she half opened the door to the dining room. Sound washed over her. There were a dozen bottles on the sideboard. Several were empty. The three women she could see were all dressed expensively, elegantly, in the new fashions she had seen at Chaffee's downtown. Dresses with hemlines just above the ankle. No bustles.Less ornamented, more simple clothes than any of the women would have owned – or worn – before the War. They seemed larger than life, they laughed so hard, talked so loud: animated, expressive and sure of themselves. They were also having a hard time standing up, and most of the party had been seated, including Mrs. Waters, who did not look prepared for a quiet conversation with Florence. She retreated to the kitchen

What was there to eat? There was most of a four layer chocolate cake in the pantry. The slices would be thin, but she could cut nine slices, and serve it with spoonfuls of Susie's pitted pie cherries. Yes, and she was sure she had cream she could whip, she knew how to do that. Plus coffee. That took care of dessert. What else?

There was nothing on the top rack of the cooler besides the cream, milk, butter and eggs she expected. That, and half a round of the sharp cheddar Florence used for grilled cheese.

On bottom, laid on top of the ice, was a waxed paper parcel of sliced bacon. Probably no more than half a pound. That wasn't going to provide lunch. Down on her hands and knees, Florence stuck her head inside the icebox so she could see all sides of the ice. What was that? There was a parcel wrapped in butcher paper, tied with twine, that had fallen on the back side of the block of ice, out of sight. She pulled the parcel out. It was squishy in her hand, but what she immediately noticed was the smell. It was fish. And it was not fresh. Florence cut the twine and laid the open package on the counter. Inside were six salmon steaks. This is probably fish, thought Florence, that Susie bought inexpensively to boil up for the cats. Normally Florence would have said the steaks were spoiled and put them in the trash. The dining room door banged open and Mrs. Waters barged through the kitchen.

"We're getting hungry out here. Oh, salmon." She stopped, swaying back and forth.. Florence could see her trying to focus on the fish. She shook her head. "Excellent idea, Florence." And then she was gone.

Florence did not think these salmon steaks were an excellent idea, but they were all she had. Quickly, she built up the blaze in the fire box. Then she hauled a huge copper casserole out from a shelf in the pantry and placed it on the stove top. She chopped all the remaining bacon and tossed it in the pot, along with a diced up onion. The bacon spit and sizzled. After a few minutes she gently set the salmon steaks on top of the bacon and onions and added cold water to cover. Then she washed her hands using the Fels Naphtha to get rid of the smell. She wadded up the fish wrappings and stuffed them in the fire box. Best to burn the evidence.

While the fish simmered, she peeled six potatoes and diced them small. The fish cooked quickly. Using a big spoon, she took the filets out of the pot, peeled away the skin and picked out the bones. She tossed her potatoes, diced, into the simmering liquid. While the potatoes cooked, she broke the filets up into smaller pieces. When the potatoes were tender she smashed them up a bit to thicken her liquid, then added the fish back to the pot. Added salt and pepper. There were a dozen eggs. In a pan with gently simmering water, she poached all twelve. While she waited for the eggs, she sliced the cake, put it on separate plates, spooned out the cherries, whipped the cream. When the potatoes and fish were hot, she poured all the whipping cream she had left, plus some milk, for a total of about three quarts, into the casserole, and removed the pan from the heat.

As far as she was concerned, all she had done so far was make a chowder. She had watched their houseboy in Victoria make chowder hundreds of times. She served the chowder in soup bowls, gently sliding a poached egg into each bowl, dusting the top with paprika.

The table sparkled in the afternoon light, and the ladies ooo'ed and ahhed over the silver, and the fine linen napkins, the Royal Doulton china and the cut glass crystal. It was all, Florence thought, just like Aunt Francis would have expected. Then they tried the soup. The poached eggs made a huge impression, becoming pretty yellow swirls when you pricked the yolk, and because it was a chowder, everyone forgave May for serving them a cheap food like fish. They said it was rich and delicious. Since Florence had no intentions of tasting any herself, she was willing to accept their opinion as gospel. Mrs. Waters even had a second bowl. Florence wasn't certain that was wise, but there was no way to stop her, so she served a second bowl, followed immediately by dessert.

In ones and twos the ladies drifted away after lunch in a haze of cigarette smoke, hugs and kisses, until finally there was only Florence and Mrs. Waters. That great lady stretched herself at full length on the drawing room sofa, and fell deeply asleep.

Florence ate the remaining two poached eggs with some toast, in the kitchen. Then she cleaned up. Her fist act was to pour away down the drain, and into the garbage, all of the remaining chowder. As she cleared the table, she could hear Mrs. Water snoring, and once, an intestinal sound that Florence had been taught polite company does not acknowledge or discuss. When everything was clean and back in its place, she crept upstairs to the children's playroom. There was a small grand piano, left behind after their childhood lessons. From memory, she played quieter pieces from Chopin and Liszt, and was quite lost to time until someone knocked on the playroom door.

"Florence?'

"Sir?" It was Mr. Waters, back from the club to pick up Mrs. so they could have dinner. He was a stocky man, powerfully built. He enjoyed telling stories of Wyoming, where he claimed to have grown up as a cowboy.

"Where's Mrs. Waters?"

"She was asleep in the living room last I saw her, Sir."

"Well, she's not there now. May," he called. He walked off towards Mrs. Waters separate bedroom. "May!" Florence could hear doors opening, being shut. Then he was back at the playroom door. "I suppose you emptied all those gin bottles in the dining room?"

He sounded quite serious. Florence never knew when he was being serious, when he was teasing her. But Mr. Waters didn't like to be teased back. Occasionally, when he told his Wyoming stories, his wife would laugh skeptically, and tell anyone listening that her husband had grown up on a potato farm in Idaho and that the only ranching he had ever done was with the family cow. Once, after company had left, Mr. Waters hit his wife, telling her to shut up. Mr. Waters frightened Florence.

"Oh, no, Sir," she protested. Then she saw he was smiling.

"Good. Never drink rot-gut gin. Drink the good stuff." Then he was gone again.

Florence wasn't certain how to respond to that advice, so she said nothing.

"May, what in God's name are you doing?" she heard him say. She walked out into the upstairs hall. There was a loud retching, gagging sound. Then Florence could see that Mrs. Waters was on her hands and knees in the bathroom. Vomiting. She coughed, choked, and it happened again. All over the tile floor. And again.

Mr. Waters pulled a bath towel off the towel bar and tossed it at his wife.

"I don't suppose," drawled Mr. Waters, "that you wish to go with me to the Club for dinner."

Mrs. Waters spewed her answer all over the bathroom floor.

"No, I didn't think so. Try and help her, Florence." He made to leave.

Mrs. Waters was gasping for air. "Poison," she said loudly and distinctly, although Florence thought she might have said, "Poissin", the French word for fish.

"I dare say, you stupid cow. How many times have I warned you not to drink that cheap gin?"

"The soup," Mrs. Waters gasped, gagging up a small sample for inspection.

Mr. Waters laughed. "May, there are six empty bottles on the sideboard in the dining room. Please, trust me. My slot machines are in the finest drinking establishments here and in Seattle. Rot-gut is rot-gut, and rot-gut will make you sick. Florence," he concluded, which startled her.

"Sir?"

"Pour out those bottles in the dining room."

"Yes, Sir."

Mr. Waters turned to inspect his wife. He wondered if it would be worthwhile to stay home. He could send Florence downtown in a cab for dinner. He would strip off May's clothes. Bathe her. Then do what he wanted to her body. Since their last child was born nineteen years ago, May had not been willing to have sex. Today, tonight, she certainly wasn't going to be able to stop him. The thought of all that white naked flesh, under his control, gave him an erection. But the smell of the vomit was disgusting And it would take too much effort for the minimal reward of revenge. God knew, she wasn't any fun in bed. He could purchase what he needed with far fewer consequences and much more pleasure. He turned abruptly on his heel, clattered down the stairs, and was gone. "It was the soup," Mrs. Waters moaned. Florence didn't say anything. She started soaking towels in the sink to clean the bathroom floor.

Driving Lessons

It was just a bit before half-past five. The sun had not risen higher than the Cascade Mountains, but the sunrise was on its way, sending a thin red glow that traced the outlines of Mount Pilchuck, Glacier, White Horse and Three Sisters. Florence sat in the kitchen, huddled over her first cup of coffee, reading the morning paper. She was very careful not to wrinkle or spill on the front page.

"WILSON VISITS EUROPE," screamed the headline. She read on with interest. The early morning had become her favorite time of day. She was the first one up and dressed. The house was quiet. The crackle of the wood stove. Although the Waters were talking of buying one of the new electric stoves. Florence didn't understand how an electric stove was going to warm you up in the morning.

There was the sound of an automobile going down the hill behind the house. It was a relatively new sound. More and more people owned personal automobiles. At six, there was a symphony of steam whistles, especially from Clough and Hartley, the big shingle mill on the waterfront. While people claimed all the whistles had a purpose, Florence thought the operators occasionally sounded off just for fun. Florence didn't really care. The whistles were part of the background of noises, along with the trains, the slamming and bangs of boxcars, the tugs and other shipping in the harbor, the whine of huge saws. Florence had seen saw blades as tall as she was with teeth the size of her fists, biting into a saw log. And the smells, the vinegar like smell of freshly cut cedar. And the cinders from all the mill trash burners. At night the domes of the trash burners glowed red. And in the morning, everything was covered in cinders. You learned to hang laundry in the basement, and gauge the direction of the wind, and only hang laundry outside on a wind out of the south.

It was a cold, clear morning, and the air had smelled of sulfur and rotten eggs when she stepped outside to fetch the paper. It was the smell of cooked wood chips, of paper being made.

"It's the smell of money," Mr. Waters would cut her off when she complained.

"It's the smell of money," he would repeat. "The fools have to make it before I can take it away," he sometimes added. He never spoke directly about his business, but Florence had concluded that it involved gambling and wasn't entirely legal.

She read on. President Wilson was to give a speech addressing all the leaders of the European countries. He was trying to convince them to form something called a "League of Nations." The newspaper was printed in Seattle. She had visited Seattle exactly once, although the Waters' traveled there once or twice a month, in her experience. Their two children went to schools in Seattle.

Carefully she folded the newspaper open. She read the advertisements. One store in Seattle fascinated her. A department store called Frederick and Nelson. So many social events were held there and reported on the Society page . Fashion shows were chronicled. The women pictured wore the latest styles that showed a woman's legs. Florence still wore dresses and skirts that swept her shoe tops. These women had shorter dresses, and in a few cases, very short hair. Her own hair still hung to her waist, although she always wore it up and back during the day. Some of the clothes pictured in the newspaper were from Paris. Her own clothes were all hand-me-downs. She longed to attend a fashion show. To buy new things. There were line drawings in magazines, and occasionally a pattern, but the fabrics described either didn't exist, or weren't available in Everett. She suspected the latter was the real situation.

She heard a door upstairs close. She carefully re-folded the newspaper, and filled the silver pot with hot coffee. She set two pieces of bread to toast. Lightly buttered, served with strawberry preserves in a small dish at the side. Everything went on a silver tray. She took the tray and the newspaper, into the dining room, and set everything at Mr. Waters' place at the head of the table. She filled his coffee cup and stepped aside as he stomped in, pulled out his chair and sat down.

"Toast?" he barked.

"Ready, Sir." He grunted.

"Two eggs."

"Right away, Sir." He didn't always have eggs, but Florence was ready. She returned to the kitchen and put two coddled eggs in individual egg cups. "Buzzz." There was an electric switch beneath the carpet that he could press with his foot. "Buzzz." Florence hated the buzzer but she answered the summons.

"Jam?" he demanded.

"On your tray, Sir." He grunted. Florence didn't understand how he could ask the same stupid questions every morning. Didn't he look at what was on the tray?

"Eggs."

"Coming, Sir."

As the buzzer sounded again, she served the eggs. She had one for herself, and she sat at the dining table to eat it. Good, the yolk was runny the way he liked, the white just barely set. Perfect.

"Salt." She passed him the salt. Mrs. Waters place at the other end of the table was empty. Mrs. Waters was seldom awake before ten, and she generally just took a cup of tea in her room, which was why Florence supposed Mr. Waters asked that she sit with him while he ate.

"Well, I see that ass Wilson is in Europe."

"Yes, I saw that."

"Damn fool should stay home and quit interfering. Who cares if all those damn foreigners kill themselves in another war."

Mr. Waters, and for that matter everyone else she knew in Everett, seemed to forget that she was a foreigner. They lapsed back into silence. Florence was surprised when he filled his own coffee cup, pushed back his chair, and sat for five minutes staring out the window.

"Florence," he finally asked, "do you drive?"

"Do you mean an automobile?"

"Yes."

"Oh, no, Sir."

"That's what I thought. Well, you're going to have to learn."

She thought of the steep hills, the twists and turns of the narrow streets on Rucker Hill, and she was filled with fear.

"Sir, I don't think I could learn."

"You're going to have to learn," Mr. Waters pressed his point, "because Mrs. Waters should not be driving. I'm spending too much time away from my business to be her chauffeur." Most afternoons, Mrs. Waters was drunk. She had had several 'accidents' with the car. Florence knew Mr. Waters had paid handsomely to hush the incidents up and leave the police and the courts ignorant of his wife's behavior.

Florence had lived with the Waters' for nearly two years, but she still hadn't puzzled out what business he was actually in. Mr. Waters said little. His wife said a little more, but it was all ridicule. When Mr. Waters chose to reply, it was to remind his wife that she enjoyed spending his money.

Mr. Waters stood up and slapped his newspaper onto the table. "I'm late. But I'll be back at three. Be ready to go for a drive." He drained his coffee cup and left.

Florence cleared the table. Washed and put away the dishes. Collected the freshly delivered milk from the stoop. Sat quietly in the kitchen, listening to the beating of her heart, waiting for Susie to arrive at eight. Hoping that Mr. Waters had not been serious, or would forget the idea, or forget to come home at three. Mr. Waters did not forget. At three he was home, and he took her by the elbow, and led her outside to the drivers side of the automobile. The engine was running.

He turned it off.

"Sit here," he said, opening the door. She sat behind the steering wheel. She folded her hands in her lap and drew up her knees, careful not to touch anything with her hands or feet. Mr. Waters sat in the passenger seat. He lit a cigar, then said through clenched teeth, "Florence, pay attention. When I was younger I trained mules. A good cigar," he blew out a stream of heavy smoke, "was always essential."

Florence didn't move, didn't look at him.

Mr. Waters shrugged. Then he swiveled in his seat, bringing his right hand across his body and hit her on the tip of her right shoulder. Hard. Florence cried out in surprise, her whole body shaking, rubbing her shoulder, and turned to look at him. He laughed.

"Now that I have your attention," he began. He explained the use of the brake, the gas pedal, clutch, gear shift. He made her operate each pedal. The he got out, cranked the engine. The motor started. He climbed back in. Reached across her to release the handbrake. On his instructions she pushed in the clutch pedal. He engaged first gear and told her, "Step on the gas." The car lurched forward twenty feet.

"Steer," he shouted, twisting the wheel. Completely confused, Florence put her hands on the steering wheel with a feeling of hopelessness. She didn't know where she was going, or what to do.

"Left," he barked, and together they executed a left turn. The street descended steeply for three blocks. They picked up speed. Florence closed her eyes.

"Brake," he said, punching her on the arm again. "Open your goddamn eyes." Her eyes flew open and with both feet she pushed down on the brake. The engine stalled as they skidded to a stop.

"Christ," he cursed. He hit her again. The same place. He shoulder throbbed. It was getting quite sore. "Are you a fool, girl? Are you stupid? Keep your eyes open." He made to hit her again, but she flinched, and cried out, and he changed his mind. He sat and smoked in silence, paying close attention to the ash on his cigar. Abruptly, he explained all the controls again. Coasting, he had her drive down the hill, getting the feel of the brake. He had her stop on the flat spot at the bottom of the hill on Tulalip Avenue, where he re-started the engine. Then they were off again. She turned right onto Pacific, lurching along slowly in first gear. Another vehicle passed her on the left and she nearly steered off the road to get out of the other drivers way. As instructed she turned left on Rucker, dangerously close in front of a four horse team hauling timbers. The two lead horses shied and the driver cursed at her. She heard him distinctly. She cringed. Mr. Waters laughed. They went north on Rucker. By a miracle, Hewitt, the most heavily traveled street in town was momentarily empty. Mr. Waters didn't bother to explain that she should stop before proceeding across, and she sailed through without a scratch, and none the wiser. They continued north. Occasionally, Florence had a moment to notice the large and imposing homes they were passing. At 19th Street Mr. Waters decided they would have to stop. A block early, he explained the sequence.

"Are you listening to me?" he demanded.

"Yes, Sir."

"Tell me what you're going to do."

"I'm going to stop."

"How?"

"By pushing the brake."

Mr. Waters couldn't fault her explanation, but he was convinced she didn't really know the proper sequence of what to do. They were traveling about fifteen miles an hour as they approached the intersection of 19th and Rucker.

"Take your foot off the gas," he instructed. She did.

"Brake," he said. She hesitated.

"Brake," he shouted. She jammed the pedal to the floor. Unfortunately, it was the gas. The Essex shot ahead

"Brake!!" Florence didn't brake, but she did let up on the gas. As they came up to the intersection, there was another automobile approaching from their right on 19th street. Unless she stopped, or turned, the two vehicles would collide.

"Turn," he screamed, lunging for the wheel and pulling the Essex into a tight right turn. Florence helped him turn. And she found the brake, so they turned sooner and much more sharply and instead of staying in the street, the car jumped the curb, crossed the sidewalk and smashed and flattened a U.S. Mail box mounted on a concrete post. And since she didn't depress the clutch, the engine shuddered, stalled and stopped. There was a moment when the only sound was the slow scrape of metal on metal, as the Essex and the former post box got comfortable, and the savage beating of her heart.

"I told you I couldn't do this."

"You - silly - bitch." And with each word he slapped her across the face. "And if you cry, I'll break your nose."

Florence had grown up surrounded by gentle women. Her father left for China when she was seven. Vaguely, she remembered him reading her an Oz book. Since then, she had grown up reading about the fight in Europe. The brutality of war. The numbers of dead, or wounded, that were now being published were staggering. Closer to home, she had seen men die the day she arrived in Everett. Now Mr. Waters had beaten her. Apparently, this was the way all men were.

Mr. Waters was out, inspecting the damage. He lit a fresh cigar from the butt of the first, then had her release the brake and the clutch with the gears in neutral. Then he and another man who had come out of his house to see what all the commotion was about, pushed the Essex back into the street.

"Thanks," Mr. Waters called.

"Good luck," the man called back, and both he and Mr. Waters laughed.

"Off we go then," Mr. Waters said smugly, tapping his cigar ash into the street and blowing a puff of smoke in her direction. "Right turn."

She turned right. The blocks in north Everett are laid out on a rectangular grid. The ground is flat. At his direction she turned right, right, right, right, right, then left, left, left, left. Clutch, brake, clutch, gas, turn, clutch, gas, gas, gas, brake, turn, clutch. Around and around and around. Stopping and starting. Stopping and starting. Then left. Around and around. When she got better on the flat, he had her drive over to Wetmore, then down to Lombard, then back up to Wetmore, slight hills that only required minimal clutch work. She bit her lip. She sniffed. She wiped away tears she hoped he didn't notice. When he didn't speak, smoking his cigar in silence, she just kept going straight. Once he took out a silver hip flask and took a long drink.

Her arm hurt. Her cheeks stung where he had slapped her. The more she drove the easier it became and she had time to think about other things. Running away. Back to Victoria. She had very little money, some coins left over from a purchase she had made for Mrs. Waters. She doubted she had enough for the fare. She thought about the classified advertisements she saw in the newspaper. Live in help. Could she move out, find work? She didn't know.

"So," he said at last. "Let's put you to the test. Left," he instructed. She turned, and saw what he meant. She was headed straight into the downtown business district. There were dozens of other automobiles on the street. She gripped the wheel harder, and prayed.

Everett High School occupied the block between 24th and 25th. She had to slow, then stop, for students crossing the street. Going south, vehicles were parked on both sides of the street. Pedestrians crossed between cars in the middle of the block, some of them practically stepping in front of her. Didn't people know that was unsafe? Didn't they know she might not see them? Might not stop in time?

Mr. Waters sent her left on Hewitt, traveling down the hill, towards Riverside. As she made the turn Mr. Waters yelled at a man coming out of the bank.

"Hey, Jimmy!"

"Hey!" Jimmy ran after them and jumped on the running board.

"No, no," said Mr. Waters as Florence slowed, "drive on. Jimmy me lad - how be yah?" affecting a bad Irish accent.

"Ah, always the best," said Jimmy in his native Irish brogue. "That's a fancy driver there," he added.

"My wife's niece. Florence, meet Jimmy Sullivan." Florence nodded hello.

"Very fancy", said Jimmy with a wink.

"And what are you doin" on this fine day?"

"Beatin" a few heads, collectin' some debts."

"Glad to hear it," said Mr. Waters, "good lad. Go forth with my blessing." Mr. Waters made the sign of the cross, like a priest blessing his congregation. Jimmy laughed and jumped off at Oaks.

"A good man," Mr. Waters offered. "He works for me."

"What does he do for you?" asked Florence.

"He does his best. So don't you worry about it. Just drive down the hill to

Riverside and then we'll turn around."

On Riverside, the streets were crowded, mostly with men, going in and out of different store fronts. Children played on the steps of the Diefenbaker Building.

"This is where I make my money," gloated Waters. "One armed bandits. Nobody beats the house." Florence didn't know what a one armed bandit was. Or what that had to do with a house. She kept her eyes on the road.

When she was almost to the river, she executed her first U turn. Then she drove back up the hill and at the crest of Colby, started down again. She turned left on Grand, and right on Pacific, and was very relieved to see she was actually headed home. But then he had her turn right onto Laurel.

Laurel circled up the west side of Rucker Hill, at the edge of the bluff. There were some blackberry bushes to the right. Otherwise, it was a long drop to the train tracks and the waterfront. Laurel is narrow and steep. The street was barely the width of her wheels. She walked this way often, the view was spectacular, looking out over the harbor and Puget Sound, the Olympic Mountains far to the west over the top of Whidbey Island, and far to the north, Mt. Baker.

The Rucker Mansion was at the top of the hill where the road turned away from the cliff and traversed east along the face of the hill, in the process passing the Waters' front door. So this was a way home, but it wasn't the way she would have chosen. The engine was beginning to stall and Florence knew she was in trouble.

"What do I do?"

"What do you think?"

"I don't know," she pleaded.

"Do something!" he shouted. She pushed in the clutch and jammed on the brake and they stopped.

"Bad choice," he said quietly, and he hit her over her right ear. She gave a yelp, and he did it again. "Stupid. Downshift, stupid." And he hit her a third time.

Florence wanted it all to end. It had been over an hour since he had hit her last, and she had been hoping the entire afternoon was some sort of mistake. He must see she really was a terrible driver, but she didn't deserve to be hit. Just leave her alone and she would never do this again. Her head felt awful. Her eyes were full of tears, and she was crying, and now he hit her because she was crying. She hated him.

Using both feet, she gave the engine a burst of gas, let up quickly on the clutch, added more gas, and the Essex leapt forward. At the same time, she closed her eyes, and turned the wheel hard to the right, towards the blackberry vines, and the cliff.

Mr. Waters lunged for the wheel. "You silly bitch." He was too late.

Florence swung her right elbow and hit him in the nose, which surprised him more than it hurt. She kicked him. She tried to poke him in the eye with her fingernails. She arched her back, and pushed him away, and since he was intent on gaining control of the steering wheel, he tried to ignore her. She pushed herself backwards right out the door and landed on her head at the edge of the road just in time to watch the Essex roll, all four wheels in the air, the rear wheels still turning, then the sounds of underbrush snapping, ripping, as the Essex continued to roll.

She got her feet under her and she ran. She didn't look back. She ran as fast as she could. Up Laurel. Past the Rucker Mansion. Then east on Laurel until she reached the Water's front door. Up the stairs. Into her bedroom. She slammed the door and locked it. Then she sat down on her bed, head in her hands. Sobbing.

The Essex had started over for a second revolution, but then the body had struck a huge stump, bringing the Essex and Mr. Waters to a smashing stop. Waters couldn't believe his good fortune. He hung there sideways for a few moments, then slowly dragged himself out the driver side door, through the blackberry stickers and up onto Laurel. His hat was missing, his suit was never going to be wearable, but the little bit of blood on his hands wiped off with his handkerchief, he was alive, and there was a very nice sunset. Count your blessings.

Florence had surprised him. He thought she was beaten, but she had fought back. He set a leisurely pace for home. There was no hurry. He intended to enjoy her final humiliation.

The house was completely dark, and very quiet, when he let himself in. No door was locked against him. A good sign, he thought. From the dining room sideboard he helped himself to a double whisky, which he drank off in several swallows. The bottle was genuine Scotch, good stuff, no doubt imported from Scotland and sold in a government controlled retail store in Vancouver or Victoria, then smuggled south. Which fit his world view perfectly. Governments didn't really care what you did, as long as they got their share of the profits. He poured a triple, which he swirled in the glass and was in no hurry to finish. He sat in the dark of the drawing room, enjoying the lights and the busy scenes of enterprise spread out at his feet. He was prepared to wait for hours.

Eventually, Florence and her bladder would have to come out of hiding to visit the bathroom. He would be waiting.

Florence struck a match and lit a candle. Her room had an electric lights, but she didn't want anything that bright at the moment. Her windup clock said it was half past nine. She must have slept for two hours. She was hungry and thirsty, but more urgently her bladder was about to burst. She blew out the candle. Out her window, she couldn't detect the reflection of any downstairs lights. She hadn't heard any one come in, or move about. Cautiously, in stocking feet, she opened her door a crack and listened.

Not a sound.

She took a step out of the safety of her room. Stopped. Waited. Nothing. She took two more steps towards the known but unseen bathroom, then two more. What? What was that? She froze. She listened. She could hear her own breathing. The pounding of her heart in her ears. She held her breath.

Finally, she could hear him. Hear him breathing. A raspy sort of sound. He was very close. Too close. She took a step backward. She started to take another. She heard two quick footsteps. "Gotcha." A hand closed over her arm. She screamed, tried to twist away and run. Another hand clamped over her mouth. His body was pressing her back, pushing her up against the wall, and his face was inches from hers.

"You're mine, now," he hissed. He let loose of her arm and pawed at her breasts, then tried to pull up her blouse. She tried to bite his hand. Couldn't. Tried to kick him between the legs. He turned aside. She clawed at his face.

"Bitch." He slammed her head against the wall. He ripped the buttons and fabric of her blouse. He gave a violent jerk to her skirt that sent her sprawling, free of his grasp, but not wearing much more than her underclothes and rags.

"Help," she screamed. "Help." She didn't know why she was calling for help since no one else was home. She thrashed on the carpet, then had the wind knocked out of her when he fell on top of her, prying open her legs. His intentions were now very clear.

Her hand, groping in the dark, came in contact with the hall table, then the cloth on the table, which she pulled off. A candy dish that sat there fell to the floor and broke. Painfully, her hand found a broken piece of the dish. She picked up the curved and jagged piece of glass, and she found his face. He screamed. She slashed at him again, and now they were wrestling for the shard of glass.

"Give it-"

"No-"

"Give it to me."

"No no no noooo!"

The hall light flashed on. Mrs. Waters stood in the doorway of her bedroom. No shoes, but otherwise fully dressed, including a small hat, as if she might be going out to dinner.

On his knees, Mr. Waters sat up straight. Florence could see his male thing sticking out between the buttons of his pants fly. With a clear target, she gave him a vicious kick, all heel, where it would hurt most. He toppled over backwards with a mewling sound and curled up in a ball. His face was bleeding from several deep jagged cuts.

"Oh, well done, my dear, well done," said Mrs. Waters, with a deep resonant belly laugh. "Oh, well done," and she clapped her hands in glee and laughed again. "Oh, my dear, this is wonderful, just wonderful." Then she shook herself, patted her hair back into place and with great gravity gave Florence instructions.

"Florence, go in the bathroom and clean yourself. Then go to bed."

Florence was inclined to argue, but she was aware of being very cold, and not wearing much clothing. Mrs. Waters sounded sober, and a bit like her Aunt Francis. Not surprising, given that they were sisters. Florence scrambled for the bathroom and closed the door.

Mrs. Waters went briefly to her room and returned with a straight-back chair, her cigarettes and an ashtray. She sat down, crossed her legs, and lit a cigarette. Florence raced out of the bathroom, wrapped in a towel, and disappeared into her own room, locking the door behind her.

"Stop moaning that way. And sit up straight, Charles, perhaps against the wall," said Mrs. Waters to her husband. She blew out a long stream of smoke. She was sober, and feeling rather well right at the moment. "We really must chat."

In the Cage

Her kitchen table was tiny. She had to fold her morning paper in half to have room on the table for a coffee cup. There was barely floor space for one chair. But it was her newspaper, and her table, and if she spilled egg on the paper no one was going to yell or make her entire day a misery. She had repainted the kitchen a pale straw color, and the kitchen cabinets a slightly darker yellow, and with the overhead electric light it was quite cheery, and easy to read the newsprint. There was only a single window that looked south at the house across the street, but she could see the back porch, and in the morning, watch the parade of their cats in and out.

At eight she prepared to leave. In the living room she sat in one of the two wing back chairs covered in dark burgundy leather that Mrs. Waters had given her. A polished pair of her black work boots sat beside the chair, and she slowly pulled them on and did up the knee high lacing. They were ugly, and she knew they made her look very old-fashioned and a bit ridiculous, but they kept her feet dry and provided support all day. She purchased three pair at Chester Beards at the same time, and always let a pair sit for two days after she had worn them before wearing them again. She kept them well oiled and polished. The room, on the other hand, pleased her. For an apartment, it was huge, with a large, five faceted bay window overlooking the corner of 22nd and Rucker, and a spreading shade tree that mercifully leafed out in the summer to dampen the sun through these windows that faced full west. Everything was neat and tidy. Mrs. Waters had given her several pieces of furniture, and money to buy more, and the room really was very presentable. She especially liked her old sofa with its scroll back and delicately carved trim.

Florence never knew when her landlady, Miss Clark, who owned the building, would drop in for an inspection. Part of the low rent, she had concluded, was having a nosy landlady and house rules intended to maintain a 'proper' establishment. She fetched her coat from the bedroom closet. There was a second bedroom, and here she kept the small grand piano from the playroom that Mrs. Waters hadn't wanted, and a treadle sewing machine Florence had purchased used. She couldn't afford to buy dresses in the new shorter style, but she could make them, and did. For all this luxury she paid more than she could afford, twenty-five dollars a month, which included steam heat, electric lights and ice.

Promptly at eight thirty she stepped out her door. She took the back stairs, out the back door, walked up Hoyt to 24th St., where she cut across the Everett High School campus. She liked looking at the building. It was one of the few buildings in town with any style, or permanence. When she had first heard someone use the phrase, "roll up the sidewalks" she had assumed they were referring to parts of Everett, and she was surprised when it turned out they didn't mean literally. She had been prepared to believe they did.

Three blocks more, at California, she always enjoyed the Indian story pole erected east of Colby, in front of the Redman's Hall. A plaque said it was carved by William Shelton in honor of Chief Patkanim, one the signers of the Point Elliot Treaty.

She hurried another block down Colby to Monte Cristo Trust and Savings Bank, arriving promptly on the dot at eight-forty-five. You didn't want to be early, there was no place to wait out of the weather. But you never wanted to be late. Girls who were late were publicly scolded and usually ended up in tears. If it happened three times in a year, you were fired.

Mr. Lind (Lindstedt before the War) unlocked the door and ushered the girls inside. Then he re-locked the door.

She spent the first fifteen minutes of the day cleaning what had already been cleaned during the night by the janitor. She checked the floor, a smooth gray marble, in front of her station, for brown stains or spit. Why people thought is was acceptable to spit on the floor bewildered her. But it happened every day.

A waist high mahogany counter polished to a mirror finish completely cordoned off one side of the room, with a high palisade-style tellers cage that stretched all the way to the ceiling. There were six tellers stations, with brass bars as big around as her fingers swooping down from the top of the palisade almost to the counter, leaving only a small opening at the bottom through which money and passbooks came and went.

Florence re-polished her brass. Sometimes the janitor left smudges. Florence stared out at her customers all day through these bars. Her customers looked back at her. She sometimes thought her view of the world was similar to a reproduction of modern French art she had seen in a magazine: all the images were slashed and fractured. She wanted the bars to be polished, with the least distortion possible. But sometimes all she saw in the shiny surface was the distorted, fun-house mirror image of herself reflected back at herself. The top of the counter was covered in the same stone that graced the floor. Generally, you didn't have to worry about anyone spitting on the counter. Occasionally, someone missed the heavy green-glass ashtray and left their ashes behind. She always checked.

Behind the palisade, she had a small oak desk and a wooden chair. Ledgers, pens and an inkstand were allowed on the desk. No framed photographs, or other personal items. Ranged behind her and the other girls were shelves filled with account ledgers, filed alphabetically.

At nine, Florence lined up with the other girls. Watched by Mr. Chase, the Bank President, Mr. Lind opened the vault. Mr. Chase was married to one of Mrs. Waters' best friends. Mrs. Waters had arranged this job for Florence, before leaving town, permanently as far as Florence could tell, for San Francisco. Which meant the only other person in town she really knew was Mr. Waters, and he wasn't supposed to talk to her. She felt very isolated.

Florence received her cash drawer from Mr. Dennison, the Head Cashier. She immediately went to her table. She had seven twenties. She counted again. Seven. Nineteen tens. She checked the count. Fine. She had forty-three fives, but only fifty-five ones. For a total of six hundred. She counted her change, mostly half dollar pieces and quarters. Another hundred. Seven hundred total. She balanced. But she would never make it through the day with only fifty-five ones, especially since today was a Friday and a payday. Taking two twenties, she locked her drawer in at her station, and returned to Mr. Dennison. He had his head down at his desk, writing something in a ledger book she did not recognize. He ignored her for several minutes, which was annoying since he really had nothing else to do, but if he saw you were annoyed he kept you waiting even longer. Florence waited absolutely still, no expression on her face.

"Problem, Miss Harcus?" he finally asked.

"I'd like to buy some ones."

"Very good. How many?"

"Forty."

"And do we balance this morning?"

"Yes." Once she replied 'of course' when he asked, but it was a response that made him frown. And once, on her third day on the job she'd had to answer 'no' when he asked her at the end of the day. She was short ten dollars, which she paid up out of her own pocket, exactly four days pay.

Florence watched him carefully as he counted out forty ones. Back at her desk, she checked his count. Forty. It was a drill you marched through every morning. At the beginning of the day, balance. At the end of the day, balance. In your head, you balanced after each transaction.

"Honey," Helen told her at lunch one day. Helen was the most senior girl, having worked at the bank for over ten years. "Honey," Helen said again. "You don't trust nobody. You don't trust me, or Mr. Dennison, or any other bank employee. And you sure as hell never trust a customer, not even if it's your own mother. Anybody - and I mean anybody- hands you money, you count it. Before you give anybody money, you count it twice. And if you push it out the slot, and they push it right back, you count it again. The only person lookin' out for you is you!" And Helen poked her in the arm to make the point. Florence spilled her coffee. But she got the point.

At nine-thirty Mr. Chase personally unlocked the front door and ushered the waiting customers inside. He had a kind word and a smile for everyone. Years ago when he was starting his bank, Mr. Chase observed the hard work and thrift of the immigrant communities, and concluded, "These people are going to be successful." He built his bank on home and farm loans for such families, and passbook savings accounts. As the community prospered and grew, so did his business.

The first customers of the day were women, withdrawing a few dollars for next week's groceries. If you farmed or fished or logged, you got paid off in the fall, hopefully with enough money in your back pocket - or the bank - to survive the winter. Florence would see these ladies later in the day, when she went to Manning's for a bowl of soup. They would sit at Manning's, three or four to a table, groceries in bags or baskets stacked around their feet, drinking nickel cups of coffee (free refills) that they nursed for hours, as they gossiped, sometimes in English, sometimes not.

Her first customer was Orla Jackson. Short, cheerful, about her own age, but already with two small girls in tow. And visibly pregnant with a third.

"Good morning, Mrs. Jackson."

"Yes. Good morning."

"How may I help you today?"

"Well," Mrs. Jackson pushed her passbook across the counter, "I need ten more dollars."

This was a little confusing. "You want to withdraw ten dollars?"

"Yes. That's what I need."

Florence checked the balance. Mrs. Jackson had a little over one hundred and seventy dollars. "There's some interest due from the last quarter that needs to be posted."

"Oh?" said Mrs. Jackson with a smile. "Well, I thought so, but I wasn't sure."

Florence posted the interest, totaling $1.70, then deducted ten dollars from the new total. She signed the book. She had Mrs. Jackson sign the book. She pulled the 'J' ledger off the shelf. She found Mrs. Jackson's account. She updated the ledger and signed it. She took the ledger and the passbook to Mr. Dennison. He examined both documents critically, but in the end signed the ledger. Florence returned to her window and Mrs. Jackson. Florence counted out two five dollar bills and also returned the passbook to Mrs. Jackson.

"I'm buying a new hat," Mrs. Jackson confided, packing away her passbook and money. "Chaffee's is having a sale." Chaffee's was the nicest and most expensive women's store in Everett.

"Good for you," said Florence.

"Thank you," said Mrs. Jackson. "Norma, Janice, we're leaving," she said to her girls. Trailed by the children, she almost ran out of the store. Florence noted it was still a few minutes before ten. No doubt the sale began when Chaffee's opened at ten. She was certain Mrs. Jackson would be at the head of the line.

Three men came into the bank and walked directly towards Mr. Chase's office in the back. Florence knew the two big, tough looking men were bodyguards. The other man was the head bookkeeper at the Hulbert Mill. Several hundred men were employed and expected to be paid, in cash, today. The three men would leave with thousands of dollars. Mr. Chase and Mr. Dennison would handle this transaction personally. It was safer not to bring that much money out of the vault until it was absolutely required.

The procedure never varied. Check the passbook. Check the passbook against the ledger. Obtain a signature from Mr. Dennison, complete the transaction. Money in a bank is like the tide, Florence often thought. It comes in, and it goes out. On Fridays, money flowed out for payrolls, came back as deposits in individual accounts. As she handled other peoples' money, she became increasingly aware of how little money she had herself. Mrs. Waters had generously given her five hundred dollars for furniture, and to set up housekeeping. Florence had over half remaining, and in a savings account, for emergencies. But anyone who worked appeared to make more money than she did. Just before her lunch break, a man in a much abused bowler hat, beard and dirty fingernails, pushed ten twenty dollar gold pieces through her window and asked for paper.

"The stores don't want gold no more," he explained belligerently. Florence didn't want it either. She locked her drawer and took the coins to Mr. Dennison. He examined each of the coins. He weighed them on a scale the bank kept for such purposes to make sure the coins were genuine U.S. mint and weren't slugs. Finally he nodded yes. He knew she couldn't use the gold in her cash drawer, so he went into the vault and came back with ten paper twenties, which he counted in front of her. Back at her window, Florence counted the bills again. Ten at twenty. Then gave them to the customer, who slid the bills into a stack but then hesitated for a moment.

"Sir?" she asked.

"Twenties? Ah - I really wanted tens."

"As you wish," said Florence.

The man pushed the stack of twenties back through her window. Florence almost put them in her cash drawer. Almost. But she could feel Helen poking her shoulder, and a voice in her head, 'don't trust nobody'. She counted the stack of twenties. There were only nine. She counted again. Nine.

She smiled pleasantly. "I'm sorry, Sir. I need another twenty dollars. "

"If I'm short," the man said, red-faced, getting loud, "it's because you shorted me."

"Sir..."

"I had two hundred dollars. You're cheating me!" He was very loud.

Florence pushed the $180.00 towards him so he could reach it. She locked her cash drawer and stepped back from the counter. "Sir," she said, "I gave you ten twenties, but that is not what you gave me back." She was shaking, but she kept her voice low and calm. She had no doubts she was right. She had double counted each step.

Mr. Dennison appeared at her side. "Is there a problem?" he asked.

The man stood staring at the two of them for a moment. "No," he said abruptly. He picked up his money and left the bank.

Florence explained what had happened. "I'll notify the police," said Dennison. "He may try somewhere else."

Florence went to lunch at Manning's. Chicken noodle soup. Bread. Coffee. Fifteen cents. She knew she should bring her lunch. Leftovers from dinner. But she had been so hungry last night, she had eaten every scrap of chicken. She didn't have things like cake or cookies. She decided she needed to use her free time on Saturday better. She sat at her table, nursing her own second cup of coffee. It was a way to ease her feet. She never thought when she was younger that her feet would hurt from standing up all day, but they did. Mentally, the work wasn't all that challenging, and she knew it could be worse. She could be working in a laundry, ironing shirts for piece work wages. Or worse yet, in a cannery. All that fish slime, plus the work was only seasonal.

After lunch, the money mostly came in. People depositing part of their wages in their account. People paying their mortgages. Or this new business, paying for an automobile with monthly payments.

She cashed several bank drafts, being careful to have a bank officer authorize the disbursement in advance. A girl who no longer worked for the bank, Rachel, had cashed a bank draft from a prominent businessman. A long time customer. She went to Mr. Dennison after the fact and was fired on the spot.

"That man is practically bankrupt," said Mr. Dennison. While the draft was eventually covered by another bank, that didn't make any difference to the bank. Mr. Dennison probably would have approved cashing the draft. That also didn't make any difference to the bank. Rachel hadn't followed the rules. You weren't supposed to think, you were supposed to follow the rules. Except, of course, for those times when you were expected to make an exception for a very good customer. Florence concluded that not making exceptions might get you yelled at, but wouldn't get you fired. As a result, she never made exceptions.

At two Mr. Dennison asked her to close her window and help Becky and Mr. Lind in the vault. They were making up a small payroll. Florence joined them. She double-checked the count, put the cash and coins in the envelopes, made sure each envelope was labeled with the right name. Twenty-three employees. Bayside Mechanical. Mr. Lind supervised, which meant he watched, but didn't help. On this particular account, Florence didn't mind. She was very curious about Bayside Mechanical.

She had strolled past Bayside Mechanical on her lunch hour. The building was awfully small to be a place where twenty three men worked. All the windows that faced the street were painted out. There was a freight dock, but it was fully enclosed by high swinging gates. She couldn't even see a door you would use to enter.

And for a place that employed twenty-three people Bayside didn't buy much. A few, very few, office supplies. Puget Sound Power and Light. West Coast Telephone. City Fuel. Occasionally a bank draft for Lloyd Hardware. Mostly large drafts for gas and oil, which Florence interpreted as multiple delivery trucks, although she had no means to determine how many. Every week she made a point of inspecting Bayside's account.

Her curiosity was straightforward. Mr. Waters was listed as the owner of the business. She never saw his signature on a draft, she never saw him in the bank, but the ledger listed him as 'Owner'. She occasionally walked past the building. She tried Saturdays, once a Sunday afternoon. She never learned anything more.

The bank closed its doors at four on Friday. At approximately half past three every Friday, the run of last minute customers began to trickle, then flood, in the door. These were people in a hurry. They made frequent mistakes with their addition, and were inclined to be rude.

Her last customer of the day was Mr. Eide. He did what he always did. He paid money in. Florence had never withdrawn money for him, although his account showed that in 1919 he had mostly taken money out. He was a curiosity. Always a clean and pressed white shirt, but the cuffs had been turned, and in other ways he had the appearance of being somewhat shabby. His suits were old, second-hand, Florence decided, after seeing him twice one week. Thirty something, but when he took off his hat, bald as an egg. His hands were clean, the nails well cared for, but rough and hard looking. Which was odd. She would have called him rich. She wondered what he did for a living. He had a balance of over twenty-one thousand dollars, and every week, like today, he added to it. She accepted his four hundred dollars in tens, updated, his bank book. He said a polite and quiet 'thank you', put on his hat, nodded and left. Shortly thereafter, Mr. Dennison locked the front door, and the day was over. With a sigh, all six girls sat down and started working over their accounts. First, balance. That way, if there was a problem, you had time to solve it. Counting cash and bank drafts, she had a great deal more money than what she had started with, so it took longer to count. But she balanced. Leaving her starting balance in her drawer, she wrapped the rest with a rubber band and went to see Mr. Dennison.

"Sir, I'm balanced."

He was intent on adding a column of figures and he didn't look up. "Very good. Leave the drawer and your excess deposits, and finish up."

"Yes, Sir."

As she returned to her desk, she heard Judy release a long sigh of relief.

Must have been a problem. That she solved. Florence had been the first to turn in her drawer. Soon the rest, one by one made their way to Mr. Dennison. Everyone had balanced. The mood lightened. Soon it would be time to go home.

No, she wasn't going straight home, she remembered. She had volunteered to help serve at the Brown's wedding reception at Church. The wedding was at seven with the reception following. It was something to do, she might talk with a few people, and the only people in town who she might eventually know besides the people at the bank, were her fellow parishioners at Trinity Episcopal. The Church was only a block from her apartment. She had attended several services, then volunteered to help with the children's Christmas program.

When they discovered she knew how to play the piano, she was in constant demand as a rehearsal pianist. She had never before known the music to 'Little Town of Bethlehem', or 'Joy to the World'. But she did now. She could play them in her sleep. And factually, nearly all the people in Everett she knew by first names were under twelve years old. But the prospect of the church picnic, and a possible outing or two, loomed as the only items on her social calendar.

At five, Mr. Dennison ushered them all outdoors. With hurried good-byes and wishes for a pleasant weekend, the girls scattered. No one walked in her direction, so Florence went on alone to her evening.

All day the date, May third, had nagged at her. She walked a block, then stopped, the window display of spring fashions at the Grand Leader reflected back at her.

"Oh, I know."

It was her birthday. And since this was 1921, today was her twenty-fourth birthday. If she was in Victoria, she was more than old enough to purchase liquor or vote. As a Canadian citizen, she couldn't do either of those things in Everett.

She stood looking at her own reflection for a moment. Tallish, long hair now cut short, in her best imitation of a bob, since she cut her hair herself, slender, carrying her light spring coat and hat. The face staring back at her resembled her father in many ways. The thought caused her to grin at her own reflection. What a recommendation. A woman who looked like a man.

She caught sight of her feet. And those stupid boots! Maybe she should walk home and change her shoes. No, she decided. She was likely to be on her feet for several more hours. She needed the boots. But maybe they'd have a pot of hot coffee on when she got there. Or she could make one. With some buttered date nut bread, that would probably be dinner. She walked on towards Trinity.

Home, 1919

In late February Hank marched up the boarding ramp of the hospital ship, the U.S.S. Henderson. The Henderson was carrying wounded men and some troops, from Brest, France to New York, New York. He rated the early trip because of his rank and his medals, but he only got to use a berth for eight hours. Two other men slept in the same bunk, in shifts. Hank got lucky. When they tossed for who got what shift, he was the winner. He slept from ten in the evening to six the next morning, and then got up to breakfast. Almost like real life, but he didn't play cards or gamble. So besides sleeping and eating, all there was to do was talk, stand at the rail, smoke, and stare out at the ocean and the horizon. After nine days of unrelieved Atlantic Ocean, Hank was thoroughly bored.

The Statue of Liberty was impressive. One of the few stories his mother told about her arrival in America was her sighting of the partially complete Statue. That, and the endless lines at Ellis Island. His father had arrived in America when he jumped ship in Duluth, with the recollection that when he got to dry land, "I ran." Hard to imagine his mild, law abiding father being a law breaker. Or for that matter, running.

The New York skyline was a sight to behold. Until you actually saw it, you couldn't really grasp how huge it really was. There was only a single tall building in Seattle, the Smith Tower, and nothing in Everett was taller than six stories, and two stories was typical. Landed, Hank had sixteen hours until his train left. He had three choices. He could explore New York. This was complicated by the fact that the ship had actually docked in Hoboken, New Jersey. Which was just a name to him. He had no idea where he really was.

His second option was to wait in the train depot. But that involved more aimless talk, and cigarette smoke. He would have five days of that on the train as he crossed the country.

His last option was to try and find his Aunt Josie, one of his father's sisters. When the family split up after the winter of 1901, in Alberta, Josie and her husband had returned to work as domestics in New York, work they had done before in the 1880's right after they first arrived in America. As a couple they were done with farming, and the only trade Josie's husband Angus knew, besides farming, was being a butler. The far west no longer held an attraction for them. Angus had passed away about five years ago. Josie still kept house for a wealthy Norwegian couple. All Hank had was a mailing address, but a smooth talking cab driver had Hank on a ferry crossing the Hudson and then across the Brooklyn Bridge and on the sidewalk in front of a very impressive brick home almost before Hank could ask, "How much will it cost?" and digest the answer.

The main entrance was pillared with a wooden portico, painted a pale cream, the stone steps scrubbed and swept immaculately clean. There's at least one Norwegian who lives here, thought Hank, as he followed a narrow walk through a wrought iron gate around the back to what he hoped was the door to the kitchen. He knocked.

A woman about his mother's age answered the door and stood looking at him in his uniform for a moment. "Well," she said at last in accented English, " I can give you a sandwich, but that's all, and you'll have to sit outside to eat."

"That's fine," Hank said in Norwegian. He smiled a devious grin. "Could I have a sandwich with two fried eggs and bacon? Please?" It had been one of his favorites as a child, and Josie had fixed him many a meal.

Josie looked at him harder. "Do I know you?"

"I haven't seen you since I was ten," he said simply. "I'm Hank Eide."

"Hank? Hank Eide? But you're…oh, Hank!" She was very embarrassed, but she threw her arms around him and hugged him all the harder.

When she got over being embarrassed, she pulled him inside and sat him down at the kitchen table beside the stove. Hank got his fried egg sandwich, and fruit salad with home canned pears, crisp apples and real whipped cream. She fixed him several ham sandwiches for the train, and set out two additional quarts of pears to take with him. She was busy, busy, busy, talking non-stop, and Hank wondered what was wrong.

"Hank," she asked at last, "have you heard from your family?'

"It's probably been more than a month," Hank answered. "At Christmas?"

Josie went to a kitchen drawer and took out a letter. "I had a letter last week," Josie said. "Hank, your brother Arnt," Josie choked, and Hank got very still. "Your brother and his wife. They got flu, Hank. They died."

Hank had witnessed scenes from hell, and not shed a tear. He had first hand experience with the randomness of death. One night he had been under a gun carriage, repairing the wheel bearings, when a shell landed among the men watching him work. Everyone standing was killed. Under the carriage, on his back, protected by the metal of the gun and the carriage, he survived, but was unable to hear a anything for two days as he sat in his tent and waited for his hearing to come back. Hadley found a bottle of cognac somewhere, and he got good and drunk for the first time in his life.

He had seen things that he never wanted to talk about or remember. But for a moment, sitting in Josie's kitchen over the remains of his meal, scenes came flooding back. Living men without legs or arms. Dead men with no heads. Draft horses smashed to a bloody pulp. He put his head down and wept. For Arnt. For Ingrid, his wife. For everyone. For everything.

Three weeks later he was home, and back in his old job in the machine shop at Two Brothers Iron Works, where he had apprenticed at age fourteen, nearly fifteen years ago. Sitting on a stool next to his lathe, in the quiet of the lunch hour, talking to his friend, Bill Lorimer.

"You've got this wedding," Bill prompted.

"Hadley asked me to be his best man, and I said yes." Bill nodded his understanding. "I decided I should try and find some Champagne. For a toast. As best man, I think that's one of the things I'm supposed to do. I asked Eddie to check around for me." Eddie was Hank's youngest brother, and a drinking man. "So Eddie, he comes back and he tells he can't find any Champagne." Bill had never had any Champagne in his life, though he assumed, correctly, that it was some kind of fancy French stuff.

"Eddie says if you want Champagne, take the train up to Vancouver, buy it, pack it in an old suitcase, and check your bag through to Everett. He says everyone does it, and no one gets caught. Does that make any sense? What's the point of all these stupid liquor laws?"

"I don't know, Hank" said Bill. "We're dry at my house. Or at least my wife is," he added with a smile. Then someone shouted.

"EIDE!"

"Our Lord and Master," said Hank, swallowing the last of his lunch coffee.

"He's new, Hank", Bill cautioned.

"Well, I'm old," said Hank, "and I don't like this raka-nena." A raka-nena was a term Norwegians borrowed from the Finns. It meant "snot nose."

Hank walked over to the bottom of the long stairway that led down to the shop floor from the upstairs office. Wearing a new looking three piece suit and a crisp white shirt and tie, Mr. Thompson stood on the third step up.

"Yes, sir?" Hank said in his best military style.

"What is this?" Thompson came down the remaining steps and held out a bolt, two inches in diameter, the length of his forearm.

"It's a bolt," said Hank, handing it back, and stating the obvious.

"I know it's a bolt, Eide, but its not the correct bolt. I specified a diameter of one inch."

Here we go, thought Hank. He took a deep breath and tried to calm himself.

"Yes, you did," he agreed.

"This," said Thompson, shaking the bolt in his hand, " is not one inch."

"No, it isn't," Hank agreed again.

"Why not, Eide? Why not? Do you know how to read a drawing?"

Thompson's shop drawings were things of beauty. Thompson had a recent college degree in mechanical engineering. Unfortunately, Thompson had never been seen operating anything more mechanical than a pencil. Einar Flatbjoe, superintendent of the machine shop, had stepped out of the office, and stood on the stair landing up above, listening.

Hank ignored the reading comment, and tried to keep his voice low and under control. "A one inch bolt in that location will eventually shear. It needs to be bigger."

"Have you studied metallurgy, Eide? Is that what the Army taught you?" He spit out the "you".

"It's not a question of metallurgy," said Hank, starting to get angry. "It has to do with how the machinery will actually be used."

"I thought these bolts were part of a pulp mill digester," said Thompson. You cooked wood chips under pressure, in a slurry of lime and sulfur, to create pulp for paper. These bolts were designed to keep the lid on the digester while the pulp was being cooked.

"They are. And the man who tightens these bolts every day will tighten them tighter as they wear, thousands of times in a year."

"But if they're tightened to specs," Thompson said, his voice dripping sarcasm, "there won't be a problem, you stupid Norwegian." Over half the shop crew was Norwegian. These men, and others, had left their food to crowd in close, and listen. Thompson's comment brought a low growl.

"The men working the digester," Hank said through clenched teeth, "won't be your top hands. They won't know a spec from apple butter. They'll hand tighten these bolts with the tools they're provided, likely to be long handled box end wrenches. They'll do it by feel, and the general notion that the tighter the better, for reasons of safety."

Einar Flatbjoe thought it made perfect sense. Hank's comment reflected an acquired knowledge of how men used machinery. Thompson apparently didn't see it that way.

"Is that so?" said Thompson, getting right in Hank face. "Is - that - so ?"

Hank was at his limit, and he knew it. He turned around and started to walk away. Flatbjoe was pleased. He needed Hank. He didn't need Thompson. Bill Lorimer put his hand on Hanks arm and started to say something to him, but he was interrupted.

"Eide, you're a dumb ass Norwegian," Thompson hissed. "And a coward. A coward, Eide." Hank stopped in his tracks.

"Hank," said Bill, very worried.

Hank shook his head. "I was going to quit soon, anyway. I can't do this job anymore. See you Sunday." After church on Sunday, Hank and Bill were planning to go out to Silver Lake, trout fishing. Hank walked back and stood in front of Thompson.

"Come back for more?" Thompson said, sneering.

Hank only hit him once. It was a right hand cross, almost a hook, but his whole body was behind the blow, and Hank hoped to break Thompson's nose. Maybe drive the cartilage up into his brain and kill the bastard where he stood. But at the last minute Thompson turned his head away just enough, and instead Hank broke Thompson's jaw, his nose, knocked him out cold, but didn't kill him. You could tell he was alive the way the blood came spurting out of his nose .

Flatbjoe slowly came down the stairs and stood looking down at Thompson bleeding all over the clean, swept floor. "Pick up your pay, Hank. I'm sorry." Flatbjoe would always feel it had been his fault. He and Hank shook hands.

"Right," said Hank. He knew he couldn't stay after hitting a boss. He also didn't want to stay, which was why he had hit the raka-nena on the nose. He headed up the stairs to the office.

Hank didn't want to go home, but he also didn't want to wait five hours for Bill and a ride home, so he walked. Slowly. Down along the river. He skipped some stones and watched them sink. Kind of what my future is doing, he thought. Sinking.

It began to rain. On past the city dump, he followed Railway Avenue. Small sawmill operators on the left, cutting western red cedar shingles and shakes. Men in teams loaded finished pallets of fragrant cedar shakes, shingles and cedar gutters in freight cars for the trip to markets in the East. A series of small boat yards and repair shops on the right, lined up along the shore of the riverbank. Hank walked past his own skiff, hauled up on shore. He walked past abandoned derelict fishing boats. Rusted out machinery. There was a dump truck parked in front of a barn-like boat house. The boat house leaned heavily to the right, and someone had done a clumsy and ineffective job of trying to brace up the near corner. It was the dump truck that really caught his eye. The dump truck had been painted a garish red, white and blue. Glum as he felt, wet as he was, he had to laugh. Even the wheel spokes were painted in the alternating paint scheme.

"And it's a five ton Packard dump truck," he marveled. Across the radiator was the wartime, factory applied, slogan, "Save a Freight Car For Uncle Sam."

Hank had worked on Packard trucks in France. The Army owned thousands of them, and they were a real workhorse. With a sixteen foot bed you could load them down with all sorts of interesting cargo. Packard was the first manufacturer to abandon the sprocket and chain drive, introducing a worm gear to replace it.

Hank had fiddled with dozens of Packard trucks. The first thing you did to one in the Army was disable the governor on the engine. Otherwise you were limited to ten miles an hour. That speed made you a tempting target for German artillery. Even if the brakes wouldn't take it, it was much better to go faster, risking a crash, to avoid being shelled.

This truck had a hand lettered flat, wooden "For Sale" sign propped up in the window, which Hank found very interesting. A man could do things, earn a living, with a truck like this. He noticed the mud puddle he was standing in was getting deeper. He moved a few feet to higher ground. There was no name or phone number on the "For Sale" sign.

An automobile, an older Ford with side curtains, splashed to a stop, and a man got out. He knew the man. It was David Engeset, an attorney here in Everett. Hank knew him because he, his wife and his son, Eric, attended Central Lutheran. What Hank knew from the Church Bulletin was that Engeset was changing professions, having recently been ordained as a Lutheran Minister and accepted a call from a church in Yakima. What was he doing here on the wrong side of town? Did he have something to do with the truck? Or the boathouse?

"Mr. Engeset," Hank called out, and Engeset stopped and looked back at him.

"Hank! What brings you down here?"

"I was interested in this truck. Do you happen to know who owns it?"

"Let's get out of the rain," Engeset suggested. He fished a set of keys out of his coat pocket, sprung open a rusty padlock on a pair of very tall barn-like doors, and put his back into pushing one of the boathouse doors open. Inside, the first thirty or so feet was a heavy, planked, wooden floor, with a ceiling maybe twenty feet high over their head. Hank bounced a bit on the balls of his feet. The floor felt solid as a rock. Probably four by twelve's on twelve inch centers, thought Hank. After that thirty feet of floor, and the twenty foot height, the ceiling opened up full height, more than thirty feet Hank guessed, and there wasn't a floor, but only a narrow walkway, skirting the sides of the building. The floor was missing down the middle, and the river end of the entire building was open, except for a huge canvas curtain. In place of a floor, there was a marine railway. Standing in the dark, it was like looking down a tunnel. Through a few torn scraps of canvas, now flapping in the wind, the river slid past, gray and dŏtted with rain in the waning afternoon light.

He was standing beside a big pile of machinery. There was a big drum winch, wound with rusty cable, powered by a two cylinder Easthope, together with some complicated gearing that stepped down the rpm of the motor for turning the drum winch. All the equipment desperately needed to be greased. The cable reel attached to a short but stoutly built wooden marine railway carriage, a thirty foot long sled with rusty iron wheels, that ran on track that sloped, partially under cover, down into the river. At high tide, you'd run your boat aground on the carriage, making sure she was secure and wouldn't just tip over. Then you'd start up the winch and haul.

Everything was designed with the intent of hauling out fish boats, say up to fifty feet, bringing them in under cover and up on the ways where you could repair plank, caulk the seams, clean the bottom and repaint the hull. The entire building was probably ninety feet long by forty wide. You could see daylight in many places through the walls, and for that matter, the roof. Swallows were obviously nesting in the rafters. All the woodworking tools, sawhorses, ladders and lumber you might expect to see in a boat shop were missing.

"You like that Packard, huh?" said Engeset, shaking the rain off his hat.

"Are you the seller?"

"I'm selling everything, truck, boathouse, machinery. I represent the owner," Engeset explained. "Her husband died and she moved back to Wisconsin." Hank could only dimly see Engeset's face in the available light. "You could buy everything, the building, the land and the truck, for $5,000.00."

"Five!" Hank repeated. That was almost all the money he had. The savings from fifteen years of scrimping , living a quiet life with his parents, doing odd jobs for others on his weekend days off, and walking everywhere. All his Army pay. Paying five thousand would leave him with very little in reserve.

Engeset was surprised when Hank didn't immediately say no. "She might carry a contract," he suggested. "You're a journeyman machinist, aren't you? Good, steady income?" Hank avoided that question by asking a question of his own.

"That roof needs a lot of work," said Hank. "and the building needs cross ties and bracing. She's leaning pretty bad." Hank pointed. The entire building was leaning north, more than six inches out of plumb.

"No argument."

"How about cash?"

"Cash? Sure. Make me an offer."

"Name a price," Hank countered.

"No, if you want to gamble, you name a price. It's not for me to say."

Hank was thinking at a furious pace. "Three thousand," he offered.

"No," said Engeset abruptly, and Hank was surprised at how disappointed he felt. Then Engeset smiled. "There's an upstairs apartment where you could live. Four thousand, five hundred."

"I get the truck, too?"

"Why not."

"Three thousand five hundred," Hank countered again.

"Cash, with a note and a contract for a thousand more, total of four-five?" Engeset was smiling.

"I'll take it," said Hank. They shook hands, sealing the bargain.

"Come by my office in the morning, Hank. We'll sign the papers, count your money, and walk over to the County and make it all official."

"I'll be there."

"Here, you lock up." Engeset dropped the keys into his open palm and departed. A truck. And a boathouse. He was beginning to get an idea. He went back out in the rain and with some difficulty started the truck. The engine obviously needed some work, but it didn't sound like anything he didn't know how to repair. The bed worked on a hydraulic lift. Invented by Gar Wood, in the workshop behind his home. Wood was now rich, and spent his money on speedboats and winning Gold Cups. Hank backed his truck inside, under cover. There was more than enough room. The clutch and gearbox seemed to be fine. The points were probably wet and in need of replacement.

Patching the roof would have to come after he got the structure standing up straight and square. How about using pilings driven in along the south side, like flying buttresses? They wouldn't have to be the full height of the building. Maybe twenty four feet? Sink 'em eight feet, leave sixteen feet standing. Then he could use cable – with galvanized wire – run through to the north side. That would tie the building together and allow him to pull the north wall back six inches to the south. He'd also need a new band saw and a lathe. Well, new for him. In fact, he would buy used. He could build a decent workbench, but better lighting he'd have to buy. Otherwise, he had everything he needed if he bought a fish boat, say thirty to forty feet and wanted to haul her and rebuild her.

Thinking about fish boats and Gar Wood was giving him another idea. An even better business idea. With relief, he sat down to think. Now, he could go home. But not quite yet. He had much to think about.

Victoria and Back Again, 1922

The alarm woke Hank at two-thirty a.m. With a groan, he rolled out of bed. His back hurt. He decided he needed to spend some of the money he was making to purchase new springs and a mattress. But time and tide wait for no man.

By the light of a single bare bulb, he dressed. Over his one piece wool union suit, he pulled on heavy canvas pants - tin pants, they called them - an extra heavy gray wool sweater that his mother had knit and still smelled like the sheep who donated the wool. A matching hat. Wool socks. Thigh high rubber boots. From the ice box, he drank a pint of milk straight from the bottle in one long, gulping swallow. Deciding not to shave, he packed a few groceries in a gunny sack, turned off the light, clattered down the stairs. A friend, a fellow Norwegian from Church, had his boat hauled out and up on the ways, under cover. But right now, all was darkness, shadows, the river sliding silently by. The railway wasn't making him much money, but he picked up a little cash doing machine work and welding, and it made him look legitimate.

Hank pushed open the swinging doors. He started the Packard, which he had decided not to paint. He had discarded the solid rubber tires and fit new rims and pneumatic tires, war surplus, which improved both speed and the ride. Stacked on the bed this morning were a dozen crab pots - each the size of a small bale of hay - sixty feet of manila and several cork buoys flaked down inside each pot.

Five blocks north, Hank crossed over the Snohomish River on the Chestnut Street bridge. He was out on the river delta, on Ebey Island, the largest area of semi-dry land. He splashed down the road. His moorage, tucked away off Steamboat slough in a backwater, consisted of a two upright pilings, three planks nailed to two semi-floating logs, and a very springy four by twelve cedar plank, eighteen feet long, that connected this collection of salvaged logs with dry land. Canary reed grass grew from the ends of the logs that formed his dock. Nothing fancy, barely serviceable. The chief virtue was the deserted and remote nature of the location. There were no houses, barns or outbuildings within sight. A few scraggly cottonwoods, stands of salal, blackberry vines and wild rose lined the banks of the estuary, a backwater off the main stem of the Snohomish River. You could load and unload elephants out here and no one would notice.

In the darkness, the Anna Marie floated quietly at her mooring. She looked just like the other boats in the fleet. A thin, chipped coat of white paint, streaked with rust, slimed with fish offal and bird droppings. While her pilot house, sweetly built with a gentle curve at the bow end, was actually brand new, and overall she was bigger than the average boat worked by just one man, at forty-two feet from stem to stern she blended right in. Which was what Hank had in mind when he bought and rebuilt her.

No one ever noticed that she never had a scrap of weed on her bottom. And everyone took notice of her owner, a taciturn, unsmiling Norski who said little, asked less, and always paid cash and expected to be paid in cash, never credit.

It was slippery this morning, a heavy dew. Since he had no intention of swimming this early in the day, he carefully felt his way down the plank ramp. Hank was pleased with how the Anna Marie had turned out. He was especially pleased with how she performed. He unlocked and slid open the door to the pilot house. At twelve feet long, Hank had twice as much cabin as most working fish boats. A small cast iron wood-burning stove made by Washington Stove Works sat to his right. A galley table that sat two comfortably, on the left. The steering station was forward, with excellent visibility. A 36 inch ships wheel, some intricate woodwork there, the spindles turned from a piece of teak Hank had salvaged, then polished and varnished. Five windows arranged in a gentle curve fit across the front of the wheelhouse, with the two side windows being openers. Below and forward there were two narrow berths tucked under a raised foredeck to create a small cabin built into the bow section of the boat.

First things first. A fire in the stove. Make some coffee. Hank had heard about the gillnet boats that fished at the mouth of the Columbia River. Long and narrow, but with a rounded bottom and comparatively shallow draft, with flatter, rounded sections from side to side and fore and aft, these boats were very different from the deep hulled fishing boats of Puget Sound, or Alaska. It only took three and a half feet of water to float this boat. A deep, roomy hull drawing five to six feet was nice if you were carrying tons of iced fish, but that wasn't the cargo Hank had in mind.

The Columbia boats were lighter, more easily driven hulls. The original hulls were designed to be pushed by sails. When reliable gas engines came on the scene the narrow design had been kept, because a small engine would push these boats at a fair speed, six to eight knots. Length had been added, and carrying capacity. Pound for pound, you could go faster in this type of hull, as long as you didn't overload it.

Hank set up the coffee pot, then put a cast iron skillet on the stove and added six strips of bacon. He had searched all over Everett and Seattle for a Columbia gillnet hull with no luck. Then he heard about a hull for sale up north, in Stanwood, twenty-five miles away. A town at the mouth of the Stillaguamish River, and the south fork of the Skagit. Two river deltas. Lots of thin water in that area. He took the train to Stanwood.

On scene, he had his choice of three hulls. He bought the third one he inspected. It had a small working engine, the hull was in good shape, and as shallow in draft as he had hoped. She'd float in three feet of water, instead of the usual five or six. The boat, when he bought her, was open with no cabin, no decking. He'd have to build what he wanted from scratch. Which suited him fine. Foss Towing was making up a tow to go to Everett. Hank made arrangements for he and the Anna Marie to go along. Anna Marie was his mother. Naming your boat after your mother was traditional.

Hank adjusted the draft on the stove. The bacon was beginning to sizzle. There were two large, hinged hatches, covered in long staves of vertical grain fir that ran fore and aft, making up the cabin floor, running almost the entire length of the pilot house. Hank pulled each half open, then gingerly lowered himself into the engine compartment. Here was the point of the lighter hull, the stretched out, longer pilot house. A V-12 Liberty engine, with nearly 1000 inches of cubic displacement. Originally based on the double V-6 made by Packard, the V-12 had been made by a half dozen manufacturers for installation in aircraft for the War. Packard themselves had built over six thousand engines, and theirs were generally considered to be the best made. Hank had bought his as war surplus in Seattle for $250.00.

The engine developed over four hundred horsepower, and was the biggest engine a civilian with money could buy. There were bigger engines the Army was using in its new planes, and he had heard Boeing was angling to buy a few, but this was as big an engine as he could get his hands on.

There were some drawbacks. Like starting. You couldn't crank twelve huge cylinders to life by hand. At the forward end of the engine Hank had installed a small, gas powered air cooled engine that started easily with a length of cord wound around the fly wheel.

When the starting engine was running smoothly, Hank engaged a simple, manual clutch that cranked the main engine. She turned over, caught and purred to life. Quickly, he disengaged the clutch and shut down the starter motor. The Liberty ran on with no hesitations, no misses. This engine ran like a Swiss watch. He devoted many hours to maintenance to make sure it stayed that way.

Installed on an airplane, these engines used an unholy amount of oil. The valves were all out in the open and pilots would come back from a mission coated in black gunk. Hank stole a solution he had read about in a magazine. Custom made valve covers that redirected the oil back into the block. He did the casting and machine work himself. Added a few improvements. Did the thread and die work for the attachment points. He cut gaskets from tire tubes.

The other drawback was gasoline consumption. At three-quarter speed, this engine burned twenty gallons of gasoline an hour. Your average fishing boat might burn two or three, maybe four gallons an hour when pressed and with a full load of fish and ice. Hank had fabricated and installed two sixty gallon side tanks made up with black iron. That gave him a range of almost a hundred miles, if he needed it. To be safe, he and the Anna Marie kept a low profile.

He would plod along all day at the expected, and much more economical, eight knots. But if it was necessary, he knew he had twice as much speed available. Maybe more. Someday it might make the difference. He didn't want to put it to the test, but he thought he might be able to outrun the Coast Guard. To keep his low profile, he spread his fuel purchases around, and packed two five gallon cans aboard on every trip he made down to the boat. With the stove lit and the engine running, Hank made his way back on shore. Two at a time, for balance, he carried the crab pots from the truck to the boat. He also brought two big buckets of fish heads on board. And his ten gallons of gas.

He untied his mooring lines, pushed off. In the wheelhouse he put the engine in gear, there was only forward, no reverse, swung the wheel to bring her around 180 degrees. Downriver. It was almost four thirty. Time and tide wait for no man, he told himself again. As the river opened up and widened

Hank left the wheel for brief intervals to tend the fire in the stove, turned his bacon, poured himself his first cup of coffee, but he couldn't leave the wheel for long. There were snags, floating trees, loose lumber and deadheads, logs lost off log tows and stuck firmly in the mud. Slam into any good sized piece of wood and he could hole his boat. It remained dark. The water was a shimmery, silvery blue. A dead head, or floating wood, showed on the surface as black. Hank steered away from those spots.

While the tide had turned and was falling, there was still enough depth of water for Hank to cross the bar, avoiding the long detour past town in the dredged channel. He was going west, past Priest Point and Mission Head, across the bottom end of Port Susan, then north up the long length of Saratoga Passage.

Bouncing back and forth between the wheel and stove, he set the bacon aside, drained most of the grease, and fried three eggs. Drank another cup of coffee. Ate the bacon, eggs, buttered bread, and drank another pint of milk. Then more coffee. Saratoga was calm when he turned the corner to head north. No daylight yet. The engine ran steady and strong, nary a miss.

The tide goes in and the tide goes out. Right now, the tide was going his way, north. A huge volume of water, thirty miles long, three to four miles wide. And there was only one narrow exit. All this water had to squeeze through Deception Pass, an opening between the north end of Whidbey Island and the mainland. Walls on both sides were sheer rock hundreds of feet high. And the Pass was less than 100 yards wide.

At peak, the current in the Pass ran as high as eight knots. About as fast as most fish boats running flat out, full speed ahead, could manage. Eight knots of speed into an eight knot current was a recipe for a shipwreck. You had no maneuverability.

Going with the current could be just as risky. He went through when it was still relatively slow, and weak. But at maximum ebb, the highest speed, the current was once again in charge. You were just along for the ride. It was impossible to avoid the whirlpools, forty feet across, that occasionally would cough up a fifty foot log right in your path. Better to transit the Pass at slack, the few short minutes when the water wasn't moving in or out, but was briefly at rest. A prudent man waited for slack. But that meant the tide, not your own version of time to sleep, or be awake, or time to eat, or daylight, or weather, set the schedule. The tide called the shots. Time and tide wait for no man.

Two hours - sixteen miles- behind him, two more hours to go before he had to do some work. He smoked a cigar. Did the dishes. Wiped down the galley. The sky gradually lightened to reveal low clouds. Opposite Penn Cove there was a light chop, suggesting that on the unprotected west side of Whidbey Island there was a pretty good breeze blowing in from the ocean down the long easterly run of the Straits of Juan de Fuca.

Just after eight-thirty, Hank was at Strawberry Point. The water stretched wide out to the east but it was very shallow, especially over towards Stanwood. On even a moderate low tide, the sea birds could either fly or walk all the way into town. You could see a few buildings low on the horizon glinting in the morning sun. One hundred miles further east, the Cascade mountain range framed the view. Another mile and Hank slowed the Anna Marie to dead slow and went on deck to ease five cups of coffee over the rail to leeward.

The hatch over the fish hold was in two pieces. He stacked one half on top of the other and began working. Slowly, popping the engine in and out of gear, he searched for his pot floats. There were dozens of different floats on the water. The unwritten rule was that everyone used a different color. No one had been using a three color combination on this stretch of water, so Hank was using red, white and blue. Not original, but effective.

He slid up beside a float and snagged the line with a boat hook. His pots had been soaking for two days. He led the line over a well greased roller block, and hauled. Sixty feet of line, the weight of the trap, plus whatever crabs might be trapped inside. No engine assist. Just muscle. The pots were sitting in forty to fifty feet of water. Pulling sixty pots in a morning was good exercise.

The first pot came up empty. Hank rebaited with fish heads and sent it back down. The second pot had seven crabs. All dungeness. All female. The kind of haul crabbers called "hitting the ladies room". He tossed them all back. Rebaited. Re-set the pot. The third pot came up plugged. Feast or famine. Thirty crabs, maybe more. Many of them were female, or too small, but eleven big males were dropped in the hold, where they scrabbled around and tried to pick a fight. He switched on a circulating sea water pump that ran off the engine. The fish hold was like a bathtub, it could only get so full, then it drained. Fresh sea water provided the crabs with the oxygen the crabs need to stay alive, and fresh.

Now, nearly every pot came up with crabs. The routine remained the same. Every five pots he stopped to drift for a few minutes and rest his arms. Twice while he was drifting he drank a cup of coffee. It was long day. You had to pace yourself. Watch the gulls now and then. At a little before two he had pulled all his pots, put the six pots that he had mended and brought back with him back in the water, and stacked four that needed to be taken home and mended on the stern. The tide had turned and now ran against him.

By his count there were two hundred and seven keepers in the fish hold. At this point, most crabbers would have tuned around and gone home. For Hank, the real trip was just beginning. Up around the corner to the left was Cornet Bay, a convenient place to wait for the tide to turn. He arrived at three. Slack was at four-thirty. He tied the bow of the Anna Marie to a piling, shut down the engine, and sat down to wait. Slowly the background noise of the engine faded away, and the silence deepened, becoming almost a physical presence punctuated by small sounds, waves lapping on the hull, wind in the trees, seagulls calling. The scrape of the line he'd tied to the piling as the Anna Marie moved back and forth. The bay was enclosed on three sides by high, steep hills covered with trees. The surface of Cornet Bay was riffled but calm, but you could look up and see the tree tops moving in the wind coming down the Straits. It was going to be a little rough once through the Pass. But he didn't think it would be awful.

He drank another pint of milk, then set the milk bottle afloat, and using what he always thought of as Hadley's Colt, fired shots at the bottle until it shattered and sank. It took him three shots. Back at the galley table he field stripped the gun, cleaned and oiled the various parts, put everything back together, then leaned back with his eyes closed, just for a moment or two, he told himself.

At five, he woke up with a jolt. He'd dozed off. Got to get going. He tossed open the hatches, kicked the engine awake, slipped his mooring, and he was off. A little bit late, he headed out through the pass. Slack was over, and the now outgoing tide was headed west, in his direction. But the velocity hadn't built up yet, and the Anna Marie skated quietly on the surface between the rocky cliffs. Quickly and briefly a whirlpool moved her rapidly twenty feet left, but Hank steered away from trouble and bouncing through a small tide rip composed of short standing waves, it was over. They were out the other side.

Hank checked his compass, taking a visual bearing on the south end of Lopez Island, and Victoria on the distant western horizon. He settled down to wait. A line of smoke on the horizon suggested a steamer, but he couldn't see her and there were no other boats in sight.

It was thirty-six miles west to Victoria. Four or five hours of motoring. Since it was May it would stay bright until nine, but there would be enough light on the water to steer by until ten. He should make it to the inner harbor before it was pitch black. The trick was to avoid falling asleep. Again.

While he traveled he pried the shells off two crab, which didn't make the crabs happy, and cleaned out the innards. He boiled up the meat remaining in the shells and set it to cool in the sink. Dinner was cracked crab, bread and butter and more coffee. The meat was sweet, tender and fresh. He ate every scrap. The shells went overboard. It was now sunset. The low overcast glowed with an intense orange light, and was reflected on the water in lighter blues and shades of orange.

Like most fishermen, he never checked in with Customs. At half past nine he made fast to the Victoria Cannery dock. He had made good time. He sold his catch for cash, and moved deeper inside the harbor to a small moorage on the south side of the harbor reserved for commercial fisherman. The Anna Marie blended right in. There was nothing to do until nine the next morning. It had been a twenty hour day. He went below, stripped to his union suit, and crawled into his bunk beneath two wool blankets. He was soon asleep.

In the morning the first thing Hank did was boil up a huge quantity of hot water. Then he started coffee. He filled a basin, stripped, and took a sponge bath. Carefully, he shaved. Dressed in a clean white shirt, tie and wearing a suit handmade by Jack Hatlen and freshly shined shoes, he drank his first cup of coffee, damped down the stove, put on his hat, locked up and left.

He kept a truck parked on shore above the moorage. One of the new Ford Double A's, designed to carry over 2 tons, it had almost forty horsepower. Not as much as his Packard, but more than enough for what he did here. The bed in back was enclosed by canvas, another essential.

He drove to the Empress, a grand and fancy hotel owned by Canadian Pacific Rail, built as a destination hotel for tourists and honeymooners. He had breakfast in the dining room. A waffle with ham and eggs on the side. Shortly before nine he was in position at Willard Imports. Doing business from a warehouse on Turner Avenue, a business and commercial area, Hank wasn't waiting out front with the other retail customers. He was parked out back, nestled snugly up against the loading dock. Two other bigger trucks were also waiting. The drivers examined each other, and Hank, and nodded, but no one was sharing a smoke or small talk. But then there were also no fights, for which you had to be grateful. Fighting meant you could lose your buying privileges.

If the staff decided they wouldn't sell to you, what were you going to do? Call a policeman? Go to court? "I'm a smuggler, Your Honor, and they won't sell me liquor." Not likely. Which was why everyone was on their best behavior.

The warehouse doors swung open. Three clerks with order books walked out, behind them crews of men with hand trucks. All the employees worked for Willard & Sons, Ltd., a family owned business, which legally imported liquor and sold from this location six days a week, watched over by the B.C. Government. Hank preferred Willard's to the Kennedy Warehouse. Willard's had a better selection.

Officially, the position of the B. C. Government was to uphold the highest moral standards and the rule of law. Plus, to collect tax revenue on every bottle sold. Unofficially, since no Canadian laws were actually broken until the liquor left Canada, enforcement was a matter for the U.S. authorities, to be carried out on their side of the border. Meanwhile, on Turner Avenue, the policy was cash on delivery. You could buy as much as you wanted of whatever was available, as long as you paid immediately, in cash. Hank was in the first three, so he was helped immediately. Gibbs, the clerk he liked best, a one armed veteran of the Battle of the Somme, came to help him.

"Champagne?" Gibbs asked him. He knew what Hank wanted.

"Ten," Hank nodded, meaning cases.

"Epernay?" asked Gibbs. You couldn't always get the same label you purchased previously, but Champagne from the Epernay region would, according to French law, be at least three years old and have that toasty-vanilla flavor with nice small bubbles that Champagne drinkers preferred.

"Fine."

"Oh," and Gibbs grinned from ear to ear. " Would you like some Aquavit?"

"Aquavit? You're pulling my leg."

"Came in yesterday. On a cruise ship from Copenhagen, all the way through the Panama Canal. Thirty cases, and I don't know when, or if, we might see some more."

"Sold. I'll take it all." He would make some extra money with the Aquavit. There were Swedes and Danes in Seattle who considered Aquavit a food, an essential part of the Swedish tradition of smorgasbord, or in the case of the Danes, smorebrod. Norwegians, on the other hand, drank Aquavit with anything, but especially pickled herring.

"Thought you would."

"Any French red?"

"Nothing you'd purchase."

"Thanks," Hank called, but he doubted Gibbs heard him. Two men were already rolling the cases into the back of his truck. Within thirty minutes of his arrival, Hank had paid - cash - and was leaving. Another truck immediately took his place. Forty cases was 480 bottles. After expenses he only cleared seventy-five cents on the resale, or $360.00 per trip, but he was averaging six trips a month. When he started he had done two trips a week. One week with fair weather, he had made three trips. He needed to earn money and replenish his bank account. He'd had to buy a few things, like the truck in Victoria, on credit. Now that he had all his bills paid he could work at a less frantic pace. There were also other ways to make a little more. For instance, his buyers would pay extra for the Aquavit.

Next month would be month seventeen. He wasn't going to be buying John. D. Rockefeller lunch, but for a son of a sod busting Norwegian farmer, as far as he was concerned, he was getting rich.

He returned cautiously to his moorage. No one followed him. He checked often. He proceeded to unload. The Wharfinger in his blue uniform with the kepi hat was collecting moorage fees, but he just waved at Hank and Hank waved back. Hank paid him by the month. Along with a bit of liquid refreshment. With two cases a trip it took twenty trips up and down the dock with a hand truck to load. Half went below in the bow. Half below decks in the stern and stacked around the engine, in among the fuel tanks and the crab tank. But out of sight, out of mind.

It was lunch time before he could start his engine and head for home. First stop was the fuel dock. Second stop, eighty miles away, was Everett. It was sunny and calm as he ran along the shore enjoying the scenery and the big expensive homes that were almost built on the beach. Victoria was sure a pretty place. He ran through the narrow channel between Trial Island and the point at Oak Bay, admiring the houses lined up along the shore, then pointed the Anna Marie east. Out in the Straits it was foggy. Hank preferred fog to any other weather. You steered into a fog bank, and for anyone watching, disappeared, and who knew where you were going, or after a while, where you were?

He veered left, as if he was traveling north up Haro Strait, but as soon as Victoria had disappeared into the fog behind him, he came back around to his right, again headed east, and towards home.

If you could read a chart, and the clock, and knew your boat speed at a specific rpm, only a fool could get lost. He had spent one entire day running time trials over a measured mile when he first re-launched the Anna Marie with her new engine. He purchased a good compass and an accurate clock with a second hand, and unlike most fishermen he made it a point to purchase the government charts. With all those tools, knowing where you were was a process of some fairly simple math. Math, and having made the trip over a hundred times before.

Hell of a thing, thought Hank, two hours later, as the shapes of Cattle Point and Goose Island emerged out of the fog and became distinct. Hell of a thing. I'm back with my Uncle Sammy in the good old U. S. of A. with a boatload of Champagne and Aquavit, both shipped here from 'over there' over huge distances, and crossing the final few miles in a crab boat.

Champagne, at least, ought to travel in style. In the private railroad car of someone wealthy, or better yet, in the plush luxury of that ocean liner from Copenhagen. Not in the bow of the Anna Marie.

Lunch, which he ate late, was an omelet, done in true French style, filled with onions, cheese and Dungeness crab. Plus coffee. He was two hours early for slack at Deception, but he pushed the throttle ahead, adding more power and speed to buck the flow against him, and he slipped through easily. He had decided to hurry. He was only half way home, and getting tired. He swooped down on his string of crab pots, pulled the first ten he found, stacked them, crabs and all, on the back deck, then charged south down Saritoga Passage.

At Everett, on the return trip, he deliberately went the long way in the dredged channel that took him past the Yacht Club, the sawmills, shipyards and canneries. He tried his best to look like any other commercial fishing boat, in his case a crabber, motoring home in the dark, working his back deck, sorting his catch, followed by a flock of diving, screaming seagulls, home late but safe and sound. Hank pitched most of the crabs overboard, but kept a dozen of the bigger males, piled into his empty bait buckets. He also hoped two of the watchers, driving a truck, saw him and would head out to his moorage and meet him.

When he arrived, Johansson and Johansson were waiting for him. He didn't know if that was their real name, or if they actually were twins, but they were as alike as two boiled white potatoes, both in their mid-fifties, both heavy set, blonde white stubble for hair, huge hands with plump white sausages for fingers, and beet red in the face, getting redder if they got angry.

Hank stopped the engine and quietly glided to rest at his moorage. One twin took the bow line, the other the stern, and tied him to the dock. Hank had heard they ran a barbershop, and sold the liquor out the back door, retail, by the bottle.

"Goddamn you, Eide, you're late," said Johansson number one.

"You are late, Eide," echoed Johansson number two.

"Get a new ramp, " groused number one. "Aren't we paying you, Eide?"

"We're paying you," insisted twin number two.

"Goddamn you Eide, are you listening Eide?" bitched number one.

"We're paying you, get a new ramp," said number two, shaking his finger at Hank. Hank was ignoring them.

"We're paying too much," said number one as Hank went inside and forward. "We have to pay you less," called number one after him.

"We can't afford you Eide. Are you listening?" Every trip he made, they tried to renegotiate the price. Downward.

"Goddamn you Eide," number one was about to go on, when Hank, back from inside below, set a case on the deck in front of them.

"You boys are right," said Hank. "The money you're paying me isn't right. I want more." Before they could respond with indignation, Hank pried open the top of the case and simply said, "Aquavit." Hank was counting on what every Norwegian believed about the Swedes to be true: Swedes eat so they can drink.

The twins stood in silence for the longest time, uncharacteristically not saying a word.

"Oh, Eide," they both breathed out in a breathless whisper together. Number one took a bottle out of the case, number two produced a pen knife, number one cut the seal, pulled the stopper, and took a drink. Number two grabbed the bottle and did the same.

"Oh, Eide. Goddamn Eide. For a Norski, you must be part Swedish."

"Swedish," commented number two, taking another drink.

"Oh, ho!" chortled number one, a huge grin on his face. " They will stand in line, Eide. They will each want an entire case, and if they have the money," he shrugged. It was clear, if they had the money they could have a case.

"They will take their Aquavit home, Eide. They will save most of it. They will tuck it away, hide it carefully."

"For Christmas, Eide. They will wait for Christmas."

"After the Lucia Queen walks, Eide, after the Lucia Queen walks." Swedes and some Danes, began Christmas with the Saint Lucia walk on December 13.

"When we are at the table, with our families Eide. Surrounded by children and grandchildren. And with our good friends. At the table. With roast pork, Eide. Potatoes and herring. This Christmas, we will toast with Aquavit," finished number two.

"Skoal!!," said number one, and he tipped back to bottle.

"Skoal!!" responded number two, hopefully, eagerly reaching for the bottle.

"Get to work," barked number one, corking the bottle and putting it back in the case. "How many Aquavit, Eide?" He meant cases.

"Twenty-nine." Hank was holding back a case for his own use. "And ten champagne."

"Fine." They quickly agreed on a price and number one counted him out his money. Everyone worked silently for fifteen minutes and the Anna Marie rose higher in the water as she was unloaded.

"Take six crabs," Hank offered as number two appeared with a gunny sack.

"Thanks," said number two. He began trying to fish crabs out of the bucket.

"Pick them up from the back," Hank instructed. Number two never seemed to learn. The man persisted in trying to pick a crab up by its claws.

"Goddamn," yelled number two, "Goddamn, I'll kill you, you bastard," he yelled down into the bucket. Swedes! thought Hank.

"Here." He quickly and expertly picked up six crabs and stuffed them in the man's gunny. The man nodded his thanks.

Cursing at each other, Hank could still hear them as they drove off into the night.

July 4, 1922

"I used to like parades when I was a kid," said Hank. He puffed his cigar. He and Hadley sat on the running board on the shady side of his truck, waiting for the show to get on the road. Hurry up and wait. It was like being back in the Army. It was a rare Independence Day, with not a cloud in the sky. Usually it rained. The temperature was already near seventy at ten-thirty and it was going to get hotter. Hank's dump truck, together with dozens of other vehicles, were being marshaled into order in the yard at H. O. Siefert, a building supply company on Riverside, located immediately adjacent to Hewitt. The parade route was west on Hewitt from Riverside to Bayside.

All of the H.O. Siefert trucks were decked out matching Hank's, with red, white and blue bunting and banners. Kids ran wild everywhere you looked, playing tag, or hide-and-seek, or simply running and screaming because it was fun. Four hundred sailors, dressed smartly all in white, added to the confusion, blatantly flirting with any woman who passed. The U.S.S. Idaho, the world's most powerful battleship, and a wonder of the age, according to the Everett Herald, was anchored in the harbor.

Five marching bands were warming up, each playing a different tune, and one of the marching societies, the Warm Beach Athletic Association, was marching circles around the other parade entries, their pretty drill mistress dressed in gold sequins and white leather boots, high stepping and calling out the cadence. The team members were already so drunk, Hank marveled they could stand, let alone march.

"Now, I hate parades," Hank went on. "It's like Remembrance Day. I don't want to remember. And the damn fireworks," Hank and Hadley both flinched as a string of firecrackers went off. It was too much like gunfire. " I especially don't like the fireworks. Next year I think I'll go fishing."

"You'll miss my speech," said Hadley, stubbing out his cigarette.

"Good," said Hank, and Hadley laughed.

"They asked me to speak this year," said Hadley.

"And?"

"I graciously declined. Said I might be gone. What the damn fools want is inspiring words about how we learned to be brave soldiers playing sports at Everett High School." Hadley lit another cigarette and blew away the smoke.

"I never attended."

"All I could think of to say," Hadley continued, "was that during the time we spent in France, when we arrived we were too stupid to know any better, and that by the time we did know better, we were frightened to death all the time." Hadley got a nod of agreement from Hank. "What was that song the Brits would sing while they were waiting to go over the top? The one with the barbed wire?"

"Oh," said Hank. Hadley wasn't surprised when Hank sang the lines in a quiet voice:

"If you want to find the old battalion,
I know where they are,
I know where they are.
If you want to find the old battalion,
I know where they are.
Hanging on the old barb wire,
I've seen 'em,
I've seen 'em,
Hanging on the old barb wire, I've seen 'em.
Hanging on the old barb wire."

"Shit," said Hadley. Hank could only agree. Sometimes at night, trying to sleep, he still heard the rat-a-tat-tat of machine gun fire. The screams of men who were wounded.

Fifteen minutes later, that's where Gertrude, Hadley's wife, found them, sitting in silence, smoking. Both men jumped to their feet, swept off their formal dress caps and stood ram-rod straight.

"Ten - shun!" Hadley barked in his best parade ground voice. Both men clicked their black polished boot heels in their best Prussian military style.

"Oh, now stop it you two," said Gertrude with affection. She kissed Hadley on the cheek, then Hank. "You both look so handsome."

"You're feeding him too well," opined Hank.

"True," said Hadley, glancing down at his stomach. Gertrude had discreetly moved the buttons on his dress tunic to give him more breathing room.

"You're the two best looking men in the entire parade," said Gertrude, straightening Hanks tie. "I came to find you," she said turning back to her husband, "because I need to know what you're doing after the parade." Hank started to leave and give them some privacy but Gertrude stopped him with a hand on his sleeve.

"Well, we were supposed to go out to the Idaho for lunch," Hadley said, "but the Parade Committee kicked up such a fuss they re-arranged the program and now we're going to the lunch at the YMCA, then out to the ship, probably for coffee and dessert." Hank nodded his agreement. That was the same as what he had been told.

"Then I'll see you briefly at lunch. But Betsy is really very fussy. She's teething." This last to Hank by way of explanation. "Mama has her now, but I'll probably have to go home fairly quickly."

"I'll see you later, then."

"Yes, and Hank, we're going out to the Club for dinner. Please, join us."

Hadley gave an imperceptible nod, yes.

"Sure," said Hank. It wouldn't be all that bad. The food was good and a decent selection of bootlegged liquor by the drink was available in the bar. He could use a drink. Or three. Gertrude fluttered about a moment more, then left.

I could use a drink right now, thought Hank. As if reading his mind, Hadley pulled out a hip flask and handed it to him. He took a swallow. Scotch. He took another. Good Scotch. He smiled. He only imported the best for Hadley.

"I heard about this fishing lodge up in Canada." Hadley sat back down in the shade. "Some of the big Hollywood people go up there."

"Yeah?"

"Painters Lodge, at Campbell River. Salmon fishing."

"Fishing here is decent." Hank didn't like the notion of spending money to go fishing.

"It can be," agreed Hadley. He smiled to himself. He had presented the lure. Now he set the hook. "They catch really big Chinook - forty, fifty pounds - on light fly rods and tackle."

"You're joking."

"Serious. Serious fish."

"My God," said Hank. The feel of a forty pound Chinook on light tackle, the surge and power, the skill and patience necessary to play a fish that size.

"When can we leave?"

"Tomorrow," replied Hadley, capping the flask. "But it's supposed to be best in mid to late August. Here come our dignitaries," Hadley pointed out. Hank was providing a ride and a platform for the Veterans of the Spanish-American War.

"Did you disable the hydraulic tilt?" asked Hadley.

"I did. I decided it would be bad form to dump them out at the intersection of Hewitt and Colby." Both men laughed at the thought, then composed themselves to be as dignified and formal as the occasion demanded.

Lunch took forever. As Hank expected the parade ran late. It was nearly one o'clock before everyone had straggled back to the YMCA. It was terribly hot. Every window in the high ceilinged room was wide open, but did little to cool off the crowd of hundreds that stood shoulder to shoulder. Extra long trestle tables, ranked in rows, took up most of the floor space. The tables were covered with a hodgepodge of tablecloths, borrowed from every church basement and service club in town. Conditions did not improve when everyone at last was seated. Mason jars filled with flowers added a spot of color. Then they all stood up and the Mayor's wife, "in recognition of all the ladies here who have worked so hard to provide this wonderful lunch," led the guests in reciting the Pledge of Allegiance. They all remained standing to sing "America, the Beautiful," and listen to a prayer. The singing wasn't very good. Hank decided the crowd was light on Norwegians. The prayer went on and on, as the man spoke in a droning monotone.

Then they sat down with much scraping of chairs, to listen to Norma Brevik, an Everett High School graduate studying music at St. Olaf College in Minnesota, sing the "Star Spangled Banner." Norma, a sturdy looking Norwegian, sang beautifully. Hank knew all the Breviks from church. She was accompanied on piano by a woman who looked familiar, but Hank couldn't think of from where.

Lunch was wonderful, if you enjoyed a hot dish made with noodles, or a salad made with Knox Gelatin. There were noodles and tuna. Noodles and chicken with almonds. Lots of noodles and damn few almonds. Noodles in a cream sauce with cheese. There was flavored gelatin with canned fruit salad. Gelatin with bananas. Fresh grape fruit sections. In gelatin. There were dozens of church ladies all wielding huge spoons like terrible swift swords, filling your plate with more food than you could eat, filling glasses to overflowing with water and lemonade, and later, coffee cups with coffee.

Sitting at the head table, perpendicular to all the other tables, Hank couldn't get up and leave when the speeches began. The Mayor blathered a welcome to the U.S.S. Idaho, the Captain, the Officers, the students from Annapolis who were on board for the summer, the men, the cooks, the stewards, and somebody's third cousin twice removed named Fred who once actually had served aboard the Idaho.

The Idaho's Captain of course had to stand up and say thank you, thank you, thank you. He introduced his officers, all of whom were paired up with "the fairest female beauty Everett has to offer." Here Hank almost laughed out loud. He had noticed dozens of sailors - and officers - roaming Riverside last night, where the fairest female beauty on offer was for sale, by the hour, at a negotiable price. But then, there were rumors that even the Mayor was known to frequent a certain establishment.

From that point on he did his best not to listen, except when Hadley kicked him under the table and whispered, "Stand up and smile." Hank stood up, but didn't smile. Still there was an enthusiastic round of applause for "our own brave hero…." Hank sat down.

It was much later when the motorcade deposited Hank, Hadley, the Mayor and other elected officials and the Captain with his Officers at Pier One, and the process of boarding the tug Irene and ferrying out to the Idaho began. At last there was a chance to light a cigar. A nice breeze was blowing across Port Gardner Bay, kicking up white caps that sparkled in the afternoon sun.

"So tell me, Sergeant, why didn't you join the Navy and see the world?" Hadley asked him, taking a pull at his hip flask and handing it to Hank.

"Well," said Hank, straight faced, taking a drink, "You know that I'm Norwegian." Hadley nodded.

"We Norwegians just love mud. It's what makes us so good at cleaning houses. And there ain't no mud in the Navy," Hank said.

"That explains their white uniforms," Hadley observed sagely.

"It must."

"It's all I could think of." They each had another swallow and emptied the flask.

It was after six before the two mud lovers were returned to dry land.

The Captain hadn't offered his guests anything stronger than coffee. With the Federal Volstead Act recently ratified and now law, Hank guessed it would be a brave man who would offer people he didn't know anything stronger. Hank had planned on Hadley driving the two of them to the Club in his automobile, but Hadley said, "Gertrude said she'd meet us there."

Hank drove. Which is why, as they slowly ascended the manicured, tree-lined drive at the Golf Club, in a five ton dump truck decorated with Fourth of July bunting, every golfer they passed stopped to welcome them with a wave and a holler.

"I don't notice the other members arriving in dump trucks," Hank pointed out.

"Wednesday is dump truck day."

"Good. I'll come back. If I'm invited?"

"Consider it done."

"Thanks." There was a maintenance shed on the far side of the parking area. Hank pulled in beside a Massey-Ferguson tractor.

"Perfect," said Hadley grinning.

The Clubhouse was set at the crest of the hill, with views north and west over the tree tops. Built of wood, and somewhat reminiscent of the tourist lodges built by the railroads, stairs led up each side to a 360 degree verandah. Lockers and dressing rooms were in the basement, dining room, kitchen and bar were on the main floor, offices and a small ballroom upstairs. Hank and Hadley headed for the bar. Hadley procured two iced gin and tonics, and they had each half emptied their glasses by the time they sat down outside at a table on the porch.

"Much better."

"Much." Hank loosened his tie. Hadley did the same, then unbuttoned his tunic, took it off and draped it over the back of his chair.

"Get comfortable, Hank." So Hank did the same, and rolled up his sleeves. Informality he regretted a few minutes later when Gertrude made an entrance with another young lady in tow.

"Hadley, darling, why don't you get us two of those," said Gertrude greeting her husband. "Florence, this is our friend, Hank Eide." Hank had stood up.

"Hank, this is a friend of mine from Trinity, Florence Harcus." Hank immediately recognized the piano player from lunch. Then just as suddenly, he made another connection.

"Actually, Mr. Eide and I are aquainted," said Florence.

"Oh?" said Gertrude, sounding disappointed.

"Miss Harcus corrects my addition when I do my banking," explained Hank. Florence was tall, slender, and very pretty, he observed, and had those long bony fingers from playing the piano.

"Mr. Eide is a regular customer," Florence added, overlapping somewhat with Hank. Both out of courtesy stopped what they were saying, leaving the silence to Gertrude.

"Call him Hank. Sit down Florence," Gertrude said, dropping in a chair. "Sit down." This to Hank. She patted Florence on the arm. "You must be exhausted after working all day on that lunch." Florence was tired, and her feet ached terribly. With gratitude she sank into a chair. Hadley came back with four fresh drinks. Hank noticed that when Florence crossed her ankles she was wearing the kind of ugly black boots his mother wore.

"Miss Harcus…," Hadley said by way of greeting, and also to convey some information to Hank.

"Listen," said Gertrude setting her glass down with a thump. "This is not some Victorian novel. This is 1922. This is Florence. This is Hank. This is Hadley. I'm Gertrude. Understood?"

Everyone smiled their agreement.

"Good. Now, where is that waiter? I want a steak."

As it happened, as Gertrude meant for it to happen, as everyone knew Gertrude meant for it to happen, Hadley had too much to drink, Gertrude said she had better take him home, and Hank ended up having to give Florence a ride home. Hank and Florence scrunched across the gravel.

"Florence, I'm sorry," Hank apologized. "But this is your ride home." Hank's Packard dump truck glistened in the moonlight.

"Oh," said Florence. "Oh."

"You can laugh. It's what I did the first time I saw it."

"You own this truck?"

"All mine."

"I've noticed it before, I've seen it around town, and I've always wondered…."

"I didn't paint it. I don't know why it's painted this way."

"Oh, Hank," she couldn't stop laughing.

"It's not a coach and four, and it also won't disappear at mid-night, I'm afraid. But if you climb up on the running board and have a seat in the cab…." Hank gave her a hand. The bench seat was really designed for one and they sat scrunched together, shoulder to shoulder, thigh to thigh. Then they were off, down the hill.

"Do you have a horn."

"My, yes," said Hank. "It's an air horn. Very loud." He gestured at a cord hanging from the roof with a wooden handle.

"May I?"

"Go ahead."

Hank knew what was coming. Florence pulled the cord, and jumped where she sat with a start as a deep ear-splitting bellow split the silence. Now Hank was laughing.

"We can wake the dead," she opined, joining his laughter. Then she pulled the cord again. Florence gave him directions, and when they arrived, Hank pulled onto the side street at 22nd and Rucker, and parked.

"Hank, I can't ask you in. But if you're willing to sit on the steps, I can provide lemonade."

"Great."

Hank sat on the steps. The breeze had died, and the evening air was still and warm, shirtsleeve weather at ten pm. Rare in Everett. Florence eventually came back with a pitcher and two glasses. Hank noticed she was wearing slippers. Much cooler.

Hank took a sip. It was blissfully cool. "Thank you. Tart. Very nice."

"I think most people add too much sugar."

"Um," said Hank, swallowing.

There was a silence. There was a huge tree in the front yard that shaded the porch. "What kind of tree is this? With those big leaves?" Hank asked.

"A catalpa. You don't see very many of them."

"I've always wondered." There was another silence. "You can see the Idaho," Hank said.

"Where?"

"There." He pointed at a gap between two houses across the street where you could see the bay. The Idaho was all lit up, from stem to stern.

"Oh, yes. The paper says she's like a little city, with a barbershop and a bakery, a laundry, everything." There was another silence. "Weren't you out there today? I know Hadley was."

"That's right. They took us out." Now Hank paused. "She's very big and impressive. Huge guns. Much bigger than anything I've ever worked on." Hank took a deep breath, blew it out. "The crew call her, The Big Spud." Florence laughed. "Unfortunately she's a spud that sinks," finished Hank. It had been his chief thought while he was aboard, one he had kept to himself.

"I don't understand."

Hank shrugged. "One submarine, with a determined crew, and the Idaho, and all her crew, is on the bottom."

"Oh. Oh, you mean like the Lusitania?"

"Exactly like." It was a gruesome thought, and it stopped all conversation.

But it gave Florence an opening for a question she had been thinking about. "Hank, I don't really know you, but could I ask you a question?"

"Go ahead."

"Well…you and Hadley…you and Hadley… everyone else talks about the War, except you two. When people came over, tonight at our table, and started a conversation about the war you were both very polite and you smiled…" Florence trailed off. "You and Hadley were the ones who went over there and fought in the war," she said lamely. "Yet you say so little."

"I don't like to talk about it." He stopped.

Florence decided she had offended him. Then quietly, in a voice she had to lean forward to hear, he said, "Too many people died. We were just trying to stay alive." He stopped again. "We were lucky. A huge number of people weren't."

"I'm sorry." She emptied her glass and poured them both another. "I'm not an American," she offered as an explanation, and an apology. "I'm Canadian. I was born in Victoria. Canada entered the war with the rest of the British Empire in 1914." She paused.

"There was a nice man who courted my Aunt Margaret before the war. He took us rowing once. He died fighting in Belgium, in 1915." She took a deep breath. "I used to read the casualty lists in the Colonist out loud after dinner. To my aunts. Usually I ended up in tears." Florence had her knees pulled up under her chin and her arms around her legs.

"I felt so sad and helpless. I think that's why they sent me here, to Everett." For a long time neither one of them spoke. He really didn't know her well enough to offer any kind of comfort. Finally, he stood up.

"When I think about the war, Florence, I feel exactly the same way." He handed her his glass. "Thanks for the lemonade." He smiled at her. "Good night. "

"Good night." She waited on the steps until she heard him drive away. She picked up her glasses and the pitcher and went upstairs to bed.

A Saturday Walk

Nearly all week, Monday, Tuesday, Wednesday and Thursday, Hank had the Anna Marie up and on the ways at the boathouse. Four beautiful July summer days, hot and calm. The air was warm, but the roof – even with all the holes – provided good shade. He re-caulked the bottom plank seams below the waterline with new oakum and seam compound. There was a rhythm to caulking. It helped if you sang or hummed a tune. He painted all the seams with red lead Tuesday night. When the seams were good and dry, it was sand, sand, sand and blow, blow, blow your nose, to get out all the sanding dust. He re-painted the entire bottom Wednesday morning and slid back into the water Thursday evening on the high tide. All this time he prayed the weather would hold for a trip to Victoria on Friday. But you could see the change coming by the wind direction. She started to blow out of the south.

Sure enough, it was overcast Friday morning when he got up. The wind had definitely come around to the south to stay for a while and it was blowing hard. As he ran up Saratoga the weather filling in behind him got worse. The sky darkened and intermittently it rained. He worked his pots, and arrived at Deception Pass bang on the slack, but it didn't look good. He poked his nose outside the Pass to see what could be seen.

He sat on the north shore of Deception Island in the lee of the wind, going up and down in what had to be a ten foot ground swell. He guessed the wind was blowing thirty knots plus, with higher gusts. It was a sea of whitecaps. Worse, the tops of the cresting waves were being blown off, and scudded off north, making this watery environment appear to be made of drifting sand. Not a chance. He wasn't going out there. Not today.

He swung the wheel 180 degrees. Better to go back inside and wait, than take a bad risk. He rafted up with a log tow moored against some pilings on the south side of Coronet Bay. He sluiced down the deck with buckets of salt water and mopped and scrubbed for an hour.

The weather got worse. The rain was constant, coming down in sheets. The tide was going out. The logs on the inside edge of the tow rose higher as they went aground in the shallow water. Which presented an interesting possibility. He took off his boots and wool socks. Rolled up his pant legs. With bucket in hand, he cautiously crept from log to log over the tow and stepped ashore on the sandy beach.

It had been ten years, maybe more, since he had scrambled around barefoot like this on a beach. The stones and the barnacles seemed harder and sharper and he danced gingerly from foot to foot. What brought him ashore were the clams in the eel grass at the water's edge. You could see the clams spitting.

Putting his weight on his heels, he stomped through the eel grass. His heel hit a lump. He reached down and pulled the lump out of the soft sand. It was a cockle clam. Another clam spit. He stomped over the area. Another clam. Another. When he had two dozen he went back to the boat. He was soaked, wet to the skin. He stripped off his wet clothes, toweled off, changed into dry clothes, and built up the fire.

The cockles were the size of a small peach, and each had a two inch long digger foot which he cut out and chopped up. He cubed some bacon, fried it up. He didn't have an onion, but he did have three potatoes. He peeled them, diced them, and fried them briefly with the bacon. He added the clams, their juice, and a pint of milk to the pan. Salt. Pepper. When the potatoes were soft he had lunch. Maybe there was enough for dinner if he put in some crab meat. He fell asleep reading an old issue of the Saturday Evening Post.

The weather was no better when he woke up. He ate his supper, left over chowder, washed the dirty dishes and wiped down the galley. He opened the hatches, climbed down beside the engine, and spent the evening hours changing the oil, cleaning the filters, the plugs, adjusting the timing, tightening hose fittings, inspecting all moving parts for wear and tear. No drip of oil, no smudge of grease went unnoticed. Satisfied, he closed up.

He opened the galley door but sat inside, smoking a cigar and listening to the rain pound on the roof, watching the small puddled rings on the bay's surface changing color as daylight seeped away and became darkness.

He thought about Florence, but he didn't know what to think. She was simply someone he had been introduced to. She was very attractive. However, he was basically a mill hand. She was educated. He was not. His sisters, his mother, his brother's wives, they all sewed. They were always nicely turned out. Very respectable to be sure. Florence, either she wore clothes that she bought at the better stores, or if she sewed, she made clothes like you saw rich people wearing in the newspapers. Simply looking at her you knew she came from money. She fit right in with the Golf Club crowd. If he hadn't been wearing his uniform, and with Hadley, he would have felt very out of place.

She wasn't like him. She wasn't his people. Still, she was very attractive. Even wearing those stupid boots, she was graceful. He liked the way she moved. He like her shy smile. He chucked his cigar butt overboard, closed the galley door and went to bed.

The weather was no better in the morning. Even if he arrived in Victoria later today, he couldn't do any business until Monday. As for waiting another day, all he had left to eat was eggs. He was nearly out of coffee. Might as well go home. Go to church tomorrow, have dinner with his parents, start north again on Monday. He started the engine. South then.

Florence slept through the storm Friday night, and woke up Saturday morning with the day off and nothing planned. Except that if someone didn't do laundry and iron, she would either have to sew up another dress, or go naked to work on Monday. With a sigh she slid out of bed. Well, it appeared it was going to rain all day, anyway. As always she began her day with the newspaper and coffee.

At two, flushed from hot water, steam and the heat of her iron, she was done. She'd polished all her boots. Sewed back five buttons and fixed a hem. The dress she would wear tomorrow to church was pressed and hanging on the back of her bedroom closet door. She considered a bath, but she was tired of being hot, wet and steamy. She wanted to go for a walk. She went for a walk. After walking for twenty minutes she was disgusted. It wasn't raining, it was pouring. Her feet were soaked. She should have turned around and gone home but she didn't want to go home.

At Fourteenth and Grand there was a steep switchback stairway that led from the top of the bank down to the waterfront below. It was there for the convenience of mill hands and cannery workers who walked to and from their waterfront jobs. But anyone was welcome to use the stairs. If she went down, maybe she could find a net shed on one of the docks where she could sit, dry out, and maybe watch the boats. She had a dollar in her pocket. She might find some fish she could purchase for supper.

At the bottom of the hill she had to thread her way through rows of stationary railroad freight cars, all with a big white mountain goat and "Union Pacific" painted on the side. It made her nervous. You never knew when a line of cars might begin to move. At Fourteenth Street, on the commercial fishing pier near the Everett Packing Company, she found shelter under a shed roof that was covering thousands, just thousands, of wooden cases of canned salmon. Her chair was a stack of empty wooden crates. On the far south side of the dock men in work clothes were brailing salmon up out of the holds of fish boats, and the dock was a knee high mass of silver salmon, streaked red with blood. Gulls swooped and dove over the pier, occasionally tried to land and steal a fish, and their raucous cries mixed with the shouts of the dockworkers and the grind of machinery. From her work at the bank, Florence knew that many of these men were from Croatia. Not that she saw the men. She dealt with their wives, who did the banking.

So far the shoulder seams of her rubber jacket weren't leaking so some of her clothing was dry. You couldn't say the same for her boots. She became aware that someone was standing in front of her, staring at her. A man, with two other men.

"Well, now," said Jimmy Sullivan in his thickest Irish, a huge grin splitting his face. "What have we here? Miss Florence, is it?"

She recognized him but decided to ignore him. He worked for Mr. Waters. The other two she didn't know.

"Cat got yer tongue, eh? Jimmy don't mind. Most people don't want to talk to me." His friends laughed at this apparent joke. He waited, hoping she'd give him some kind of opening, but she sat silent and looked away.

"Boys, this fancy lady is some kind of relation to Mr. Waters. These is my boys, Miss Florence, Bobby here, and Jack. Say hello, boys." Both men muttered a hello. Florence didn't respond, or even glance their way. Jimmy decided there was no hurry.

"Funny place to see you, Miss Florence." He tipped his hat. "Mind how you go, now." Jimmy and his friends walked off.

Florence didn't want to know Jimmy, and she didn't want him to know her. He reminded her of Mr. Waters, and those memories always made her very angry and uncomfortable. She stood up and moved quickly in the opposite direction, out towards the end of the dock.

Hank tossed the last two crab into the crate. He gave the thumbs up sign. And the man topside winched the crate up to the dock and out of his sight. He came back in a few minutes.

"Total of six hunret six three pounds," the man called down. "Cash or credit?"

"Cash," Hank called back. The man waved. Come on up.

Hank climbed the slimy wood ladder. Several of the rungs creaked when he put weight on them. He was glad to get away from the stink. The tide flat area under the dock was a mess of rotting fish carcasses. The dock man counted cash and coins into his hand, then went back inside his shack where it was warm and dry.

Hank stuffed the money in his shirt pocket. Crab was up two cents a pound. If he wasn't careful he might make money crab fishing

"Hank?" He had to look twice. It was Florence Harcus. Dressed like a Newfoundland cod fisherman in knee length foul weather gear and a Sou'wester, worn properly with the long bill down the back. Only cod fisherman usually didn't wear bright yellow slickers. Nine dollars mail order from Sears and Roebuck, last time Hank checked. Although he preferred the olive green. Regardless of color, it was still a wet bedraggled Florence. He should have known her instantly from the ugly black boots.

"You look wet."

"I am wet. What are you doing here?"

"Selling crabs. That's my boat." He gestured and it was clear he meant down below, at the bottom of the ladder. Florence walked over to the edge. Down below was a fish boat that appeared to her untrained eye, much like all the others, except…

"You don't have those long wooden poles."

"No. Those are trolling poles, you use them fishing for salmon. I fish for crab. And no nets. The smaller boats with nets are gill-netters. Although this boat was a gill-netter when I bought her. I use crab pots." He used his arms to approximate the size. "I'd show you one but all of them are in the water. Hopefully catching crabs."

He was getting soaked standing out in the rain. He had an idea. "Come up the river with me and I'll show you a crab pot when we get to my moorage."

Florence had to admit it was an original line.

"Will you bring me back here?"

"No," Hank shook his head, "I'm headed for my moorage, but I can provide you a ride home from there." Florence was tempted. It seemed harmless. Plus

Jimmy and his friends were somewhere on the dock behind her. It was also a long wet walk home.

"Fine," she said. It might be interesting, she thought.

"Fine," agreed Hank. This could be interesting, he thought. He made for the ladder. Then had a thought: She was wearing a skirt. "Please," he indicated she should go first. "You first."

Florence hesitated, then climbed down the ladder, Hank following. Her hands were filthy and slimy when she got to the bottom. As the Anna Marie motored away from the dock, she glanced back. Was someone watching? She couldn't tell.

"You can hang your wet things on the back of the door," Hank called from the wheel. "If you want to clean your hands, there's water at the sink, soap and a towel. Just work the pump handle."

Florence stepped into the cabin and pulled the door shut behind her. She hung up her rain gear. Washed and dried her hands. The towel was an old sugar sack, feather stitched around the edges. The cabin was cozy and warm, a fire in the stove.

"Coffee?"

"Yes. Please." It was very strong, and hot. She wondered if he had any sugar. Mug in hand, she stood beside him at the wheel.

"I've never seen Everett from the river."

"It does look different." The engine hummed right along, sending vibrations up through her feet.

She pointed. "What's that mill?"

"They make millwork. Doors, windows and sashes, things like that." A gust of wind and rain hit Anna Marie, spattering the windshield. The cabin heat should be making her feel a bit drowsy, yet suddenly she felt very relaxed and at ease. The hot coffee was having an effect and the passing scenery was new and interesting. She felt revived. Hank was wearing a wool cap on his bald head. He looked very young.

"What kind of engine does your boat have?"

Hank usually wouldn't talk about the Anna Marie, but he saw no harm in Florence. He explained about the Liberty engine. The hull. Building the new cabinhouse and decks. Silences were awkward, so he filled them. As they moved up the river and into the backwaters, they saw more and more Great Blue Herons.

"I like the Herons," said Florence. "They seem so serious and solemn."

"They're good fishermen," said Hank. "But they have to be. Catch fish or starve. Speaking of which…."

Hank mentioned that he had two small fish. Would she like one - or both- for her supper? They ended up at her apartment.

She couldn't remain on the boat for very long. His place was out of the question. She asked him to hers. When they crossed town, they stopped at West Dependable and purchased a few groceries. When they arrived at her apartment he did notice she carefully propped the door to the hall open.

Her apartment was what he expected. Clean and elegant. Like Florence. Hardwood floors. Polished furniture. Oriental rugs. Pictures in nice frames on the walls. Florence lived much the same way as Hadley and Gertrude. There wasn't a hand crocheted doily or tablecloth in sight. He also noted two pair of boots arranged neatly beside a wing chair. That meant, along with the sopping wet boots she had just taken off, she had three pair. Curious. Hank stood at her sink with a long thin filleting knife he'd brought with him.

"What are those?" The two small fish were white on the belly, but a dark mottled brownish- green on top. Both were the size of a dinner plate.

"I don't know their real name. We always call them Sand Dabs." Each fish yielded two thin filets the size of his hand off the belly side. Then he cut the white skin away from the filets. He wrapped the bloody remains in newspaper.

"I'll take that with me so it won't smell up your place."

"That's all the meat?"

"That's all. The rest is bones and parts you wouldn't want to eat. Unless you're a crab."

"And they swim into your pots?"

"Occasionally. Not often. But with sixty pots, I usually catch something besides crab. Lots of fish swimming along the bottom. Say, when the potatoes are done, I'll cook the fish for you. " Florence had a dozen small white potatoes on the boil.

"Thanks. I'm not much of a fish cook. I guess I cook it too long."

"Most people do."

"You cook?"

"Some."

"Did your mother teach you?"

Hank laughed. "Yes and no. Bacon, eggs, coffee, she taught me those things. But when I was 'over there', the French, they have a different way of doing things." He stopped.

"Go on."

"After the Armistice there wasn't much for an Artillery Brigade to do. Most of our equipment had been loaned to us, and it all went back to the French. Heavy equipment that we had shipped over was being sold, or given, to the French, or the Belgians. Christmas, 1918 I was told to take thirty days leave. Hadley left with the staff, so I found this inexpensive place to stay in Paris. Up on this hill, called Montmartre." He poked a fork into a potato.

"Getting close."

"I stayed on this little street called Rue Lepic. Dozens of tiny cafés and bars. Green grocers, bakeries, shops that sold nothing but birds, even little tiny song birds that you eat, or fish. Places that sold nothing but hundreds of different cheeses. It was very different."

"What did you do?"

"I slept a lot," he admitted ruefully, and laughed. "And I ate." He considered, then confessed. "And I drank. Champagne and red wine."

"Wine?"

"Three times a day. Not with breakfast," He added hurriedly seeing her concerned look, "but with lunch, dinner, and in these little places that sell nothing but glasses of different wines, and maybe some light food, until they close around midnight. Some of these places had music, or people who played, then passed the hat."

He paused to see how she was reacting. Some people were very unforgiving on the topic of alcohol. Also jazz music. Saw both as part of Satan's master plan to corrupt America. He decided not to mention the jazz.

"What does this have to do with learning to cook?" Florence sounded more curious than disapproving.

Hank laughed. "These places were small. Four, six, maybe eight tables. The kitchen was usually right out front with the tables, where you could watch. And it was never the women who cooked. Always a man. I watched, I asked questions, and I learned."

"Do you speak French?"

"Oui," Hank answered, and Florence laughed appropriately. "Maybe eighty-ninety words, and most of that is spark plugs, tools, truck parts. But I had this little book with some words and phrases, and sometimes you found someone with a little English, and you could always point and say 'please'. Believe me, I ate very well."

He set her cast iron frying pan on the heat and added a huge glob of butter. When the butter started to brown he added the fish. He counted slowly to one hundred and twenty, and turned it. He counted again, and moved the fish onto plates. Florence didn't think he had cooked the fish at all. He dropped a big handful of chopped parsley into the brown butter, along with the boiled potatoes, which he rolled around to coat them on all sides, then divided the potatoes and the sauce between the two plates, and added a generous squeeze of lemon, salt and pepper, to each plate.

"That's all?"

"Well, the French would add some flaked almonds to the sauce, but for Everett, that's all. Come on." Hank carried the plates and they sat down quickly at her dining room table and ate.

Florence was impressed. "Hank, this is delicious."

"How you gonna keep them down on the farm," he sang quietly, "after they've eaten French food?"

Florence put back her head and laughed.

Hank wished he'd brought a bottle of Champagne.

A July Picnic

Hank sat aboard the Anna Marie, drinking a cup of coffee. He looked around at the interior. It was all shipshape, everything in its proper place, all neat, clean and Bristol. But. "Damn." What was he going to do? He had invited Florence to go on a picnic. To spend the entire day on the boat. Next Saturday. And she said yes. Hallelujah!

But if a woman spent the entire day aboard, she would expect to be able to relieve herself. Where? Did he build an outhouse on the stern? It was an amusing picture, pages of the Sears catalog fluttering off into the wake. It was also stupid. Could he provide a bucket? Look the other way?

None of these solutions seemed suitable for Florence. His parents' home was very nice, very comfortable. Florence's apartment was also very comfortable, but it was also elegant. What was the comfortable and elegant solution? What did rich people do? Not urinate?

He went to the library. Then he drove the Packard to Seattle. That took all morning. There was a ship chandler in Ballard that advertised in "Rudder", a boating magazine that catered to the yachting crowd. This chandler in Seattle declared in their advertising that they sold Wilcox-Crittenden yacht fittings to the "discriminating yachtsman".

Hank was certain he wasn't the "discriminating yachtsman" their advertising had in mind. He didn't own a double-breasted blazer, but they gladly provided him a truck load of equipment for cash. He drove back to Everett, which took the balance of the day. With the picnic planned for Saturday, he had four days to work. He hoped everything he'd bought worked as advertised. There wasn't room in the schedule to go back and forth to Seattle again. Certainly there would be no trip to Victoria this week. Johansson and Johansson were not going to be pleased.

On Saturday morning, Hank picked up Florence early. As promised, she brought the picnic lunch. At the boat, Florence watched Hank lift the engine hatches.

"I wondered where it was."

"Right here," Hank said, standing on the bilge-stringers.

"It's big. Four hundred horsepower?" she recalled their earlier discussion.

"Four hundred horsepower," Hank confirmed. He put the glass cover back over the points. Everything was fine. He pulled the rope cord on the starter motor. It ran rough for a moment, then smoothed out. He continued to listen for a moment, then engaged the clutch and the Liberty turned over, then roared to life. He adjusted the throttle. She settled down and purred. He shut down the starter motor.

"Hooray!" cheered Florence.

Hank laughed. "She better run. She has to run every time. Otherwise we swim or walk home." He climbed out of the bilge, shut the hatches, and it became much quieter, a noise you could easily speak over and be heard. Florence noticed as they pulled away from the dock they were towing a small skiff, flat bottomed, painted dark green. Hank called it his duckboat.

Going north up Saritoga, Florence cooked breakfast. Bacon, eggs over easy, fried potatoes, coffee. Hank watched, and ate. It was all very good, except the coffee, which to his taste was weak. Hank pushed their speed up to twelve knots an hour. He burned more gasoline, but he didn't want to spend the entire day motoring. Florence took her turn at the wheel, and Hank got to sit and watch the miles go past. The rising sun lit up the Olympic Mountains with a red glow, and the bay stayed flat and calm.

Hank had told her he needed to pull his traps. He explained the colored corks, showed her how to work the controls, and Florence ran the boat while he did the heavy lifting. With two of them the job went quickly. "You work hard, Hank," Florence observed, as he tossed the last pot back in the bay and played out the line.

"These pots have been soaking for a week. This was a very good haul." He took off his hat and wiped the sweat off his forehead, and smiled. "Normally, they aren't quite that heavy."

They had the time, so Hank ran up around the corner, past Cornet Bay, to the approaches of Deception Pass.

"The tides running pretty hard against us, so we won't go through," he explained. "But over there, about thirty-five miles, is Victoria. You mentioned you grew up there."

"I did. I haven't been there in years." She sounded very sad. "I never realized it was so very close."

There was a big boom log on the loose, headed right towards them. Hank spun the wheel. "We better get out of the way." Florence turned, and watched Victoria disappear from view.

They motored back a mile east, and anchored off the north shore of Hope Island. Florence was becoming uncomfortable. She had restricted herself to one cup of coffee, but according to the ships clock it was nearly half past eleven.

"Can we go ashore?" she asked, looking hopefully at the sand beach in a small cove, then over some logs along the shore, then an easy climb up a low bank to some dense shrubbery.

"We will. But you might want to use the W.C. before we go ashore."

Her eyes widened, but she didn't speak.

"Forward. Below? In the bow?"

When she was steering, she had noticed what she thought was a new wall in the cuddy cabin forward, but she went down the three steps very surprised. Where there had been two berths and a floor, now there was one berth on the right, not much floor, and a wall, about chin high, to her left. A wall with a narrow door and a brass handle.

She opened the door and stepped inside. "Open Sesame," she breathed. There was a half-sized toilet, a mirror above a small sink with a pump handle, a brass soap dish mounted to the wall above the sink, with a bar of Ivory soap, two bright white towels and a washcloth on a brass towel bar, and a roll of toilet paper on a brass holder. Conveniently, there was a brass plate with instructions mounted where it could easily be read. As she pumped the bowl dry she giggled as she watched the wash water swirl down the drain. She couldn't imagine many fishing boats being as well equipped.

Hank was kneeling on the stern, setting picnic things into the skiff. Florence came out the cabin door laughing.

"Hank, is it all new?"

He sat back on his haunches and smiled. "It is."

"And you did all that for me?" She said it as a joke, but immediately realized it was a very awkward question.

Hank's smile faded a bit, but he looked her in the eye. "I didn't install the toothbrush holder." He paused. "I wasn't sure we needed it."

Conversation stopped.

Then Florence surprised herself and Hank again. She went to him, leaned down and kissed him on the cheek . Her lips were warm.

"Thank you. It's very thoughtful." She stood up, and backed away a step. But her hand remained on his shoulder, where she had placed it for balance.

"You're welcome."

"Are we going ashore now?" she asked.

"We should take lunch with us."

"Good idea." She went back in the cabin to retrieve the rest of her picnic food.

The afternoon was long and relaxing. They went swimming. They ate. Florence had boiled up a small piece of corned beef. They had sandwiches on rye bread with mustard and horseradish, with good pickles, and peach pie for dessert. Hank was impressed. Her pie crust was as good as his mother's, the woman generally regarded as the best pie maker at Central Lutheran Church.

The day was hot. After lunch they both felt drowsy and they fell asleep in the sun. Both got sunburned. They swam again to cool off. Finally, when Hank guessed it was after five, he said, "Florence, we're four hours from home."

Slowly they packed up, rowed back to the Anna Marie, and were on their way. Hank ran at eight knots. He was in no hurry for the day to end. He boiled up three crabs, and with the sunset turning the sky pink and red they ate supper. Again, Hank had been tempted to bring a bottle of Champagne, but he didn't want Florence to misread his intentions. Even though, after that gentle, soft kiss, and seeing her in a wet bathing suit, he was absolutely certain what his intentions were.

With Hat Island and Everett in sight, Florence fell asleep at the galley table. Hank covered her with a blanket and she continued to sleep. When he made the turn into the harbor mouth, Florence woke up and insisted he stop to sell his catch, so he did. She fell back asleep as he unloaded, and he woke her as he approached his moorage.

"Florence, wake up.' He gently shook her. "We've got company."

Three men he didn't recognize were standing in the glare of the headlights of an automobile. Clearly they wanted Hank and Florence to see them. Florence came and stood next to Hank at the wheel.

"I don't know these men," said Hank.

"The man in the middle. I think…he's Jimmy Sullivan. He works for my Uncle."

"Who's your uncle?"

"Charles Waters." The name didn't mean anything to Hank.

"What do they want?"

"I have no idea." Hank continued to stare at her, but she had nothing to add.

The Colt wasn't on board. There was also nothing incriminating on board, like liquor. Hank glided into the dock, shut down, stepped off and made the Anna Marie secure. The three men, each carrying an ax handle, crossed down his board ramp, the man Florence had identified as Jimmy leading. Four people on his two log float sank the logs lower and made moving a problem.

"Help you?"

"Probably not," said Jimmy. "Miss Florence, let's go."

Hank turned to look at Florence. "Do you want to go with these men?"

"No."

Hank turned back to Jimmy. "I'm sorry, the lady said no. I think you should leave."

"I'm not ready," said Jimmy. He swung his ax handle at Hank's head. Hank ducked, and grabbed Jimmy's handle, and Jimmy, overbalanced, either had to let go or fall in. He let go.

One of the men had gotten around behind Hank, and Hank stuffed his handle into the man's stomach, which doubled him over. Then Hank hit him in the head. The man went down and Hank thought he'd stay there for awhile. But Jimmy and the other man charged him, and Hank was swarmed under. The last thing he remembered was Florence screaming, then being hit hard on his own head.

Sunday

Hank had waited all day for Waters to show up. He had spent part of the night standing guard outside of Florence's apartment. He sat on the grass and smoked several cigars. When he saw her lights go on, he concluded she was as fine as he could do anything about at the moment, and he left. He'd talk to her tomorrow.

Waters came bumping down the rutted dirt road that led to his dock an hour before sunset. Hank found it ironic that Waters arrived in a four door Packard Coupe. New, they sold for over $6,000.00. Florence was right, this man was rich.

Hank was standing on dry land. He had picked the ground for this meeting carefully. He stood with his hands clasped behind his back. Waters got out of his Packard, and walked up to him. He was wearing a hat, and an overcoat, with his hands in the pockets. It seemed a little warm for such clothing. Waters stopped five feet away.

"Eide."

"I don't think I know you."

"But you know who I am."

"Yes."

"So you know me. I didn't drive all the way out here to shake your hand."

"And here I thought this was a social call. I made coffee."

"Eide, the hospital called me this morning. You had a busy night."

Hank didn't speak.

"The Doctors figure Jimmy was hit with something like an ax handle in the mouth, and on his arm-"

"It was a baseball bat," Hank interjected. "I made it myself on a lathe when I was an apprentice." Waters got redder.

"I'm so glad," he said rigidly, "that you're so talented. What they can't figure is how his legs were crushed." Waters stopped and waited.

"Too bad. I was hoping he'd remember. Next time," Hank offered, "I'll run over his head."

Waters turned to examine Hank's truck. He noted the big back wheels. His patience was gone. "There won't be a next time." He took his right hand out of his pocket. He was holding a revolver.

"You're a hard man, Eide. I like hard men. I wish you worked for me. But it's too late for that. You're in my way."

Hank took his right hand out from behind his back, and raised it to eye level. Waters was staring down the barrel of Hank's Colt .45 automatic.

"You made a serious mistake, Waters." Waters did not yet understand. The Colt was cocked, the hammer was back in the firing position.

"What's that?" he said sneering.

"Your gun isn't cocked. I see your trigger finger move, and you're dead." Hank slowly walked up closer to Waters, stopping when the Colt was eighteen inches from Waters' head.

"Decide. Asshole." Hank was trying to provoke him. "Dead, wrapped in old anchor chain, at the bottom of Puget Sound, I figure they won't ever find you, Waters. Will anyone miss you?" Hank wasn't eager to kill the bastard, but it seemed like the simplest solution

Waters wanted to stare Hank in the eye, but his attention was riveted on the Colt's hammer. They stood there, each frozen in position, for several minutes.

Swallows chasing dinner flew all around them. There wasn't a cloud in the sky. Waters was facing into the sun. Hank was all back lit. His eyes crinkled at the corners, and he was smiling slightly. His eyes were blue and steady. Waters could feel his hand start to quiver, and a tiny trickle of urine escaped and ran down his leg. He clamped down hard on all his muscles. Except his trigger finger.

"Let me drop this," he said. He almost said please.

"Go ahead."

Waters moved his arm to the side and let go of his gun. It seemed like Hank's smile got bigger.

Hank adjusted his aim. And pulled the trigger. Waters screamed in pain. Hank stepped aside, aimed, and fired five more shots.

Blackberry Pie

Sunday night about seven p.m. Florence made one phone call. She went downstairs and asked Miss Clark if she could use her telephone to make a local call.

"Of course, dear. It's in the kitchen."

Miss Clark remained in her sitting room, which gave Florence some privacy. "Hello, Central? I need to speak with Blue 368. Thank you."

"Hello," Mr. Lind said. Florence was glad he had answered instead of his wife.

"Mr. Lind, this is Miss Harcus."

"Florence? Oh, yes. What is it?" He got straight to the point.

"Mr. Lind, I'm sorry to bother you." Florence knew he didn't like business on Sunday. "I'm not well. I won't be in tomorrow."

"Oh? I'm sorry to hear that. But are you certain? We hate to have our girls miss a day of work."

"Mr. Lind, I won't be in."

"We really don't like this, Florence."

"This is the first time, Mr. Lind."

"Nevertheless, Florence-"

"Thank you Mr. Lind. I have to go back to bed." She hung up. She was in tears as she climbed the stairs back to her apartment. It was so frustrating, these men who had nothing to do with her, always telling her what to do. She hadn't left the house today. She was too frightened. She wasn't sleepy, but she went to bed and read.

When she woke up Monday morning it was barely light out. She had been in bed for hours. She felt restless. She knew she had to walk. Better go now, before anyone would see her. She got up.

Wearing an old dress and a ragged sweater, she went down the alley to the end of the block. There was a vacant lot growing wild blackberries. The little ones. She filled a kettle, scratching and staining her arms, then went home. It still wasn't eight. She ate a light breakfast, read her paper. Then instead of leaving for work, she made pie crust. She put her pie in the oven, noted the time, and went to her back bedroom. Here was her piano.

She was working on a piece by Greig. A concerto for piano. It was giving her fits, and most days she didn't have the patience to work on it. But today was going to be the day. Grimly, she started to break the piece down. Measure by measure she worked out the fingering. Phrase by phrase by phrase she tied the measures together. She added timing. Tempo. Tone. Then she went on. Then back to the beginning. Over and over and over. Again. Again. Again. She almost clawed at the keys. It was drill. It was mostly mechanical. It was boring. It was also a relief, a release, an escape. The music drove all other thoughts out of her head.

Hank came by a little after nine thirty. The door was open. He heard piano music. He rapped on the doorjamb. There was no answer. The music was coming from her apartment, but he didn't remember a piano. He decided to wait, and listen. He was wearing a suit and bow tie. His shoes were shined. Hat in hand, he arrived both fearful and hopeful. He had all day, and so apparently did Florence.

His nose told him there was a problem. There was something burning. Something in the oven. He knocked again. Louder.

"Florence?" There was no answer. The piano playing continued.

He took three steps into her apartment, which allowed him to peek into the kitchen. Maybe he could easily solve the problem. Whatever was burning was in the oven. He opened the oven door, and smoke billowed out. It was a pie, and it was boiling over. There wasn't a damn thing on the countertops he could use to reach in with and pick up the pie. Not a towel, not a potholder, nothing. He considered opening drawers, but that seemed presumptuous. The music was coming from down the hall.

"Florence!" No answer. Frustrated, he walked down the hall towards the sound of the piano and slowly pushed open the door.

She was sitting at her piano, a small grand piano, not an upright he noted, bent over the keyboard, eyes closed, very intense. She was wearing a blue jumper, no blouse, her arms and shoulders were bare.

"Florence!"

She froze. Her eyes flew open and she sat looking at him in total fear, uncomprehending.

"Florence, your pie is boiling over."

"What?"

"Your pie."

"Oh." Then it came to her what he was saying. "Oh!" and she brushed past him and was off down the hall. He followed her, and stood at the front door again, as if he had just arrived, waiting. He heard the oven door slam, and he heard her talking, but he assumed she was talking to herself. Eventually, she emerged from the kitchen and stood examining him.

The evidence of Saturday night was written on his face. A purple and red bruise on his right cheek, that spread and circled his right eye. It was where Jimmy had kicked him. The blow that knocked him out.

"Hank. Come in." She hesitated, then closed the door after him. "Sit down." Hank sat in the wing chair, beside the boots. Florence sat opposite him. There was so much unsaid. There was so much to say.

"Are you all right?"

"I'm fine." She barely spoke above a whisper.

He tried to pick his words carefully. "They didn't hurt you."

" No." That was all she intended to say, but he waited and presently she offered more. "They drove me here. They didn't hurt me. They scarcely touched me." She hoped she had answered his concerns. She didn't want him to pursue that topic any further.

He was trying to think of how he could open his next topic when Florence stood up, retrieved her newspaper from the dining room table and brought it to Hank. She pointed to a short item in a feature called, 'The Police Blotter'. She sat back down.

"Was that your doing?"

Hank read that Jimmy Sullivan, an Everett resident and employee of Bayside Machine had been found Saturday night on Riverside, unconscious and badly beaten, and had been taken to the Sisters of Providence Hospital. Hank finished reading, but made no comment.

"Did you do that?" she persisted.

Hank didn't answer. This was not going the way he had hoped.

Florence was certain he had done it. And that he had done it for her. She couldn't find the courage to tell him that he must not. But she sat in silence, listening to the pounding of her own heart, not knowing what to say.

"Would you like some pie?" She finally asked.

"Sure."

"I'll make some coffee." She went into the kitchen.

For a while he sat listening to the sounds coming from the kitchen, then he went to the kitchen door and asked her a question.

"May I look at your piano?"

She didn't turn around. "Go ahead."

He went down the hall to the back bedroom. It was a small Chickering. What they sometimes called a Baby Grand, about five feet. Standing, he tried the action. It was light, very responsive, with a nice feel.

"Do you play?" Florence was standing behind him.

"Some."

"Play me something." She was serious. She nodded yes. He sat down on the bench. Tried the pedals. Thought for a moment. Then he played. Scott Joplin's 'Maple Leaf Rag'. He knew his playing erred on the side of being too mechanical. But the syncopated rhythms of Joplin also demanded a certain precision, and the music flowed from beneath his hands. When he finished, he turned around and she was gone, but she returned immediately with a piece of blackberry pie on a plate, and a cup of coffee on a saucer. She left, but returned quickly with her own. Facing away from the piano, she sat down on the other end of the bench beside him. For five minutes the only sounds were the scrape of a fork, the sipping of coffee. The coffee was stronger, getting closer to the way he liked it. He set his empty cup and plate aside and played again, "St. Louis Blues" by W.C. Handy. Florence didn't move, make a sound or say a thing, so he went on and played "Honeysuckle Rose" by Fats Waller.

Then he really gave in to temptation and played a 12-bar classic, "Frankie and Johnny", in a slow, insistent, stride piano style. He had heard the tune done this way by a black piano player in Paris, where the right hand seems to retard the tempo, the left adding rhythm and the occasional chord. He always remembered it.

Hank played. The fact that he played at all she found surprising and endearing, but while he didn't play the classics, he definitely played with technique. Mostly, Florence read in the magazines and press about the evils of Jazz music. She had never had the chance to watch or listen to anyone who was any good   Hank was very good, but 'Frankie and Johnny' was too close to home, and tore at her heart. She put her hand on his shoulder, and said. "Stop." He did. She leaned her head on his shoulder for a moment, then took their dirty dishes to the kitchen. Hank followed her.

"Florence-"

"Hank, will you stay awhile longer? Sit down again." He sat down in the wing chair again.

Florence sat opposite him again. It was now or never. It had to be done. "Hank, Mr. Waters is my Uncle. I lived with him, and my Aunt, for five years in their house on Rucker Hill." She stopped to breathe, went on. "He and his wife no longer live together. I moved out and she helped me find a job before she moved away." This was all new information to Hank.

"Mr. Waters and I did not get along. We still do not speak to each other. I don't like him." She spit this out. "He thinks he owns me." You could hear the hate in her voice. "He is not a nice man. He hurts people. He'll hurt you. If he thinks it will hurt me to hurt you, he'll do that, and if he thinks it will hurt you to hurt me, he'll do that too."

"Florence, I know how to take care of myself." He stopped, then went on. "I can also take care of you."

"I was afraid of that."

"Of what?"

"That you thought you could protect me."

"I can."

"Hank....", she ran down. "Hank, he is rich and powerful. He does own people. He has people who work for him who hurt people. He does what he wants and no one stops him. If he complains to my boss, I'm out of a job. Without a job, I have no place to live. I'm a Canadian national living in a foreign country. I know it doesn't seem that way to you, but you were born here. If I'm deported I have absolutely no where else to go."

"Florence, there are some things you don't know."

Now Florence got right to the point.

"Hank, because I work at the bank I know what you have in your bank account. It's very impressive, and much, much more that I've got. But I've seen what you make fishing for crabs, and you didn't make all that money crabbing. How did you get it?"

Now he was really boxed in.

"Jimmy said," she paused, "Jimmy said you were a bootlegger. Are you a bootlegger?"

Hank clamped his jaw shut and ground his teeth, but there was no way to avoid answering.

"Yes." It slipped out between his teeth and was all he could say.

"Oh, Hank." It was a long sigh. Disappointment, disapproval, despair.

"Hank, what you're doing," she struggled to find the words, "what you're doing is outside the law. Outside the law. That gives all the advantages to a man like Mr. Waters."

Hank wanted to say that the advantage was with the man who had the most courage, but how do you tell the woman you love that you're a bigger bastard than the other bastard? That you're tougher, harder, and five times as mean.

"Florence, when you're with me, do you feel protected?" It was a shrewd question, and for a moment turned the argument around.

"Yes. Yes I feel protected. But what I know, what I know, is that Mr. Waters will bide his time, then kill one of us, or both." She was very angry.

"And he'll make as much trouble for both of us as he can. He can have you arrested, put in jail. Can you deny it? No, of course not. If my employer knows I'm mixed up in bootlegging, they'll fire me on the spot."

She stood up. She was strong. Intelligent. And probably right. She was also beautiful, her shoulders bare, her head erect, tears, running down both cheeks.

Hank stood.

"I think you'd better go. Good-bye." She quickly left the room, went into her bedroom, and quietly closed the door.

Hank watched her leave. Heard the door close. With nothing left to do or say, he quietly left. He couldn't imagine an outcome more opposite to what he had hoped for.

That afternoon, Hadley left work early and drove down to the boathouse. He wanted to find Hank and talk to him about fishing for summer run steelhead in the lower reaches of the Snohomish River.

Hank was sitting in the dark, in the main workshop area, on a rickety chair at a table made from two boards laid across sawhorses, staring out at the passing river and the late afternoon sun shine. His suit jacket and tie were tossed aside, but he was still fairly dressed up for someone sitting in the dark eating a late lunch. At his feet was a tin milk pail full of chipped ice and a green bottle. Hadley figured it was Champagne. He was surprised to find Aquavit. The bottle was about one-quarter gone. Hank was eating smoked fish, plus some pickled herring, a cut up apple and crisp flat bread with butter.

"Skoal." Hank tossed back a shot of Aquavit and followed it with a beer chaser.

"This looks like some serious drinking."

"Have some." Hank poured a shot into a jelly glass, and Hadley drank it down.

"Ohggh!" Hadley choked and coughed. " I always forget about that strong licorice flavor. An acquired taste I'm afraid, and one I haven't acquired. May I?"

"Help yourself." Hadley filled up his jelly glass with beer. Home brew he assumed. He took a taste of the smoked fish. Salmon. Hank's own smoked. Sweet and peppery.

"Pretty good."

"Thanks."

"What's this all about?" Hadley waved at the food and the liquor. There was no response. He thought he changed topics when he asked, "How did your picnic with Florence go?" He waited for an answer.

"Who is Charles Waters?"

"Who?"

"Charles," Hank said slowly, "Waters." He knew Hadley had heard him the first time.

Hadley dragged over another saw horse and sat. "He's a crook. Like most people, I give Waters a wide berth."

"Why?"

"It's just safer."

"But what does he do?"

"Hank, people don't have conversations about people like Waters. If you know anything you keep your mouth shut, and if you don't know anything, you still keep your mouth shut because you don't want Waters to hear you've been asking questions about him."

"What does he do, Hadley?"

"I don't know anything. I couldn't prove one single thing in Court. I have heard that he owns all the gambling in the county. Slot machines. Cards. Women, probably some liquor, but retail, in his clubs. I've never heard he was a bootlegger."

Hank took another shot of Aquavit. Then he drank some beer.

"Why are people frightened of him?"

Hadley sat silent, watching him for a long time. Then he answered.

"Hank, he owns politicians. He's well connected. He has money to burn. It isn't healthy to get in his way."

"He got in mine."

"How so?"

"Did you know he's Florence's Uncle?"

"No. Is he really?"

"He is really. He came to see me. In so many words, he told me to back off."

"Oh, God. What did you tell him?"

Telling Hadley the truth was a little too dangerous. After all, Hadley was a respectable member of the Bar. Hank didn't want to confess to a crime, so he gave Hadley an approximation of what he did to Waters.

"I told him to go fuck himself." Hank downed another shot and said, "in those exact words."

"How did he react?"

"I was very convincing."

Hadley could imagine. He really didn't want to know more. "Hank, he's a very dangerous man."

"So I've been told. So am I."

"What?"

"Dangerous."

"Be careful, Hank. Don't get Florence hurt."

Hank nodded. "It's a problem." He was feeling drunk. If he got up and tried to walk, he'd fall down. "I'm working on a solution," he confided.

Hadley decided he should go. Hank kept Hadley supplied with scotch and wine, and he had some guesses about how Hank procured his supply, but he had never asked. It seemed best. Plus, Gertrude had dropped several unsubtle hints regarding how she hoped things would turn out between Florence and Hank. He was groping in the dark, but Hadley tried to put two and two together.

"Hank, I hope things with Florence work out the way you want them. But Hank, a girl like Florence, you can't expect her to come down here to live," he gestured at the huge open space of the boat shed, "or spend her life riding around in a dump truck." Hadley stopped.

"Go on," encouraged Hank. His voice was hard.

"Hank, you're my best friend. I owe you my life. I'm trying to help."

"Go on."

"You have to be able to offer her more than all of this and more than just yourself. You have to be offering her a way to live, and that has to be the way she wants to live."

Hank didn't say anything. Hadley started to leave. Hanks voice stopped him at the door.

"Hadley."

"Yeah?"

"Thanks." Hadley barely heard it, but it was there.

Sawdust and Scrap Lumber
Fall, 1922

Long, shredded strands of tree bark were still clinging to huge long poles that had been driven as pilings into the tide flats at the edge of what had once been the beach. Poles that still rose forty feet to support an extensive shed roof.

This part of the mill was part of the original building at the waters edge where the mill had begun. Fill, dumped in and around the pilings, sawdust, shavings and dredge spoils mostly, had been spread and pushed into the bay every time the mill needed to expand. Filled tide lands were basically free. Since the mill was built from saw logs on hand, used with minimal processing, it was easy and cheap to expand.

The original shed was probably the size of a circus tent. From there, this sawmill had grown additions in every direction, in a hodge-podge of different construction techniques, overlapping roof sizes, and floor heights. The multiple support timbers, cut over different decades, had faded and been weathered by rain, dirt, rust, lubricating grease, dust, wet sawdust, and dirty hands stained with the same, to reveal every shade of brown, gray and tan in the harvested timber rainbow.

Minimal light seeped in under this chaotic big top, and the few dim light bulbs, swinging bare on long wavy wires, were only capable of creating illuminated shadows. A maze of wooden board walks, cat walks and site built ladders tied the mill together, and made it possible to move from work station to station. Provided you weren't afraid of heights, the lack of railings, and machinery grinding away inches from where you were walking. A flapping shirttail caught in a moving chain might pull you off balance. You were either very careful, or dead.

Under the tallest roof, right in the center, was the head rig, the tall vertical blade, like a band saw, used to slab up big saw logs. From the head rig the slabs were moved on to other, smaller, gang saws and planers that cut the slab down into dimensioned framing lumber. The noise from the variety of machines was deafening, an unsyncopated melding of high pitched whines that occasionally varied in intensity, but went on without stopping sixteen hours a day, six and sometimes seven days a week. Mixed in was the thud and bone shaking vibration of twenty thousand pound saw logs being tossed around and dropped like two-by-fours. The rickety walkways bounced and shook as you tried to pick your way through the mill.

Hank watched as the head sawyer strained to engage the clutch lever. With no warning, a long linked chain that ran through multiple sets of sprockets, a huge version of a bicycle chain, dripping with grease and coated with sawdust, came to life and dragged a massive cast iron carriage forward towards the whirling sawblade. Clamped to the carriage was a huge log, six feet in diameter at the butt, thirty feet long, from a tree hundreds of years old.

The blade entered the wood, and the whine of the blade took on a deeper note. Sawdust filled the air. Hank continued to watch as the cut was finished and a giant over-sized board, four to five feet wide, thirty feet long, and five inches thick fell away with a bounce and a thud you could see, and feel up through your legs, but couldn't hear. Vertical grain Douglas fir, thought Hank. Crisp, clean, a beautiful pale, rosy-gold color. There were no knots that he could see.

The company that owned this mill also owned, and operated, a development company that built houses. They told prospective buyers the company would pay them one dollar, cash money, for every knot you could find in their framing lumber. The company seldom paid out a cent on their offer. Which was why Hank was here.

Hank waved at the sawyer and walked off in a different direction towards the back end of the mill. Much of the machinery in the mill had been cast, machined and installed by Two Brothers Iron Works. Having been part of the manufacturing, Hank had been on the call out crew for repairs for years, so he was a familiar sight to both the foreman and the crew. He knew his way around, and in this sawmill, it was unlikely anyone would think he was somewhere he wasn't supposed to be.

Trees don't grow a uniform diameter, straight up and down, from the ground to the top. The trunk of a tree tapers from bottom to top. But framing lumber is square. Boards cut from the taper have to be squared up. The offcut was waste. Lumber was manufactured - and sold - in uniform sizes. Pieces that didn't conform to uniform sizes were also waste.

Eventually, inside every huge log, there are going to be knots, the remains of branches from when the tree was young. Even on the biggest trees, there would be more knots towards the top. Some of this lumber could be sold, but with a surplus of trees, plus a surplus of high quality clear lumber selling at competitive prices, much of the lumber with knots couldn't be sold, or even given away. So it was burned. Along with all the other waste.

Hank followed a small conveyor belt of waste, like a small stream, he thought, until it joined other small waste streams to make up a river of waste wood. The river moved out from under the roof and became a very wide conveyor belt, rising on stilts forty feet into the air, then dumping the scrap into a mountain of wood. Hank was staring at a pile of scrap with enough wood for ten houses. Provided you were willing to do some work.

Two men, both black, pulled scrap pieces out of the pile and fed another belt that carried the wood up an almost a vertical slope to the top of the conical shaped wood burner and dumped the wood inside. The burner was shaped like a cone, sixty feet tall, and almost that wide at the base, the sides made of iron plate, rusted to a deep, deep red-brown.

The job of the two men was to burn the waste, but at a rate that wouldn't clog up the conveyor belt, or the feed hole at the top, or create a fire so big in the burner it got out of control and burned down the mill. When you had sparks the size of dinner plates floating away on a southwest wind over houses and buildings with cedar shaked roofs, it was time to slow down the feed rate and thus the burn. Standing where he was Hank could feel the heat from inside the burner.

"Help you?" one of the men asked.

"I hope so," said Hank. He waved at the pile of scrap. "The foreman said I could take wood out of this pile."

The man nodded, his expression unchanged. "Help yourself." He turned back to work.

Hank stood quietly another ten minutes, watching the two men work. This job would be a long, hard day, he thought. Probably for the lowest wages in the plant. These were the only two black men he'd seen in the entire plant, and they were all the way back here, doing the worst job. The two men wore bib overalls like everyone else, including Hank, and faded blue workshirts. The one man was big, six foot six at least. The other man was shorter, and wiry. They both worked steadily and got a lot done.

Hank lit a cigar and stayed where he was. Finally, the short man walked back and said, "Problem, boss?"

Hank offered the man a cigar. "You want to earn some extra money?"

The man ignored the cigar and shook his head. "Can't do nothin' the foreman doesn't tell us to do."

"That's fine, but I'll pay you ten dollars a night to pull what I want aside." Hank inspected the site. He could get his truck real close on the north side. "Stack it over there." He pointed.

"Over there," the man repeated. "Ten dollars?" he asked.

Hank could tell he was now listening. And thinking.

"Ten dollars. Each." Hank answered, doubling his offer.

"Each." The man nodded. He examined Hank more closely.

"How much of this wood you want?"

"I'm going to re-mill it," Hank explained. "Enough for a house. A big house. But I have to be able to cut out enough framing lumber, get enough clears for the finish work." He offered the cigars again. The man nodded, yes. He understood. And the cigars were being offered as part of the negotiation. He took two.

"Wait," the man said. He went to confer with his partner. They talked. Hank couldn't hear what they were saying. Both men examined the cigars, the single leaf rolled wrapper. Sniffed the tabacco. Twirled the uncut end in their mouth, tasting the tabacco. They talked some more. At random intervals a particularly large piece of scrap would belly flop onto the pile with an ear-splitting slap. Both of them came back.

"You square it with the foreman?" the smaller man asked.

That meant they didn't want to have to pay off the foreman. Which meant that he would have to do it. Probably cost him another five dollars a day.

"I'll square it," said Hank. He estimated it would only take a week to pull out all the wood he would need. Less than one hundred and fifty dollars for all the lumber for the house he had in mind was still a bargain. He fished out his billfold and handed each man a ten dollar bill, which they took and quickly tucked away in inside shirt pocket.

"I'm Hank Eide," said Hank, holding out his hand.

"I'm Billy," said the short man. "This is Samuel." Hank shook hands with both men. Tough, hard hands.

"Good cigar," said Samuel. "Thanks."

"Get them at Culmbacks." Chris Culmback ran a cigar store. "Two-bits each." Most cigars cost a nickel. Billy and Samuel were impressed.

"Anything else you need, boss?" asked Billy.

Hank thought about it a moment. "You ever dig a basement?" he asked.

"How deep?" Samuel asked quickly. He was smiling.

Some days Hank felt all he did was make sawdust. Piles, wind rows and carpets of it. Wet sawdust stuck to everything, especially your clothes and the back of your neck. It was November, and nearly every day it rained. With Samuel and Billy working mornings for him part-time, Hank had moved his 36 inch bandsaw, a big heavy industrial machine, from his boat shop to his building site. He powered the saw off the rear wheels of his truck, a trick he had learned in the Army.

But the wet sawdust kept packing up on the guide wheels of his saw. When it started to get real bad, everything stopped while he took the saw apart and cleaned the guide wheels. After the blade came all the way off the guide wheels and ripped itself to pieces in a shower of splintered steel, Hank called a longer halt. The three men spent the next three mornings constructing a temporary long, narrow open sided shed to protect the saw, their resawn lumber, - and themselves - from the weather.

They still made sawdust, but now it was dry, and didn't clog up the machinery. They kept a small fire going with the sawdust and scraps, and it was possible to eat lunch, drink a hot cup of coffee and smoke a cigar without getting soaked. Hank had started buying his cigars by the box. Samuel especially considered a good cigar essential to work.

Using only a pick ax, shovels and a wheelbarrow, Samuel and Billy dug the hole for the basement. At the same time, they spread the dirt - or mud, depending on how much it had rained - evenly over the site. Some of the sawdust was disposed of the same way, and would eventually rot and provide a good rich dirt for growing a lawn.

Hank had no experience pouring large quantities of concrete. Billy had done some sidewalks, but when he saw Hanks sketches and the quantities involved he said no thanks. Hank also didn't own the tools to mix concrete, or a set of building forms for pouring walls. His solution was to hire a local builder, Ned Reinell, to pour the footings, the basement floor and the basement walls. He figured that if Ned started him out square and level, he couldn't make too many mistakes.

He had all but given up pretending to be a crab fisherman. To maintain his cash flow, every week he did make a trip to Victoria. One day up. One day back. To keep the Johansson twins happy, he packed twice as many cases into the boat, stacked cases out on the stern under canvas, covered and surrounded by a stack of crab pots. It wasn't a great solution, it added to the risk, but so far it had worked.

In addition, he tried to time his run home through Deception Pass so it was dark. The Coast Guard had taken to posting watchers at the pass. Some nights that meant he fought the tide. He knew the risks of running in the dark would eventually catch up with him. So far he had been lucky. He ran the engine hard, and used much more gas. The evenings he spent in Victoria he devoted to engine maintenance, and a few hours sleep.

He drank more coffee. Strong coffee. You could almost stand a spoon up in the pot. He didn't manage to add anything to his bank account. He was spending money faster than he made it.

The days he wasn't on the water he spent re-sawing scrap into useable lumber. "You take big pieces," Samuel summarized, "and you make little pieces. And sawdust." Hank, or his crew, could do this every day, except Sunday. The neighbors complained the one time he sawed on Sunday. So on Sundays, after church and dinner with his parents, he trucked the clear boards they had cut out from the scrap down to the boathouse. He used a thickness planer to smooth all four sides. Then he set the pieces to dry under a shed roof he had Samuel and Billy add to the north side of the boathouse. While they were at it, he had them re-shingle the entire boathouse roof. It was years overdue, and he was weary of fighting the leaks. In addition to wages, and shingles, the roof cost him one box of cigars. The boathouse roof provided a peaceful view of the river. Hank ended more than one Sunday sitting on the roof with Samuel and Billy, smoking a cigar, watching the sun go down.

During the summer, after the wood had had a chance to season, he would have enough straight grained vertical fir to make twenty-eight four panel passage doors, six sets of French doors, not to mention numerous windows, thousands of lineal feet of fir flooring and molding bases for kicks.

Straight grain vertical fir was a beautiful wood. It was easy to work, easy on tool steel. Hank loved the way it looked, the golden red hue of the grain. Instead of paint, he would finish it all clear

He had seen a front door on a residential building in Paris that impressed him at the time and remained in his memory as an example of fine craftsmanship raised to an art. He set out to duplicate that door. It would be made from oak.

Three inches thick. A full ten feet tall, six feet wide, with a curved, rounded arch on top. Six beveled, recessed panels, with leaded colored glass filling in the arch. The joinery would have to be perfect. He would cast and machine all the hardware himself. By itself, it was a project that could take weeks.

Late at night, exhausted, he sat over the remains of his supper and made lists. Lists of materials. Lists of things he had to do. Lists of money he had spent. A much longer list of money he needed to spend. He hated the book work. Then he tried to guess how long this job would take, how long that job would take. All his lists kept growing. Longer and longer.

No matter how he allocated his time, even if he quit making the run to Victoria, he was going to have to work on this house all of 1923 and probably into 1924. Which was ridiculous. It hadn't taken the Romans this long to build Rome. However, they did have more help.

Which was why, in March of 1923, he hired Ned Reinell and his crew to come back and finish the building and the roof framing, nail up the plaster sheets, a new product replacing plaster over lath, and nail on the cedar siding. Samuel and Billy could do the shingle roof, and then the three of them could install windows and doors.

"I was hoping I could do it all myself," Hank explained to Ned Reinell, "but there aren't enough hours in the day or days in the week to get it all done in a reasonable period of time."

Ned, who had seen it all and learned the same math the same way Hank was learning it - the hard way - just smiled. He did agree that if Hank and his two helpers made and installed the windows and hung the doors maybe, by late May or June, they could have the house closed in and dry. Maybe. Ned did wonder where this Norwegian was getting his money. The man paid cash on the nail.

"What are you gonna' do with this fancy house?"

"Live there," said Hank, figuring the topic was closed.

"You have a wife? Or other family to live there with you?"

"Reinell, I'm paying you to build a house. Let me worry about the rest."

"Sure. Sure, but you could save some money and time easy, here," said Reinell, waving at the figures and lists laid out on the table. "That's a big house, you need all those rooms?"

Hank saw his point. It did all appear a little strange.

"Well, you may be right, but on the other hand, you never know, I might marry some pretty widow with six children."

"I'm startin' to see the light, Eide, I'm startin' to see the light."

A man who lived alone in a boathouse might be looking for some home cooking and companionship as he got older. Probably he was tired of that kind of life. Eide must know he wasn't any prize as far as looks went, but offer a widow with kids a nice house like he was building, sure, sure, you could see that kind of thing happening, that kind of thing, sure. Sure. You betcha.

Withdrawals

Sixty seconds after she left Hank sitting alone in her living room and closed her bedroom door, Florence began to regret her decision. She sat on the bed, watching the door, hoping he would knock. Willing him to knock. When she heard the door to the hallway open and close, and his tread on the stairs, she almost ran after him.

Instead, she stayed where she was, trying to convince herself that it was all for the best. All for the best, she kept saying, all for the best. If it's all for the best, why do I feel so miserable? was the thought that kept intruding and disturbing her peace of mind.

On Tuesday, the day after her conversation with Hank, she returned to work at the bank. Mr. Lind didn't exactly welcome her with open arms, but he did smile, once. The other girls were glad to see her and they insisted they would all go out to lunch together. At Mannings. She ate the special with the other girls. Meatloaf, mashed potatoes and gravy.

For weeks she waited and watched for Hank to come in to the bank. She never saw him. She monitored his bank account daily. Strangely, there was no activity. No money deposited, or withdrawn. Then in early October his balance declined by three thousand dollars. A bank draft had been presented by a Mr. Maulsby against Hank's account and paid out in cash. The other girls thought Mr. Maulsby sold real estate, but they weren't certain. At that point she concluded Hank wouldn't be back, or at least not while she was working.

In December, one week before Christmas, this was confirmed when she noted he apparently had been in and withdrawn ten thousand dollars.

The withdrawal was signed by Mr. Lind and initialed by Mr. Chase the bank president, and had taken place at lunch. Ten thousand was an unusually large withdrawal for any of their individual customers, and it was unlikely that she or any of the other girls would have been asked to handle this transaction even if it hadn't happened at noon. Since the funds had been paid out in cash, there was also no way to even speculate on what he might be doing with the money.

Gertrude invited her to a dinner party on New Years Eve.

"Let's ring out 1922 and welcome 1923." Her enthusiasm was contagious, and Florence looked forward to it.

In hope of seeing Hank, on the Saturday before New Years she took the electric trolley to Seattle and visited Frederick and Nelson's, which claimed to have the newest and best fashions for women. They also had the highest prices. She spent almost all of her savings, but arrived in a taxi for the party, dressed to the nines in a new dress, new shoes, new hat and coat and new leather gloves.

She rang the doorbell.

"My, my," Hadley said, ushering her in. "My, my, my, my, my," he went on as he accepted her hat and coat and inspected her new dress.

"He's so eloquent," Gertrude said, coming to greet her with a kiss. "But Florence, darling, my, my as Hadley might say. You look stunning."

Florence did a pirouette and ended with a small curtsy. "Thank you. Both Mr. Frederick and Mr. Nelson also send their thanks," answering Gertrude's next question before it could be asked. "The very latest design, tubes of silk organdy, all the way from Paris."

"I wondered, I did indeed. Come in," she said slipping her arm under Florence's. "I think you know everyone, but let's find out."

The house was small. Living room, dining room, and kitchen on the main floor, bedrooms upstairs. They were renting, but Gertrude had worked miracles with a few nice pieces of furniture, dramatic floor length curtains and a huge mirror in an antique gold frame over the fireplace.

The dining room table crowded the room, and was set with eight places. It sparkled with the gifts accumulated from their wedding three years ago. Polished sterling silver, gilded china, cut crystal candlesticks, a beautiful snow white Irish linen cloth and napkins. And gleaming wine glasses, Florence noted. Champagne flutes and two other cut crystal goblets at each place. One for water, the other for wine. The wine was a hopeful sign, and suggested Hank might be coming.

The guests who were present consisted of two other couples: Bob, Hadley's law partner, and his wife Vivian, and another couple, Harold and Alice, who

Florence knew from Church. The missing eighth guest who had not yet arrived remained unidentified. But Florence became even more hopeful when Hadley served French Champagne as an aperitif. The talk was of children, houses, golfscores and the Christmas just past. All inconsequential, animated, stories told to amuse and entertain. Relaxing holiday chatter.

As the clock on the mantle neared eight, Florence noticed that Gertrude was glancing at the mantle clock rather often, and seemed to be getting upset. As the clock struck eight, Gertrude took Hadley aside in the entry hall, and they could be heard by everyone. "Where is he…." She couldn't hear Hadley's response.

"Did you say anything to him?" Again she couldn't hear the response, more so when Bob boomed in her ear, "Four hours to go!" Since some sort of response was called for, she was dragged back in to the general conversation. Hadley returned a moment later, and Gertrude disappeared into the kitchen.

Gertrude returned, but Florence did note a woman in a starched white uniform, hired help for the evening, in the dining room clearing away one place setting and re-arranging two others. When the woman had finished the guests were called in to dinner.

More Champagne was served with the first course, a pureed chestnut soup. Dinner was roast wild duck, four of them actually, shot, Hadley said, by my very own self. A statement Gertrude appeared to want to contradict, but she remained silent.

"My compliments on the Champagne and the red Bordeaux, Hadley," offered partner Bob.

"Very nice," contributed Harold. "Where did you get it?"

"A friend of ours," answered Hadley.

"A friend of Hadley's," added Gertrude, glaring at Hadley down the length of the table.

If Florence had any remaining doubts, now she was certain: The unknown guest had been Hank. Why didn't he come to dinner? She felt tears welling up in her eyes. She quickly excused herself. Was he deliberately avoiding her? If so, why was he avoiding her? Why wouldn't he talk to her? Was he that angry? Why was he doing this? Was he that stubborn? Or disappointed? Which? Did it matter to her which? She didn't know, but she wanted to find out. Most of all why, why, why? She had to find him, talk to him.

As the days lengthened, spring arrived late in May, after a cold March featuring six inches of wet, sloppy snow, and soggy April showers. It even rained on Easter. She told herself she wasn't searching for Hank, but she began taking long walks into parts of town she normally didn't visit. Riverside. Lowell. Pinehurst. The neighborhoods surrounding Jefferson Elementary and South Junior High School. More than once, she explored up and down Railway Avenue, carefully inspecting Hank's boathouse. She never saw his truck. She did notice the new construction and the new roof, but she never saw anyone working. Once, she saw smoke coming out the chimney, and she gathered her courage and knocked, but no one answered.

Five Sundays in a row she attended services at Central Lutheran Church. To her it seemed like they sang hymns most of the service, or listened to the choir. And there was always coffee and cookies set out after the service. She never saw Hank. She did see many of her customers from the bank, people like Orla Jackson, who greeted her warmly. One Sunday she was introduced to an older couple named Eide. No one said so, but she assumed they were Hank's parents. He was short and stooped with an impressive mustache that dipped into his coffee with every sip. She was very talkative, very outgoing. That same Sunday the Pastor asked her if she would like to join the church. She avoided an answer, but the next Sunday went back to services at Trinity.

Where was he? Had he left town?

One Saturday in July when it was dry, she stuffed a lunch in her pocket and hiked miles, all the way out on the river delta to Hank's Ebbey Island moorage. The Anna Marie appeared the same as always. Well cared for. Recently used.

There was an empty coffee mug on the window ledge beside the wheel. But no other sign of Hank. The cabin door was padlocked, and she was forced to crouch down behind an abandoned automobile, pushed off in the scotch broom, to relieve herself.

How could one person vanish so completely in such a small town? She began to have the eerie sensation that he was only two steps ahead of her, standing out of sight around the next corner, dodging and hiding and barely managing to remain hidden. If she could walk a bit faster, run at unexpected moments, double back quickly and sprint around the corner, she would catch him, corner him, find him. Much to her embarrassment it never worked. She felt like a fool, which made her angry. She also felt very alone.

In September, after months of being asked, she agreed to attend a Saturday afternoon book club meeting with Gertrude at the Carnegie Library, a trim brick building on Oaks behind the Courthouse and the jail. She was hoping Hadley would drive them, and might make some mention of Hank. She was resolved to ask him about Hank if he didn't volunteer anything. But Gertrude drove, never mentioned Hank, and Florence decided not to ask.

A woman named Beverly gave a long droning report on a book she had obviously not read, The Sheik, by Edith Hull. Beverly kept referring to Rudolph Vel-en-tino. Florence didn't think Mr. Vel-en-tino had appeared in the book. However, Mr. Valentino had been the leading man in the motion picture of the same name. The talk over tea was of children and domestic concerns, and Florence ended the afternoon with a crashing headache. In disappointment, and hoping to clear her head, she declined the offer of a ride home and told Gertrude she would walk. She went down the hill to Hewitt, and continued south on Oaks.

Kitty corner from the fire station was the Armory. Adjacent to the Armory was a vacant lot. Parked on the lot was a red, white and blue dump truck. Hank's truck. Florence stopped and stared. Was he at the Armory? The Armory appeared to be locked up tight.

A man and a woman hurried up the steps of Norway Hall, across the street and disappeared inside. The Norwegian and American flags in front of the building flew at half mast. What was going on? She crossed the street and entered the lobby. Orla Jackson, and several other women she didn't know, were busy setting food out on long trestle tables. Cookies, buttered date nut bread, egg salad finger sandwiches with a stripe of anchovy, and coffee cups. Dozens and dozens of coffee cups. Most people were going up the stairs. Florence followed them.

There was another, smaller lobby. She could hear someone praying. She stepped through another set of double doors that were standing open, and she was in the hall proper. A large open space, but like an auditorium, there was a stage at the far end.

"In Jesus' name we pray. Amen."

"Amen," several hundred people murmured in return, and sat back down on their wooden folding chairs. The man who was doing the praying also sat down. There was an open casket at the front of the room. It was a memorial service. People shifted in their chairs and coughed quietly as a long line of men dressed in white dinner coats, black pants, white shirts and black bow ties filed out from a side door and began to line up in three ranks stretched across the front of the room.

A woman with a crying baby brushed past her and went into the lobby. Who were these men, and why were they all dressed the same? Florence tried to count them, but she kept getting lost in her count. More than fifty. Maybe seventy?

The ranks of men faced the audience, standing closely together. The last man in a white coat entered and stood facing away from the audience. He was bald. Then he turned around. It was Hank. In a white dinner coat? Yes, it was Hank. With a small bow he acknowledged the audience.

"Please stand and join us," he announced in a clear, carrying voice Florence had never heard him use before, "as we sing 'America the Beautiful.'"

As the audience stood, Hank took a small round pitch pipe out of his pocket. He blew a note, got a hum back in response, raised his arms. And began.

While the singers up front provided the lead, it was the first time Florence had ever been in an audience, at church or elsewhere, where people sang right out, knew all the words and articulated every one of them. No slurring. No hanging back. No drop in tone, all the way to the end. It was well done. Then the audience sat down. Hank took out his pitch pipe, blew another tone. The singers - they had to be some kind of organized group, Florence thought, they were so good - sang, a cappella, a stunningly quiet and heartfelt version of the hymn Florence knew as 'Fairest Lord Jesus'. Hank had announced the hymn as 'Beautiful Savior'.

"Beautiful Savior," sang a young blonde tenor, in a clear, pure voice.

"King of creation." The tenor took a breath.

"Son of God and son of Man." The singers hummed, singing in the background.

"Truly I'd love Thee, Truly I'd serve Thee, Light of my Soul, my Joy, my Crown."

The volume increased a little.

"Fair are the meadows, Fair are the Woodlands, Robed in the Flowers of blooming Spring...." Florence had tears in her eyes. The words were slightly different from the hymn she knew, but oh, it was so heart piercingly wonderful.

At the end the soloist and the singers came together and the volume swelled. Now they all sang the words: "Beautiful Savior, Glory and Honor, Praise, adoration, Now and Forevermore be Thine!"

It was beautiful and moving. There was a man, seated in front of where she was standing, weeping openly. There was no applause, it wasn't appropriate for a memorial service, but Florence felt like the audience wanted to applaud. Loudly and at length. Hank took out his pitch pipe again. Blew a tone. Apparently he wasn't satisfied, because he blew the tone again. Listened. Nodded, yes. He raised his arms. Began.

"Ja vi el-sker det-te Landet, Som det sti-ger frem,"

From the "Ja" everything was different. Bold, clear and ringing. The voices male, strong and on key. Florence didn't know it, but this was the Norwegian national song . ("Yes," they sang emphatically, "we love with fond devotion, Norway's mountain domes,")

"Fu-ret, vejr-bidt o-ver Vandet, Med de tu-sind stjem." ("Rising storm lashed o'er the ocean, with their thousand homes.")
Hank quieted them with his gestures. Now they sang much more quietly.

"Elsker, elsker de tog taen-ker, Gaa vor Far og mor," ("Love our country while we're bending, Thot's to father grand,"
Hank re- built the volume:
"Og den Sa-ga nat, som saen-ker, Dramme-me paa vor Jord." ("And to saga nights that's sending Dreams upon our land,")
Now he really built the volume, and the voices built, swelled and climbed to become even bolder and stronger. These men were the sons of the Vikings, part of a tradition of singing together that stretched back hundreds of years into the past. They sang with pride. They sang with strength. With conviction and tradition in every note.
On the last line Hank slowed the cadence, balled his fist, and if Florence thought she had heard volume before, now they sang from the gut. The sound came welling up through their bodies, sixty voices, breathing together.
The sound overwhelmed her: There was only the singing.

"Og den Sa-ga nat, som saen-ker, saen-ker Drom-me paa vor Jord." ("And to saga night that's sending, sending, Dreams upon our land.")
Hank made an ax chopping motion and the singing stopped in an eye blink. The last notes hung in the air and resonated off the walls. She hadn't understood a single word. Now she was crying. No one moved or made a sound.
Hank turned to face the audience, and gave a small bow. When he raised his head, he stared her right in the eye. It was physical, and Florence felt a shock run through her body. Several people turned to try and find who or what Hank was so intently looking at.
Then he turned and filed out, following the other singers. Florence left immediately. Her knees felt weak. Yes, she had finally found him, but she didn't feel strong enough to face him.

Finishing Touches

Bam! Bam! Bam! Someone was pounding on her door. She looked at her alarm clock. It wasn't even six am. She slid out of bed and pulled on a robe. Her heart was racing. Was this Hank? Probably not. More likely Miss Clark, her landlady, with some sort of problem. Was there a fire? She hurried.

"Florence," said Gertrude breezing through the open door, "get dressed."

"What is it?"

"Florence, get dressed!"

"Gertrude, it's six in the morning. What do you want so early? This is a work day."

"This is more important than work, and you're wasting time."

Frustrated, Florence started for the kitchen to put on coffee. Gertrude took her by the shoulders and pushed her in the direction of her bedroom. "We don't have time for breakfast. Hurry!"

Florence pulled on clothes, combed her hair, brushed her teeth, all the time with Gertrude urging her to move faster. Gertrude's Oldsmobile was parked out front, the engine running.

"Gertrude, where are we going? I have to be back in an hour."

"It's a surprise. Trust me, I was surprised. Hush now, we'll be there soon." Gertrude drove straight north on Rucker, as if she were going home to her house, but then she turned left on 19th and right on Grand, and kept going north. After they passed the stairway at 14th Street, Florence was in unfamiliar territory. These were new, expensive homes, that got even more expensive on larger building lots the farther north they traveled. Homes that lined the bluff and looked out over the harbor, Gedney Island and at Whidbey and the Olympic Mountains beyond. Many of the lots were vacant, growing blackberry bushes and second growth alder. Just after Eighth and Grand, Gertrude turned into a driveway of what looked to be a very new, very large home, the lawn not yet established, the brick paving the driveway clean and unstained. The house was large, two stories, with a high gabled roof. The house was painted white, the gable ends, and some faux shutters, were a light blue. The roof shingles were new and hadn't yet weathered or faded. There was a house number over the door: 868. That made the address 868 Grand. Gertrude parked and got out.

"Come on." Florence dutifully followed. Gertrude boldly walked up to the front door. It was twice as wide as a normal door, made out of oak, with lights of leaded and colored glass in the arched top and varnished a rich honey brown. A wide brass kick protected the base of the door. Gertrude pushed the latch and walked in. Florence trailed behind.

There was no furniture in the entry, although there was a nice oriental rug to protect the new floor. A curved stairway went upstairs to their right. The railing was ornamental cast iron, the newel post a massive, beautifully turned piece of clear fir. There was a small den-like room to the left. The living room was straight ahead, with two large windows framing a beautiful view of the harbor and the Olympic Mountains.

The floors were wood. Varnished fir, like the floors in Hank's boat, Florence thought. The small den room on the left was quite charming, with a fireplace, built in book shelves, clear lead paned glass in windows with a diamond pattern. In the short hallway leading to this room, there were two other doors leading to a coat closet and a tiny bathroom, with only a sink and toilet. But it was in a very convenient location. The living room was large, with the views of the Olympic Mountains and the Sound, and since you were facing west, the view would include sunsets. The dining room was a pleasant size, and would accommodate a good sized table. French doors led out to a brick patio. A swinging door led to the kitchen. The breakfast room was cozy, painted a pale yellow, with a built in jam closet and a view as nice as the dining room. It would be a wonderful room to sit in, in the morning, to read the paper and enjoy a cup of coffee. The kitchen was all electric, including one of the new electric ice boxes. Florence would have liked to stop for a moment and inspect the appliances, but Gertrude was racing away in front of her.

Florence opened a door in the back hall. A set of stairs leading down to what appeared to be a full basement, but Gertrude hadn't gone that way. Florence could hear her clicking up the stairs and she walked faster in an effort to catch up.

"Gertrude, this is a beautiful home. When did Hadley show it to you?"

Standing at the top of the staircase, Gertrude stopped in her tracks and waited for her.

"Hadley? What has Hadley got to do with it?"

"Isn't this house yours?"

For some reason Gertrude found this tremendously funny and began to laugh. "I wish it was. I would love to live here, but this" she finally managed to get out, "is not my house, nor is it ever likely to be." And she was off again.

The three bedrooms on the view side each had a set of French doors leading to separate small balconies. All the bedrooms, four in total, had huge walk in closets, with lights that came on when you opened the closet door.

"Gertrude," Florence persisted, " surely you and Hadley could afford a house like this."

"Oh, yes, but with this house, it's not a question of money. More a question of love, I would say." Florence could make no sense out of any of this. In the hallway, double doors opened to a cedar lined linen closet with multiple shelves. The two upstairs bathrooms were pretty with yellow and white tile, with green tile accents.

There was one piece of furniture in the entire house. In the upstairs bedroom, on the cool, morning side of the house away from the view , was a grand piano, a new Steinway , a concert grand. The piano was all black, in the latest clean, unadorned style. There was sheet music on the music stand. Florence sat down. The sheet music on the stand was "Dipper Mouth Blues," in C major, a tune she had never heard of, published by Gennett. She looked for the time signature. What she found was a statement that said it was a jazz tune.

Gertrude was watching her. "Gertrude?"

"Yes?" Gertrude answered, her voice full of amusement.

"Gertrude, who owns this house?"

"Someone you know very well. Hank Eide."

Florence took in the room around her. "Hank bought this house?"

"Heavens no," Gertrude laughed. "Hank built this house."

"How long," Florence asked feebly, "have you known?"

Gertrude examined her watch. "Ten hours?" she suggested.

"I see." She ran her fingers over the keyboard, but didn't play a note. She walked out in the upstairs hall and across to the corner bedroom on the view side. She stood in the room for a moment, aware that Gertrude was watching and waiting. Then she pivoted on her heel, went down the stairs, running her hand along the wrought iron railing. She caressed the newel post on the landing.

Turned from one massive piece of clear fir, it was probably twelve inches in diameter. She continued on down the stairs. Went back to the kitchen. The only thing being kept cold in the refrigerator was nine bottles of wine. French Champagne.

She switched on the lights, and carefully stepped down the basement stairs. All very functional. A twelve foot long lathe stood by itself in one corner. Some tools were chocked off on the wall. There was a metal dust pan and a push broom. A new, oil burning furnace. A closed door which when opened revealed a fruit room, stocked with unusual fruit. Red French wine, with cases of Champagne stacked on the floor. Any doubts she had that Hank owned this house disappeared.

She went back upstairs. Gertrude was waiting for her.

"I need to get home, so I can go to work."

"That's all you have to say?"

"Oh, Gertrude, it's a beautiful home. Stunning really, so very elegant and comfortable. But Hank and I no longer see each other. I haven't seen him since last September, over a year now. Obviously, he's been busy," she waved her hand at the walls, " but it has nothing to do with me. "

"Florence, Hank built this house ."

"Yes, but why?" Florence argued. "He doesn't need this house."

Gertrude came and took her by the shoulders. Staring her straight in the eye, Gertrude said, "Florence, don't be dense. He built this house as a gift." Florence didn't react, so Gertrude shook her. " He built this house for you!"

Barlow Bay

Hank woke up out of a sound sleep and sat bolt upright. It was early morning, still dark. He smelled smoke. His first thought was of his wood burning kitchen stove. He hadn't cooked anything here at the boathouse in two days. He came home late last night after a trip to Victoria. He got out of bed. All he was wearing was his wool long johns. He followed his nose. He opened the door and stood at the top of the stairs. There was much more smoke. What was worse, he could hear the snap, crackle of burning wood. He raced down the stairs, no shoes or socks on his feet. There were flames as tall as he was to the left of the double entry doors, creating ample light to see. The floor was burning, and part of the wall. He frantically searched and found a bucket. Ran sixty feet to the open end of his boat house for river water, dipped his bucket in, ran for the flames, tossed the water at the base of the fire but didn't wait to judge the effect, just ran for more. Thank God for the high tide, which brought the river high up the bank. At bucket seven he thought he might be having an effect.

He kept running. At bucket eleven he tripped, and went sprawling, and slid across the wood floor. He got wood splinters in his hands, and it felt like his left knee was bleeding. He slowed down, but didn't stop. His heart was going like a freight train down hill, and his breathing was ragged, more like great gasps of air dragged in and forced out. At bucket fifteen he noticed it was getting darker. The open flames had disappeared. He still had to deal with red coals in the charred wood.

He turned on the over head lights. Tracked down his small hatchet.

Chopped out a hole in the floor. Burned his hands, but filled his bucket with glowing coals of wood, chucked the coals in the river, took back more water, used the hatchet again. Chopped more wood. Dumped it in the river.

He now had some time to think. To ask himself: How the hell had this happened? He did an inventory of all his activities since arriving back from Victoria. Cigars and cigar butts was all he could come up with. He took another bucket full of mostly wet but blackened wood to the river and tossed it in. He stumbled and almost fell. He already hurt like hell. He sat down on the floor to breathe. He was covered in sweat. As it dried he got cold. He struggled to his feet and went back upstairs to put on some clothes.

First, he cleaned his cuts. Poured on some iodine. Then a shirt and coveralls. Then a heavy wool sweater. As he pulled on socks he noticed his cigar butt from last night in the empty salmon can he used for an ashtray. He considered this evidence for some time. Laced up his work boots. Went back down the stairs. Swung his double doors wide open.

The stars were out. It was so clear you could see the Milky Way, but his interest was drawn by the glint of his inside lights on a brown glass jug lying on the ground just outside his doors. He picked it up. Sniffed. It smelled of gasoline. There was a small amount remaining in the bottom. He carried the jug back inside. With three more buckets of water, he made sure the fire was dead out. There was no indication the fire had spread to the foundation. He went back upstairs. The Colt was in his footlocker. He took it out. The bullets were hidden on the top shelf of his ice box. He loaded the Colt, put a handful of extra bullets in his pants pocket.

Back downstairs, he started the Packard. He had a very bad feeling about what might be going on. He considered going out to check on the Anna Marie, but the road to Ebbey Island this time of night had a hundred places to ambush a man and kill him. He decided that would be stupid. Instead, he went to check on Florence.

When he arrived at 22nd and Rucker, he parked half a block away. Turned off his engine. Cautiously he got out. Tried to stay in the shadows as he moved closer. He didn't like what he found. Nearly all her lights were on. Even for Florence, it was way too early for her to be up and about. Except if something was wrong.

When her lights abruptly went out, he felt better. Up until the moment when she came out the front door of her apartment building in the company of four other people, all of whom were men, men wearing long raincoats. It was too early in the fall for raincoats. His guess was that they were carrying weapons, probably shotguns. He stayed put, out of sight on his side of the Catalpa tree. The men pushed Florence into a waiting enclosed sedan, and left rapidly. Hank ran back to his truck. Lights off, he followed at a discreet distance. When the sedan began the climb up Rucker Hill, Hank had a pretty good idea where they were going. There was no satisfaction in being right when they drove directly to the big white house owned by Charles Waters and turned up the steep drive. The bastard's back, thought Hank. I guess I should have killed him when I had the chance.

Over a year ago, Hank had adjusted his aim, and instead of shooting him between the eyes, shot a hole in Water's right ear. Then he put three bullets into the radiator of Water's $6000.00 Packard Coupe, and two more bullets in the front tires. The Packard hadn't been removed and remained at his moorage on Ebbey Island, pushed off to one side in the tall grass.

On that day, a year ago, Hank had hauled Waters back into town and dumped him out, so to speak, at the hospital, telling him to get out of town or die. As far as he knew, from that day to this, Waters got out of town.

Hank considered Waters' house. A few lights were on, one upstairs. At a minimum there were five men inside. Five men who were probably expecting him. But that wasn't the problem. Florence was the problem.

He could shoot the five men. Kill five men. Or six or seven. They would also be trying to kill him. Fair was fair. But if he shot anyone in front of Florence, or while she was within hearing distance, regardless of his intentions, or who was shooting at whom or what they might have done to her, she would insist on notifying the police. Excepting Florence, any survivor could expect to spend a considerable amount of time in jail. Explaining his motives might also land him in jail, for bootlegging. He needed to rescue Florence. He had to figure out how to do that without killing anyone. Rushing right inside, blundering around in the dark with a gun, sounded like a very bad idea.

He fingered the Colt, he warmed the gun in his hands. He cocked it and locked the safety. But he stayed where he was. Then before it got light he moved the truck three blocks away so it couldn't be seen from anywhere in Waters' house. There was a spot between two neighboring houses where he could stand and have a pretty good view, but where he was also shielded from the view from the house by trees. At least, he hoped he couldn't be seen.

Whistles sounded as shifts changed. People got up and went to work. Hank waited. If someone challenged his right to be where he was, he would have to move. His nerves got worse as the morning got longer. At what he guessed was around ten, two men – but no Florence - came out of Waters' house, got in the four door sedan, and drove away. Hoping that Waters was one of the men, he ran back to his truck and followed. Maybe Waters would go for a nice quiet drive in the country. Since it was late September, Hank told himself, the season was open for sitting ducks. Even if it wasn't Waters, he might be able to corner the two men at gunpoint and ask some questions. He was disappointed when the sedan took a short trip, no more than eight blocks, to Bayside Machine. Waters got out, but he was met at the gate by two men, both carrying rifles. All three went inside

Shit! Now what should he do?

The man in the sedan took an even shorter trip, three more blocks, to the waterfront. Down to the Yacht Club moorage. The man got out carrying a tool box. Hank parked the Packard on the other side of a warehouse and walked back to see what he could see.

The man was down on the docks. He had put on a coverall and opened the hatches on a speed boat Hank had never seen before. Barrel backed, maybe thirty-five feet long, shaped more like a torpedo than a boat, built for nothing besides pleasure and speed. There was a low windscreen, then a single cockpit. What seemed like an acre of varnished mahogany. Hank didn't think she actually was a Gold Cup boat, but she had that sleek, streamlined appearance of a boat built to go fast. What he could see of the intake and exhaust ports suggested twin engines. Hank took a wild guess.

"Probably has a pair of Liberty's in her." A Liberty was a converted aircraft engine. "Flat out she might do thirty knots, twenty knots without even working hard." The stern was narrow and raked back into what Hank thought was called a drake's tail. There was a name painted on the stern, in gold. He had to get closer to read the writing.

When he did a chill went through him: Florence. The name was Florence. For a moment, he thought he was seeing things. He started over: Florence.

The man with the coveralls was working hard with a big wrench. The man had his back to him, and Hank moved in much closer. The man was pulling the head off the engine block. That was an all day job. This boat wasn't going anywhere for a while. Hank went back to his truck and drove back to his vantage point to watch Waters' house. There were two cars he had not seen before. Both were black coupes, and at a guess, were Fords. After a while three men came out, two got in a car and drove away, the other man went back inside.

The changing of the guard. How many were inside? There was no way to know, but the problem of trying to do anything inside the house still had the same name: Florence.

He went back, got in his truck and left. If he kept hanging around in this neighborhood he was going to get arrested. He drove back past Bayside Machine. There was nothing to see. All the windows were painted out. The access to the loading dock was fenced and screened. He considered continuing north on Grand to 868. Billy and Samuel were no doubt wondering where he was. He decided against it. They were just going to have to work on their own today.

Waters had come home to Everett in force. What Hank had observed spoke of a well planned campaign. Waters had Florence. He must know by now he hadn't burned Hank out. But maybe, just maybe, the fire wasn't intended to burn me out. He wanted to wake me up. Get me to do what I'm doing right now.

Maybe his problem is the same as mine. He has to kill me somewhere else, and in such a way that suspicion doesn't focus on him. Worse, maybe he wants Florence! But she was his niece. What kind of man was he? The boat was named Florence. That was the clue. You name your boat after your mother, your wife, or a sweetheart. The man was sick. But it might explain Water's reaction, like a bull elk in heat. Hank made his decision.

He drove to his parents home over on Virginia. He avoided his mother. Down the basement, he recovered two pickle jars. Both held cash. He left without speaking to anyone.

He went back to his boathouse. Up stairs in his apartment, he found clean clothes. Another warm sweater. He stripped the blankets off his bed. They were the only ones he owned. He drove out the road to Ebbey Island. He drove slowly, the Colt beside him on the seat, the safety off. No one surprised him. The Anna Marie bobbed quietly and undisturbed at her mooring. He went aboard. He used his nose to carefully check the bilge for gas. He checked the gas lines for leaks. He examined every part he could conceive of anyone trying to sabotage. There was no sabotage. Nothing had been tampered with. He started up, pushed off. His destination was the harbor mouth back at Bayside. He ran down the river toward the mouth, but instead of going straight out over the bar, he swung hard left, and headed south going past the big dock at 14th Street, his destination the docks at the foot of Hewitt. He pulled in at the commercial fuel dock where he topped off the tanks. They had one five gallon gas can for sale. He bought it and filled it up, then wedged it firmly in place in the engine room. It was the best he could do. He continued south down the channel towards the Yacht Club. American Towboating had a dock near the Yacht Club. He got permission to tie up and wait for a few hours. The Anna Marie couldn't be seen from the Yacht Club. He tied up, shut down, and cautiously walked over towards the Yacht Club. The man in the coveralls was still working.

He went back to the Anna Marie and made a pot of coffee. There was a kid fishing for piling perch. Hank gave the kid two dollars to go up the hill and buy him three sandwiches. When the kid came back, he tipped him fifty cents. For another two dollars he bought the kids fishing outfit, a hand line, some piling worms and a bucket. He also gave the kid one of his sandwiches. The kid hung around for while, giving him fishing advice, then left.

He tried not to fidget and fuss, but it was hard to wait. He went back to the Anna Marie to eat his food. He spread his charts on the galley table, and marked off some courses, counted the miles, converted true courses to magnetic. What if Waters ran south, down sound, towards Seattle or Tacoma? He plotted courses for that possibility. Hours passed. He went back to the Yacht Club. The man in the coveralls still fiddled with the engine. The afternoon whiled itself away.

He took a position where he could spy on the Florence but also where he could sit comfortably, fish, and hopefully not be noticed. He fished and he waited. He even caught two perch. He tossed them back. Or maybe he caught the same fish twice. Hard to know, with perch. The mechanic finally packed up his tools and polished the mahogany back to a shine, got in the sedan, drove away. It was getting on towards evening.

Having made his own bet on how events would play out, Hank did his best to wait patiently. Which wasn't easy. He needed to be doing something. Waters waited until it was full dark. The four door sedan came back, Waters got out. The coverall man got out, pulling Florence out after him. Two more men also clambered out, and took what Hank could only call guard positions. Waters, Florence, and the coverall man went down the ramp to the boat. Florence was wearing a scarf. Hank couldn't see her face. The coverall man climbed in the boat and started the engines. Then reached back for Florence. The two guards basically hoisted her on board. Waters got in and sat on the other side. The two guards untied the lines, and the good ship Florence was off.

Hank tossed the hand line in his bucket, left the bucket behind on the dock, and ran for the Anna Marie. Quickly he untied his lines and got underway. The Florence was clearing the day mark at the mouth of the channel. Hank pushed his throttle forward and tried to make up some of the distance. Waters was running a stern light. Hank ran dark. No lights. There was a pretty good chop, and Waters must have told his skipper to open her up. Hank could see spray as the Florence bucked into the chop and porpoised through the waves. Hank tried to keep pace, pushing his throttle to the maximum, but he would lose this race. He didn't have the hull or the horsepower to keep up.

Hank didn't know what to do. Waters was going north, up Saratoga on the west side, the outside of Camano Island. He had to be headed for Deception Pass. On the route Waters was taking, it was a forty mile run. At the speed Waters was making, it would take two hours, or less. Even running flat out, it would take Hank two and a half hours, and that would mean Hank would be eight to ten miles behind. With that much distance to make up, Waters would be so far ahead of Hank, that he could safely disappear into the San Juans and Hank would never find him. Or Florence.

He decided he had to take a chance. He had checked the mileage carefully. The route Waters was taking was basically a big arc, part of a circle. Hank could shorten the distance by cutting across the circle on the diameter. Sure, if he ran on the east side, on the inside of Camano Island, up through West Pass and then out into Skagit Bay, he would save close to eight miles. He would also be out of the chop if he hugged the east side of Camano most of the way. Calmer water and a shorter distance. The risk, and it was very real, was the very shallow water at the head of Port Susan, immediately west of Stanwood. The trick would be finding his way into the approach to West Pass in the dark, and then the danger of actually running the narrow channel through West Pass in the dark. He was unlikely to make up all the distance Waters was gaining, but it would keep him close and give him a chance. Right now Waters was gaining ground at the rate of something like four miles an hour. If he didn't try something Hank would never catch him.

He decided to take the chance. He swung the wheel to the right and headed north up Port Susan. His heart sank as Waters stern light disappeared. What if he was wrong? Well, if he was wrong, and if anything happened to Florence, he'd burn down Waters house, and kill the man at the corner of Hewitt and Colby, in full day light on the Fourth of July, if necessary, and to hell with the consequences.

But there wasn't much comfort there. He ran with one eye on the compass, the other on his chronometer. Up the east side of Camano, the water was calmer and he did make better time. There was less wind, less wave, and less current to slow him down. In under an hour, he was at the head of Port Susan. The channel into West Pass was marked, in a way.

Tree branches had been pounded into the tidal mud, then a scrap of cloth. or a colored glass bottle tied to the top. The trick was getting two of the markers lined up in the dark. Entering West Pass, the problem was not current, it was depth. And staying in the channel. Fortunately, the Anna Marie was shallow in draft. Twice he steered away from almost submerged pilings. Once, he bumped something, hard, in the dark, but the Anna Marie bounced off. The closeness of the call left him with weak knees. The prudent thing to do would be to slow down. He kept his hands away from the throttle. Full speed ahead.

Exiting West Pass he set a course directly for Deception Pass. He swept the horizon over and over, trying to find Waters and his boat. The wind had really kicked up. It wasn't terribly rough yet, but it was coming on to blow. He saw something out of the corner of his eye. He jerked back the throttle and the Anna Marie slowed. It was a boat. Far to his left, maybe a mile or more over towards Oak Harbor. He waited. The stern light finally pulled ahead of him. Hank couldn't really see the other boat, but the stern light was bouncing up and down. Waters may have bought himself a fast boat, but she didn't like this rough water. In the wide open spaces of Skagit Bay it was getting much rougher. He pushed his speed back up. He didn't quite have to run at top speed to keep up. While his risk had worked, it hadn't been necessary: Waters was being slowed by the weather. He heaved a sigh of relief, and followed. Waters ran straight through Deception Pass and kept going West. But now it was really getting rough. There was a set of waves before you got to Deception Island that were steep and quite big. Hank slammed into three, taking water over the bow and clean over the wheelhouse before he could get the throttle back, slow down, and coast through the rest. If he had taken green water over the cabin top, he couldn't imagine what Waters had experienced in his speed boat. Now, he only caught occasional glances of Water's stern light.

It was that rough, with big swells rolling down the Straits of Juan De Fuca out of the Pacific Ocean. Both the Anna Marie and the Florence were bouncing up and down, motoring into the troughs, then up the face of the advancing waves, hesitating for a brief moment at the peak, then down the back side of the wave, sliding into the trough. Up and down. Only when he and Waters were both up could Hank pick out the Florence on the horizon.

Waters was heading directly for Iceberg Point, the southern most point on Lopez Island, and Hank began to suspect where Waters was headed. He'd have to be very careful. This end of Lopez Island was nothing but a rock infested obstacle course. Extensive, tangled beds of kelp. Run through one of those and you could choke off your cooling system. Low reefs, some of them exposed at high tide, some just submerged. Hit one of those, and you could ruin your boat if not the rest of your life. When the Florence disappeared, rounding at Iceberg Point, Hank was certain Waters had turned north. He eased back on the throttle, and let the distance widen. He stayed well off shore. Iceberg Point was at the end of a long fishhook of land, that stretched south, and hooked west and then turned back north, creating a sheltered bay on the inside of the curve called Barlow Bay. It was the only harbor of refuge at the south end of Lopez for fishermen, tow boats, or yachtsmen. And bootleggers. Normally, Hank avoided Barlow Bay at all costs. Too many competitors, too much law enforcement, too many people. Some of them were the modern equivalent of pirates. Plus, if you were inside the bay, there was only one way out: the way you came in. Even on good days, Hank considered Barlow Bay a trap waiting to happen.

And Waters was leading him into the trap. Hank was under no illusions. He didn't think they knew he was right behind them. He didn't think they expected him tonight. Even so, they would be waiting. They wanted him to follow. Maybe not tonight. And somehow they would have made sure he followed. Maybe a message delivered directly by one of Waters men: Dear Mouse, come get the cheese. He would have to be very careful.

He backed off the throttle even more, and when he finally made the hard right turn around the point to run south into Barlow Bay proper, he entered at dead slow, mostly drifting. There were a few fishing boats tied off to mooring buoys, but none of these boats appeared to be actively in use. There were a dozen small boats, skiffs, swinging at anchor. Probably boats owned by men who lived on shore, who went out for a day, or two, to fish. Sold their catch to the local cannery.

And anchored behind the headland, in the most sheltered spot possible, was a large fan-tailed motor yacht, at least one hundred feet long, he estimated, mostly by comparing the yacht's length to Waters' speedboat, the Florence, moored alongside. A long, elegant yacht. Even in the dark you could see the rounded, overhanging transom, the sweep of the sheer from the high bow forward, running aft to the flag staff on the stern. In a way, it was a relief to see the Florence at rest. He couldn't see any people profiles in the speedboat. They must be on board the yacht. So now what?

He let the wind drift him off to the east, away from the big yacht, using the engine as little as possible.

What he was trying to do was get inside, and approach the anchored yacht from an unexpected direction. His engine sounded too loud to his ears. He shut down. He kept one pair of sixteen foot oars on board. He used them now, standing and facing forward to row. Not that he could see much over the wheelhouse. Not that he made much progress. Moving the Anna Marie against the wind was slow going. But the progress he made was quiet. There was a slight sound of water slapping against the hull, the bleat of a Heron working the shallows. Otherwise silence. Slowly Hank approached the stern of the big yacht. He could read the name now. The Persephone. He knew that Persephone was the Queen of Hell. Also the source of springtime. Kind of a split decision for the Greeks. Hank went with the Queen of Hell. It would keep him careful.

The Anna Marie nudged the hull of the Persephone. He shipped his oars and reached up to grab the lower rung of the railing that ran along the deck. No one shouted, no one shot at him. He tied the Anna Marie to the railing, bow and stern, with slip knots for a quick release, so she wouldn't swing or bounce against the big yacht. He took off his boots and socks. Better to be barefoot. Certain to be quieter. Then, climbing up on the cabin top of the Anna Marie, he was up and over the railing. He was aboard. The Colt was in his coat pocket. He took it out. He thumbed the safety off.

Staying low, he crawled forward. He heard voices. He heard the clink of glasses. Bottles. Waters must have arrived and poured himself a drink. Or drinks.

"So keep a sharp lookout. Like I told you, I don't expect him tonight," said Waters, "but he'll come tomorrow for certain, for the girl. Don't take any chances. Start watching now. He's tricky and he's tough. Don't underestimate him. Remember, I want to kill him, but if you have to do it to stop him, you go right ahead and take care of it."

"...any chances," another male voice said.

"That's right," agreed Waters. "Don't take any chances. Now, I'm going to bed."

Whoever was aboard apparently scattered in different directions. A light in the wheelhouse, forward, came on. All but one of the lamps in the main saloon went out. Hank heard a door open. Two men talking. He couldn't make out what they were saying. He risked a quick look into the cabin. Two men were outside on the deck directly opposite him, but he was seeing them through two sets of windows, smoking and talking.

Where was Waters?

He took another peek. There was a curved stair railing in the saloon, right side, towards the stern. He ducked back down. That couldn't be the only way below. It was unlikely you would access the engine room from the nicest room on the ship. No one would want you tracking grease on the carpet.

He crept forward. Tried another window. My God, a formal dining room. Brocaded chairs. A sideboard. Mirrors. A crystal chandelier. Very nice. But no stairway below. He moved farther forward. Took a peek. The galley. The next set of windows was frosted. Probably the bathroom. He went back to the galley. There was a door. It was unlocked. He stepped inside. There were carpets on the floors. Gently he lifted his feet and set them down softly, like walking on ice. He didn't want to make any noise or trip. He held the Colt at the ready, prepared to fire. He inched across the floor. He was standing in the passage that lead forward to the bath, and up a few stairs, presumably to the wheelhouse. With relief he saw there was also a set of stairs on the left that went below.

He took the stairs down. Slowly, one by one, careful where he put each foot. Stopping frequently to listen. Nothing but the sound of a ship at anchor. The stairs ended in a narrow hallway. About every six feet there was a small, dim electric light. Probably six or twelve volt, thought Hank. He crept aft. There was a door at the end of the corridor, on the centerline. Holding his breath, he turned the latch. It was the engine room. He stepped in, leaving the door open behind him.

There were two massive six cylinder diesel engines, each as big as a small automobile. Made by Enterprise Diesel. Very interesting. The casting and machine work made these engines a thing of beauty if you were an engineer, or someone who appreciated damn good work with castings, taps and dies, a lathe and other machine shop tools. The rocker arms and valve lifters were all out in the open. With a 12 inch bore and a 15 inch stroke, you would have over six hundred horsepower at 600 rpm. Hank wished he had more time to admire the work. These engines might push the Persephone at speeds faster than the Anna Marie. Certainly, the Persephone with her long and narrow hull, graceful lines, and tucked up transom, could outrun anything the Coast Guard patrolled in. He needed to disable these engines. He quickly had an idea, and it only took a moment to pull the magneto wires off the small gas engine that provided the compressed air you needed to start these diesel heavy weights. He stuffed the wires down the front of his coveralls. That was the best he could do to make certain they wouldn't be coming after him.

He left as quickly as he had arrived, and closed the door. He continued, but now moved forward. There was a cabin on his left. He listened. Someone was moving around. This must be Waters. Noting the location, he kept going forward. There was a cabin on the right. He listened. There were no sounds. He opened the door. The cabin was empty. Well, sort of empty, if you didn't count the cases of liquor stacked wall to wall and floor to ceiling. There was one more door on the left. Was that where Florence was?

He moved in slow motion, being extra, extra careful to be quiet. Slowly, slowly, oh so very slowly, he depressed the door latch, and barely daring to breathe, he inched open the door, no squeaks he prayed, no squeaks. There were no squeaks. With the door more than halfway open, he stood in the passage and tried to see what he could see. The dim light from the passageway spilled into the room.

There was a bunk opposite the door. Florence was tied hand and foot, with her back to him, stretched out on the bunk. There was a cloth around her head, which he guessed was some kind of gag. Her breathing was noisy, sounding labored. Because of the way she was breathing, he almost made a serious mistake. But the man made a snore type snort, and there he was, as big as day, asleep in a chair. A handgun cradled in his hands.

How nice, thought Hank. Company. Now what do I do?

He considered a shot to the head. But that was going to create other problems. People who would come running. More people that he would be forced to shoot. In addition, if he and Florence had a future, he couldn't shoot anyone.

Florence's big, black clunky boots were sitting on the floor beside her bunk. Hank began to smile. He thumbed the safety of his Colt to the 'on' position. He tucked the gun back in his pocket. He picked up her nearest boot. It was the left. As he hoped, it was heavy, with a substantial heel. He took the boot back high the way he had see golfers take back a club, and he swung down and through, pretending the man's head was that little white ball on the tee. Mouth open, the man slumped over in his chair, and fell towards the floor, the gun falling out of his hands. Hank caught the gun before it could hit something and make a noise. He put the gun in his other pocket.

He rolled Florence over onto her back. Her eyes snapped open, and she tried to scream in spite of the gag. He took off his hat. She saw who he was. She stopped bucking and kicking. He took out his pocket knife, and cut the rope tied around her ankles, then did the same with her wrists. Before he could stop her, she put her arms around his neck and held on like she would never let go. Hank tried to stand her upright, but it was difficult. On her feet, she did let go, and tore at the gag.

"Hush, now," Hank whispered. "Hush." He pulled the gag away.

"Hank," she said in a full voice. Hank tried to cover her mouth with his hand, she tried to hug him again, and she won.

"Florence," said Hank holding her close, whispering into her ear, "you have to be quiet. Waters is sleeping next door. Come on." He picked up her boots and handed them to her, offered her his other hand, which she took. Out in the corridor, he moved towards the stairway. Going past Waters' door, the door opened, and Waters stood there, wearing yellow and black checked pajamas with his toothbrush in his hand. Without thinking Hank hit him on the nose. Waters went reeling backwards, and Hank was on top of him. There was a discarded white shirt over the back of a chair. Hank ripped off a strip of fabric, wound it twice around Water's face and neck and tied it as a gag. Like a prize fighter down for a partial count, Waters shook off the punch to the nose and tried to stand and fight. Hank kicked him hard in the testicles, and with a groan, Waters went down slowly on his knees, hands to his groin. Then Hank got Waters right arm in a hammerlock, and used increasing pain to boost Waters to his feet.

"Are you all right?" Florence whispered. Hank's answer was to point to the stairs. Florence went up first, followed by Waters with steady pressure from Hank. Hank stayed right on Waters' heels, and kept him moving fast. Hank didn't want to give Waters any time to think, or act. In the galley, Hank hustled Waters out onto the side deck.

"Florence, you go first. Use the cabin top as a step."

Florence made the leap. Hank heard voices. There wasn't time to be nice about it. He picked Waters up and dumped him over the rail. Waters landed with a thump on the cabin top, bounced off and with a loud moan, arms reaching out to cushion the fall, ended up on the back deck of the Anna Marie.

Hank hurried over the rail after him. He pulled his slip knots and pushed the Anna Marie off and away from the other ship. He raced inside, went through the starting sequence as quick as it could be done, and as the engine came to life, he engaged the clutch and slammed the throttle to maximum. Turned the wheel over hard.

With a roar the Anna Marie slewed around in a turn, Hank straightened out, and concentrated on putting as much distance between the Anna Marie and the ship from hell as he could. Shots rang out. He didn't hear any hit, but Florence was standing on the stern.

"Florence," he yelled. "Get in here."

Florence thought something was wrong, and came running.

"Get below," Hank commanded, "It's safer."

There were more shots. The glass in the galley door shattered. Somebody had a rifle. No way was that a bullet from a handgun. Florence ducked below, and Hank continued to swing the wheel back and forth, fishtailing the Anna Marie, making her a harder target to hit. There were more shots, but no hits that he heard. Unless they had shot Waters.

Wouldn't that be sad! Hank almost laughed at the thought. He swung to the left on a new course that should take him out of Barlow Bay and back to the main channel. He still needed all the distance he could get. They had the speedboat, and could catch him easily if they tried.

"May I come out now?" Florence asked, poking her head up topside.

"Should be all right," said Hank. "Check on our guest, see if he's alive."

"I couldn't believe it when you dropped him."

"I was in a hurry."

"I'll keep that in mind for the future." She went out on the back deck.

Hank kept an eye on her. Waters was sitting up. He'd torn off the gag. Florence was talking to him. He took a moment to consult the chart, changed his course slightly.

When he looked again, Florence and Waters were in some sort of struggle. Hank pulled back the throttle and went to help her. Waters was still sitting and had one of Florence's boots and was trying to defend himself. Florence had the other boot and was swinging at him wildly and often.

"Stop it!" Hank shouted, drawing the Colt and pointing at Waters. Waters stopped, and casually tossed the boot overboard.

"You bastard!" Florence screamed, and swung her boot once more, hitting Waters in the head and knocking him over.

"Florence, whoa there. Whoa!" Hank grabbed her and pushed her towards the cabin.

"Waters, open that hatch." Waters was sprawled over the hatch top. He rolled to his knees and opened the hatch. "Now, crawl in."

Waters gave him a murderous look.

"Yes, I know it stinks and you'll ruin your nice yellow pajamas, but don't argue." Waters crawled in.

"I see you still have your ear?"

"I had it re-done in San Francisco, after they butchered the job in Everett."

"Travel is so satisfying. Get your head down." Hank closed the hatch with a bang. He went back to the cabin.

Florence was sitting at the galley table with her head in her hands. "Sorry," she said.

"Florence, it doesn't really matter to me, but I thought it might matter to you. I'm trying hard not to give in to the temptation to shoot the son of a bitch in the head." She didn't respond. "Did he say something to you?"

"Yes."

"What did he say."

"I won't repeat it. Where are we going?" she added, changing the subject.

"I thought Waters might like to visit Goose Island."
"Where's that?"
"Very close. About three miles"
"Where?"

Hank lit the kerosene lamp over the stove. He kept the light low, and handed her the chart. "We're here," he pointed at the chart. " This is Goose. That distance is approximately three miles. Twenty minutes, we're there."

Most of the San Juan Islands were lush with vegetation, trees, grass, wild flowers. In the darkness, Goose Island was a mere thirty feet away and in the dark it didn't look very inviting. At high tide, maybe two acres of rounded rock. Florence said so.

"It doesn't look any better in the daytime."
"Why is it that streaky silver color?"
"I'd guess bird shit."

Florence snickered. "How long before he gets rescued?"
"Should be tomorrow. There's plenty of traffic going past, fishing boats, steamers." Hank released the hatch. "Come on, Waters, out."

Waters climbed out. He was cold and cramped. He moved slowly.

"Take off your pj's," Hank told him. The command was backed up by the Colt. Waters took off his pj's.

"Behind you Waters," Hank pointed, "is Goose Island. Swim for it."
"I can't swim."

"Too bad," Hank said. He fired the Colt a few inches over Waters head.

There was a great squawking from Goose Island. "Dive in and learn."

Waters turned to face Goose, but hesitated.

"Waters, I'm going to hand the gun to Florence if you don't get going."

That did it. Waters did a very nice dive.

"Come get your pajama's!" Hank yelled. Waters swam back, Hank tossed him his pj's, and swimming one handed Waters dog paddled his way to dry land, pulled himself up out of the water and Hank and Florence could see him taking small steps to higher ground.

"Nice dive," called Hank. "You should try out for the Olympics."
"Fuck you," screamed Waters. "Fuck you both."

Hank waved, went back in the wheelhouse, put the Anna Marie in gear, and they motored away, leaving Waters screaming abuse in their wake.

"That's what he said earlier."
"Not very original."
"Yes," agreed Florence. "How long will it take to get to Everett?"

"We're not headed for Everett."

"Where are we going?" She was almost plaintive.

"Victoria."

There was a long silence. "I wasn't at work yesterday. If I don't report for work today, they'll fire me for certain."

"Florence, the men who work for Waters will try and kidnap you again."

"Wonderful. What do I do? Get to a phone, call Mr. Lind and tell him I can't come in because I know I'll be kidnapped. I'm sure," her voice dripped sarcasm, "that will save my job."

"Florence, we can't go back tomorrow. Maybe in a few days."

"What do you suggest in the meantime? What do you suggest I do for employment? Are you willing to support me, pay for my food and rent?"

Hanks answer to that was an unqualified yes, but he wasn't ready to discuss it.

"We can't go back now. It's too dangerous. I suggest we talk things over in the morning. If you want to yell at me, you can do it then. But I haven't had much sleep lately, and my guess is you haven't either." He quickly stood aside as Florence brushed past him. She went below. She used the bathroom. Crawled into the single bunk, pulled a blanket up over her head. She was asleep in minutes.

Hank pushed the throttle forward and started trying to find the lights of Victoria on the horizon. His night wasn't over yet.

Victoria, September 1923

Florence woke up. Her wrists and ankles hurt from where the ropes had been tied. The skin was red and raw. She was thirsty. She wanted a bath and clean clothes. She wanted something to eat. She wanted to be in Everett so she could go to work and keep her job. She used the toilet.

"Hank?" He wasn't in the galley, although the stove was burning and there was hot coffee. She helped herself to the coffee. Still no sugar. She stepped outside on deck. "Hank?" No answer.

Now what was he doing?

With the stove burning, the cabin was far too warm. Carrying her coffee, she went out and sat on the stern, sunning herself. It was going to be a glorious day. The Anna Marie was tied up to a low floating dock among other commercial fishing boats. It was very quiet. If there were other people on the other boats, they were still sleeping. Hank found her like that when he came back, sitting on the aft deck, her skirt rolled up over her knees, enjoying the sunshine.

"Hi."

"Hi yourself. I hope that's breakfast."

"Sort of." Hank handed her a white box tied with string. She broke the string.

"Sausage rolls! I haven't had them in years. Mmm…." She ate one, took two more, handed him the box. Hank got himself another cup of coffee, a refill for Florence, and one by one they cleaned out the box.

"What else have you been doing?"

"I went to the Empress and made a long distance call. It took them about ten minutes to build a circuit and connect me."

"Who did you call?" She was curious.

"The San Juan County Sheriff received an anonymous phone call this morning."

"He did? How do you know?"

"Because I was the caller."

"Ahh! And what did this caller have to say?"

"That there was a motor yacht in Barlow Bay loaded with liquor."

"Wouldn't they have moved her last night?"

"They might have tried." He set his coffee down, got up, went in the cabin, came back, and dropped a tangle of wires on the deck beside her. "It takes compressed air to start the diesel engines on the Persephone," Hank explained. "They have a small Easthope gasoline engine that turns the compressor. Those brass fittings on the end have been custom machined for the Easthope, probably on a jeweler's lathe. They're designed that way so they won't vibrate loose. I'd be very surprised if they have a spare set. And I doubt you could order new ones and receive them in anything under a week. If you can't start the Easthope, you can't start the main engines," Hank concluded.

Florence picked the mess of wires up and examined the very precise machine work on the ends.

"Is this hard to do?"

"If you have the right training and the tools, no, not if you know what you're doing." She handed the wires back to Hank.

He dropped them into the harbor and they sank out of sight. "The Sheriff also learned that the owner of the Persephone might be stranded on Goose Island."

"What did he say to that?"

"He had a number of very boring questions."

"Questions?"

"What's your name? How do you know this? Those type of questions. I knew you were probably getting hungry, so I hung up."

"Thank you. I was hungry. But Hank," Florence had to shade her eyes to look up at him, " isn't Waters likely to tell all?"

He sat back down beside her. "Very likely. So my bootlegging days are probably over." In Seattle, there was a man named Olmstead, a police Lieutenant, who was building an organization, buying off his old friends in the police department, and pushing independent bootleggers like Hank out of business. Maybe it was time to get out.

"Probably over?"

"All right," Hank conceded with a sigh. "They're over, over ." He paused. He thought for a moment. "I don't know what I'm going to do."

"You're already a crab fisherman."

"Not much money in crab. Not enough, anyway. And not in this boat." He kicked the deck. "She burns way too much fuel."

"You built a very nice home. Sell it. Build another."

"I want to live in that house." He didn't say, 'with you', but Florence heard the thought if not the words. She changed the subject. Or thought she did.

"Gertrude really does want a house like yours. If you build her, and Hadley, a house, you can hire me and I'll keep the books. Although, I warn you. Lately, I'm not very reliable. I get kidnapped rather often."

Hank laughed, even though it wasn't really funny if you stopped to think about it. "You've seen the house at 868?"

"It's beautiful."

"Could you live there?" She didn't answer. "Florence, that house is a gift. For you." He paused. He took her hand. Looked her right in the eye. "Florence, will you marry me?"

She was silent. Then she smiled, she leaned forward, brought her lips to his and kissed him. She stayed there, as he held her, cheek to cheek.

"Hank, I don't know. I know that when I'm with you, I feel safe, and when I'm not, I feel alone. But I don't know if that's love."

"That seems like a good place to start."

"I agree, but I need to think about it." She pulled back." Ask me again later. Let me think about it. She paused. "Would you do that?"

"Yes."

"Thank you."

"Now what?"

"A bath? Clean clothes? More food? Do you have any money with you?"

He laughed. He took her inside and handed her a pickle jar. Florence shook the contents out on the galley table, then was sorry she did. Money spilled off the table onto the floor.

"I used to do this for a living," she said, as she rapidly sorted the denominations, then counted and tallied each stack. "Two thousand, three hundred and forty-five." He had some rubber bands. She banded each stack. "Care to bet if I'm right?"

"I never bet against the house."

"That's good advice. I think this will be enough," said Florence. Hank wasn't certain. He took the contents of the other jar with him. He didn't have her count it. It was almost twice as full. Hand in hand, Florence wearing a heavy pair of Hank's wool socks as slippers, they walked up the dock. He explained about his Victoria truck.

"Hank, if we got married, I can't spend my life driving your dump truck, or even a truck like this, though it is smaller."

"I know where we can get a used Packard sedan. Cheap." Florence demanded an explanation, which he provided as they drove to the YMCA where in separate parts of the building they each took a shower. The Y provided clean towels and soap. There were several very nice shops selling men's and women's clothing on Government Street. They agreed to meet in the lobby of the Empress in three hours.

Hank bought two wool suits, one blue, one charcoal. The suits were quality goods, imported from England, and cost him well over one hundred dollars each. He could hear his mother scolding him as he paid the bill, which included shirts, socks, shorts, ties, cufflinks and two pair of shoes also imported from London, England.

He wore the blue suit. At an adjacent shop he bought a leather suitcase. And a wide brimmed hat, imported from Italy. He stopped at a barbershop for a shave. He was early arriving at the Empress. He asked if there were any rooms available. "But of course. For how many, Sir?"

"For my... wife and myself. Do you have a suite?" He was remembering hotel rooms he'd seen in Paris. "Something with a bedroom, say, and a small sitting room." He stopped to consider. "Maybe on the Harbor side. With a view?" The man raised his eyebrows. "Costs a bit more, Sir."

"That's fine."

"Certainly, Sir. For how many nights?"

"Through next Monday."

"Very good."

"How much? I'll pay you now, in cash."

The man named a terrible figure. Hank paid. He had his bag sent up.

"One key or two?"

"Two. My wife will want her own."

"Very good, Sir."

"In the bar or the dining room, can I just sign for things?"

"Absolutely."

"Thank you."

"Thank you, Sir."

There were some little shops on the inside of the Hotel, down a short hallway. Hank went for a walk. The second shop he strolled past sold jewelry. He came to an abrupt halt.

He went in.

There was a well dressed older gentleman, with a neatly trimmed white beard, sitting behind the counter, examining a ring through a loupe.

"May I help you, Sir?"

"Do you have wedding bands?"

"Of course." He wrapped the ring he was examining in tissue, and set it under the counter.

Hank bought a simple gold band. He had to guess at the size, but he couldn't be too far off the mark. The man put the ring in a ring box and wrapped the box in unadorned silver paper, tied with white ribbon.

"What was that ring you were examining when I came in?"

"You have a good eye." The gentleman pulled a flat wooden tray out from beneath the counter. Wrapped in tissue was the ring he had been studying. The style was Art Deco. Over thirty stones. Reminding him of rings he had seen in Paris.

"Is it French?"

"It is indeed, Sir. Cartier. Made in Paris. This is called a bullet shape. "

"Is that white gold?"

"No, Sir. Platinum. These diamonds have superb clarity and are very white. Another metal would diminish their sparkle."

"And are those stones all diamonds?"

"Of very high quality."

"How much?"

"Quite a bit, I'm afraid." The gentleman smiled a shy smile. " Four thousand."

You could purchase a very nice home in Everett for that kind of money. A very nice home.

Hank sat down in the lobby to wait for Florence. Twenty minutes late, she rushed in, totally transformed.

"Sorry." She was wearing an extremely simple two piece wool suit. No ribbons, bows, or lace. A creamy, off white wool, accented with charcoal piping. A skirt much shorter than Florence normally wore. Very revealing, fitted through the bodice and waist. The suit had silver buttons, the buttons worked with some sort of design. And no boots. White and tan pumps, with a short heel. She looked elegant and stunning. And, Hank didn't know how, but the suit showed off every curve. She looked like the wife of some very rich man. She carried a small leather case, and a cashmere coat folded over her arm.

"You look ..." Hank began, "You are," he amended, "beautiful."

"Thank you, she said. You're too kind." She blushed and smiled.

"Actually, I don't know about me, but the suit is a Paris original. Not Coco Chanel, but close."

"I should be impressed?"

"Especially if you knew what it cost. But I'll never tell."

Hank laughed. He was happier than he had ever been in his life.

"No harm done. I checked us in." Florence wanted to ask if 'checked in' meant one room, or two, but he took her gently by the arm. She watched as Hank took her coat and carrying case, gave it to the man behind the desk and asked that her things be "sent up". Hank turned back and took her arm.

"Lunch is being served. In the Bengal Room. With the palms in pots, and the lions and the tigers. But I, Hank-yi, your faithful guide, will escort you."

Florence laughed. "Have you been waiting in the bar?"

"No, but I think a drink with lunch is a great idea. Two please," he said to a young man in an ill fitting gold jacket, carrying a handful of menus .

"We're guests here at the Empress." He dangled his room key, and they were seated immediately. The colors were lush. Ornate gold leafed moldings, heavy brocaded furniture, and a jungle of dark green potted palms.

"Where did you learn to do this?"

"From watching Hadley. In Paris. You want to be polite, you want to tip very well. But you also want to act like you own the place. Excuse me," Hank said to a passing waiter, "could you bring us a bottle of Champagne?"

The man came to a stop. "Certainly. What would you like?"

"Henriot? Brut? And an ice bucket?"

"Right away, Sir."

"What else," Florence slyly asked, "did you learn in Paris?"

"I've sworn an oath of secrecy, and besides, Hadley would kill me if I ever told." There was that great laugh again. Hank loved that laugh.

He reached into his pocket, and brought out the wrapped silver box, which he handed to Florence.

"So, I'm asking again."

Florence unwrapped the gift wrap and opened the box. Saw the simple platinum wedding band. Hank had exchanged the gold band for one that was platinum. She couldn't look at him.

"Hank...." She thought about what she had just said. "Is your given name Hank?"

"No," said Hank, puzzled. "It's Henry." That meant if she married him, she would be Mrs. Henry Eide.

"What are you going to do for work?"

"If Gertrude and Hadley want a house, I'll build them a house."

"Where?"

"The two lots north of us are for sale."

"Would we really live there? On Grand?"

"Yes, unless you'd rather live somewhere else."

"Could I," she finally looked him in the eye, " have that little room, with the fireplace, the one to the left as you come in, as an office?"

"The house is all yours, Florence. You can do what pleases you."

Florence reached out and took the ring, handed it to Hank and held out her left hand. He slid the ring onto her ring finger. There were tears in her eyes.

"This is a yes," she explained. The waiter came back with their Champagne and they toasted one another. Hank couldn't stop smiling. Florence was smiling through her tears. The waiter came back with menus, they ordered, and when the waiter was gone, Hank produced his other surprise.

"I'm very glad you said yes. I didn't want to have to try and return this." He handed her a crushed up wad of tissue paper, which she unfolded.

Her hands flew to the side, as if the contents of the tissue paper were hot, burning her fingers. Her color deepened. She was having trouble taking a breath. She was stunned. Then her fingers crept back to the tissue. She put the ring on her finger with the wedding band. The diamonds and the platinum gleamed. It was the most beautiful thing she had ever seen. All the way through lunch, she couldn't take her eyes off the two rings. She remembered the roast beef as being very good, but later she had no real memory of what she ate. She kept dabbing at her eyes with her napkin. She was hungry, and she ate with good appetite, and they finished the whole bottle of Champagne, but she scarcely said a word.

They went up the main staircase arm in arm, hip to hip, hyper aware of each other physically. At the door of their room, he took her in his arms and held her, and she pressed her body close into him. She looked up at him. "Thank you," she said quietly. His response was a very long kiss.

In their room, Florence nervously exclaimed over how nice everything was. The furniture in their sitting room was French Provincial. They had a wonderful view of the harbor, and the manicured grounds and the regimented flowerbeds in front of the hotel, where precise rows of blooming geraniums marched towards the harbor.

There were two rooms. The second held the double bed. Hank went into the bedroom, drew the drapes, took off his suit coat, shirt, tie and shoes, and laid down on the bed. Crunched up a pillow to get more comfortable. He closed his eyes.

Florence came in, saw what Hank was doing. If he felt as tired as she did, she was in total agreement. Took off her shoes and carefully hung up her suit, and lay down at his side. Pulled a blanket over them both. Snuggled close.

It was still daylight when Hank woke up. Florence slept beside him. He watched her for a while, and dozed, just drifting. Finally, he rolled towards her and kissed her on the nose. She smiled and opened her eyes. Hank ran a hand up and down her arm. Up her shoulder to her neck, where he kissed her. Then his hands strayed over her breasts, then under her camisole, and she pressed closer. They kissed. For quite some time. Then she sat up and pulled the camisole off over her head. Hank kicked off his trousers. Kneeling in front of her, he removed her silky underwear. The next few minutes passed very quickly. Sweaty, but in a pleasant way. Florence knew she was a novice. Hank lead her, and in other ways, showed he was experienced. She suspected she was the beneficiary of his time spent in France.

They took a bath together, which was silly. And fun. They studied each other naked. Which was embarrassing. Florence grabbed a towel and tried to cover up. Hank wrestled it away from her. Then she tried to cover him up. It ended with Florence straddling Hank and sloshing water all over the floor. Hank learned a lesson from Florence, about passion, tenderness and intensity. Dressed, they went down to a light supper, and returned to their room for a repeat of the afternoon's program, as if trying to confirm that it was as good the third time. It was better.

In the morning, after breakfast, they bought a license at Victoria City Hall and then convinced the Clerk of the Court to try and persuade one of the judges to spend part of his lunch hour conducting a marriage ceremony. The Judge came out in his robes. It was very brief. Hank promised to take Florence as his lawful wedded wife. Florence promised to take Hank as her lawful wedded husband. The Judge invoked his authority, and the bargain was sealed with a kiss.

"Mrs. Eide," the Judge said at the conclusion of the ceremony.

"Yes, Sir."

"Was your father James Harcus?"

"Why, yes."

"I knew him. Actually, I knew them both. They were marvelous people. You're just as pretty as your mother. Congratulations, Sir." The Judge shook Hank's hand, then went on to his lunch.

Outside, the sun was shining. Half a dozen horse drawn carriages were lined up in front of the Provincial Parliament building. Hank chose the first carriage in line.

"Where to, Sir?" The man sounded very English.

"We're in no hurry," Hank said. "There's a park near here."

"Beacon Hill Park," Florence informed him.

"How about Beacon Hill Park," Hank looked to Florence for agreement, "then out along the water, towards Oak Bay?"

"Fine," said Florence. "I miss the horses."

"Many people says that, Miss. Many people," said their driver, setting his horses in motion.

"I don't miss them at all," said Hank. "Good riddance."

"Why is that?"

"You grow up on a farm, horses are just a lot of smelly, dirty work."

"I thought you grew up in Everett."

"I was born in Hope, North Dakota. My parents tried to homestead. Farming, on one hundred and sixty acres. Some years it was so dry we couldn't even grow grass." Hank stretched out in the sun. There were swans swimming on a small pond in the park. The grass was a lush green, and barbered. "The winters in the Dakotas are damn cold. Some nights we all slept in the same bed because it was the only way to stay warm." They exited the park, and turned left, moving slowly along a road that followed the shoreline. South, across the Straits, the Olympic Mountains gleamed in the sunshine.

"When did you move to Everett?"

"I was ten, so that would make it 1899 or 1900."

Florence did the math. That made Hank 34 or 35.

"Hank, I don't even know your birth date."

"July 31st. What's yours?"

"May 3rd."

"And I missed it."

"Yes, but you can give me two presents next year. Although," said Florence sliding across the seat to sit closer, "you're doing fine so far." And she held up her rings for him to admire.

"It's nice to know how I'm doing." The horses clopped along at a sedate pace, the sun was shining, and there was only a slight breeze.

"Not many people." The beach was deserted, and there wasn't another carriage in sight.

"No, but in the summer there are crowds of tourists. And many couples" Florence added archly, "visit as part of a wedding trip. Usually, after the wedding."

"I don't think that would have been practical with my wife."

"You're probably right," Florence said, but she sounded distracted.

"Hank…." He didn't say anything. "I used to walk this way."

"Wh-"

"We're very close," she said, almost to herself.

"Close?"

"To my house. Where I grew up."

"How close?"

"Driver, can you turn to the right, here?" The driver looked at Hank, and Hank nodded. The diver turned. It was a short street, with the homes to the right built on solid rock but as close to the water as the owners dared.

"Stop," asked Florence, and the driver stopped. "It's smaller than I remember. Our house is much bigger." Hank noted the trim brick house in front of them, but what he really liked were the words Florence had used: Our house. He made no comment. He would, however, have to buy a double bed. He wondered which bedroom at their house Florence liked best.

"Come on." She got out. Hank arranged for the driver to wait, then followed her. The front door was sheltered by a partially enclosed porch also made of brick. She had decided to wait for Hank. "They haven't seen me in eight years." She took his hand, and he rang the bell.

They waited, but no one came. "Ring it again." Hank did. A key turned in the lock, the door scraped in its frame, then swung open.

A woman dressed in a calf length skirt and a short, belted plaid coat peered out at them through the screen door. She didn't speak.

"I'm Florence," said Florence. It was all she could think of to say. She sounded very shaky.

"I know you're Florence, dear. Come in." She pushed open the screen door. The woman held out her arms, and Florence rushed forward. They embraced.

"Oh, my dear, my darling," the woman kept saying over and over.

"But who is this gentleman?" asked the woman. She isn't very old, thought Hank, although she was wearing glasses. She doesn't look much over forty.

"This is my husband, Aunt Margaret."

"Rather bald", she observed to Florence, inspecting Hank from head to toe. "Nice to meet you, Sir." They shook hands. The resemblance between Florence and Margaret was remarkable. They could have been sisters.

"Margaret, who is that at the door?"

Margaret, wiping her eyes, walked to the bottom of the stairs and called up. "It's Florence and her husband."

There was a shriek, and Francis flew down the stairs. Francis was made from different clay, shorter and plumper. Also older. She didn't say a word, ran to Florence and took Florence in a convulsive embrace like she would never let go. Neither seemed surprised that Florence was back with a husband in tow.

"She was always so pretty, of course she'd be married," was how the woman called Francis put it.

Hank was mystified. They had sent Florence away, never went to visit her, and had never had her back to visit. They left her alone, and without friends or support in a strange town, yet when Florence appeared on their doorstep, they welcomed her, certainly, but it was almost as if she'd gone down the street to the grocery store and finally come back.

"They're not my relatives," he concluded. And, "don't make Florence feel worse."

They sat down to tea. Arrangements were made to take tea out to their driver. Hank also thought he noticed some carrots on the plate Margaret carried out the front door.

"The carriage driver eats carrots," Hank observed quietly to Florence. She smiled, but otherwise ignored him.

"And what kind of work do you do, Mr. Eide?" Francis asked.

"I build houses."

"So you're on holiday."

"Yes. We came over by boat."

"By boat. Yes. On a steamer. There's no other way to get here."

"We came on our own boat. I also do some commercial crab fishing."

"Crab?" said Margaret coming back and sitting down. "I love crab."

"Do you ever fish for salmon, Mr. Eide?" asked Francis.

"Not commercially, no."

"But do you fish for them? With a rod and reel?" Francis persisted.

Margaret was sitting forward in her chair, paying close attention. Florence didn't know how to discreetly warn Hank of his peril. Both her Aunts were avid anglers. Florence didn't realize - yet - that she was the one in peril.

"I love to fish," said Hank.

"Really?" said Margaret.

"What a coincidence," observed Francis. "How remarkable."

"How long were you planning on staying in Victoria, Florence?" asked Margaret, maneuvering indirectly towards her goal.

Florence leaned close to Hank, and whispered in his ear. "Ask them to go fishing."

"They're having so much fun landing me," Hank whispered back. "I hate to hurry them." He filled his mouth with a cookie. In the end, he made them ask. It was more fun.

On the way back to the Empress in the carriage, Florence asked Hank, "Is this fishing trip all right?"

"Those bamboo casting rods with the Hardy single action reels are works of art. I wish I knew how to do that kind of fishing."

"You can do anything you decide to do, but I meant taking my Aunts out on the boat."

"It should be fine." And it was.

The next morning, Hank first bought Champagne, and then drove Florence to several stores where she bought the makings for an elaborate picnic. Not to mention a tablecloth, napkins, cutlery and inexpensive glassware. And sugar for the coffee.

In the afternoon, the tide was coming in, and running hard, and Hank motored to a point where the current created a back eddy off Trial Island, at the east end, just outside the kelp beds. There was a nice riffle. This spot had always looked fishy to him.

They had live herring for bait, and used very little weight. Hank set the Aunts up to fish, then sat down in the cabin beside Florence. They were sharing a bottle of Champagne.

"Hank, could you add another bunk forward?"

Hank thought about the space available. "You might have to re-work the existing bunk, but I think you could end up with two bunks. You thinking about coming bootlegging with me?"

"No! but it would give both of us a comfortable place to sleep."

Hank had already decided to sell the Anna Marie. His savings were sinking faster than a crab pot, and he could use the money. Now he reconsidered."I would like to keep her, but I hate to keep her if she won't get used. You know," he went on, "Hadley has mentioned these places up the inside passage you take to get to Alaska. Hunting lodges and other places you can stay. It might be fun to see those places."

"Let's keep her," suggested Florence. "We can always sell her later."

"True." There was a yell of excitement from the aft deck. The whine of a

Hardy reel as the fish - it sounded like a big fish to Hank - stripped line off the reel and ran.

"I'm coming, Margaret, I'm coming," called Francis, winding in her own line, and moving closer to Margaret to coach her. "Tip up," she called. "Tip up!" Florence and Hank downed their Champagne and went out on the back deck to watch. The reel screamed. The fish was still running. It was a really big salmon. At least thirty pounds, Hank guessed, from the bow in the rod.

"FISH ON," cried Margaret. "FISH ON!"

ACKNOWLEDGEMENTS

My deepest debt here is to my parents, Janice Ringman and Don Kane. Both were born and raised in Everett. Both told me stories about Everett, about people, places and events. My mother graduated from Everett High School in 1942, St Olaf College in 1946. My father graduated from Lakeside in 1940, Whitman College in 1944. Most of his life, he worked for Kane & Harcus, Printers and Lithographers, Everett, a firm founded in 1908 by Lawrence Kane and Will Harcus. He taught me to fish, clam and crab. Both my parents lived, worked, were married, died, and are buried, side by side, in Everett.

Other family members would include my paternal grandparents, Lawrence and Mary Harcus Kane. They died in 1954 when I was five. Lawrence moved to Everett from a farm in Zillah sometime during 1900. He was twenty. Mary came to Everett with her family in 1903. She was sixteen. They married, in Everett, in 1915.

All of my maternal great-grandparents were Norwegian. My maternal grandparents were Henry Ringman and Orla Jackson Ringman. In 1962, King Olav of Norway awarded Henry the King Olav Medal, for outstanding service in promoting Norwegian culture, primarily through the Everett Norwegian Male Chorus. He died in 1969. Orla came to Everett with her family in 1910. They moved from North Dakota. Henry and Orla had three daughters, Norma, Diane and my mother, Janice. Orla's second husband, Eric Engeset, grew up in Everett before his family moved away to Yakima. While he didn't go "over there", Eric did serve during WW I. He lived to be one hundred, passing away in 1998.

Helen has been my wife since 1969. It must be love. Couldn't have done any of this without Helen.

Her parents, Tauno and Jenny Hendrickson, taught me many lessons. Both lived rich and full lives. Tauno served with a construction battalion in the Pacific during World War II. Jenny spent World War II in Finland farming and taking care of her mother while her brothers were away fighting the Russians. She emigrated in 1947. When Finns talk about *sisu*, they're talking about Jenny.

Susie Walters worked for my Kane grandparents, and my parents, for many, many years. She cooked, she cleaned, she made cookies, jams and jellies. She told me stories. A committed evangelical Christian, at one time she worked for the railroad at a remote cabin in the Cascades, following the Wellington railroad disaster. She died in 1992 at 105 years old. "Precious in the sight of the Lord is the death of his saints", (Psalm 116:15). She especially enjoyed my son, Cameron, who was born in 1980.

Beth Ramsay (Aunt Beth) and her sister, Jean Ramsay Harcus (Aunt Jean). Both grew up in Victoria. Beth never married, taught school all her life in Victoria. Ramsay Machine Works Ltd., founded in 1903, still operates in Sydney, B.C.

Margaret Harcus and Francis Harcus. Francis was a public health nurse. Margaret was the bookkeeper at Kane and Harcus. She seldom remembered to bill customers or take the deposit to the bank.

David Dilgard and Margaret Riddle. I've known them and counted them as friends since 1972. THE experts on Everett history. The posters of the complete set of the Historical Markers are still the best history of Everett I know. Honorable mention must also go to Mayor Bob Anderson, who planted the seeds that grew into the Northwest Room at the Everett Public Library.

Margaret 'Penny' Buse, historian, for 25 years of conversation about the history of Snohomish County, Port Susan, Warm Beach and Stanwood, WA. Not to mention many years of friendship with both Penny and her husband, Mike.

Captain Gary Baker, USMC (retired). Gary was an historian. He was also, among other things, an aficionado of the "short count".

SOURCES

Everett, Washington. The City, its own self. The Everett I grew up in, Everett north of 41st Street, 1949 to 1967, was very little changed from the town that existed in the 1920's. Other than wallboard, paint and window frames, Everett High School has hardly changed at all from when it was built in 1910. I graduated, along with my wife, Helen, in 1967. My mother graduated in 1942, her mother in 1917. Two great-aunts in 1909 and 1911, respectively, plus many other family members in the years that followed.

The J.J. Clark Mansion. At 2129 Rucker. Built in 1892, it is one of the oldest residential structures in Everett. It was converted into apartments in the 1920's. Florence lived here, on the second floor, in Apartment 4. So did Helen and I, for 12 years, 1971 to 1983.

Sandy Point, Whidbey Island. My life-long love of saltwater and Puget Sound started here in a summer beach shack Lawrence Kane bought, next door to a another house purchased by his brother-in-law, Will Harcus. In addition to being business partners, they also owned houses side by side in Everett. It was family, family, family 24/7 in the Kane & Harcus households.

My father's uncle, Will Harcus, taught me my most important fishing lesson: Fish where the fish are. It's not as easy as it sounds. I remember Uncle Will always rowing and fishing out of clinker-built, round bottom skiffs. Always painted green and white. During the summer, his boat was usually anchored out in front of his house on a trip line. To this day, I wonder who built these boats and where he bought them.

My father remembered Tulalip Tribal members, including William Shelton, paddling over from Hermosa to dig clams on the Point. Interestingly, Kane & Harcus published, in 1923, William Shelton, The

Story of the Totem Pole. Early Indian Legends as Handed Down From Generation to Generation. Shelton always said Sandy Point was his birthplace. I remember when one of Shelton's story poles stood at 44th and Rucker.

The Everett Herald. At one time, you could page through the dry and faded originals. Now, its all on fiche. At some point, it will all probably be scanned and digitized. The Northwest Room at the Everett Public Library also has a good collection of oral history tapes, Polk Directories, and photographs.

The Snohomish County Labor Journal. Archives of the Everett Public Library.

The Daily Colonist. "Vancouver Islands Leading Newspaper Since 1853".

Victoria B.C. Public Library, fiche on file.

Mill Town and The Dry Years, by Norman Clark. Mill Town focuses on the
background of the Everett Massacre, and events the day of the Massacre.

Timber, by Edwin Parker. Parker was a Progressive, a Kellogg Marsh Grange member, and a radical in his day. His account of the Massacre was highly controversial. As a high school Senior, I had to get my parents permission to read this book, held on restricted reserve, at the Public Library.

Everett, Washington: A Picture Post Card History, Jack O'Donnell. Terrific visuals.

Everett, Past and Present, by Larry O'Donnell

Everett and Snohomish County, by Robert Humphrey

Voices from Everett's First Century, by the Snohomish County Historical Association.

Riverside Remembers, Vol. I and II, by the Greater Riverside Organization

Seattle, Now and Then, by Paul Dorpat

Northwest Legacy: Sail, Steam & Motorships, by Jeremy S. Snapp

Seattle: An Ashael Curtis Portfolio

Steamers Wake, by Jim Faber

The Experience of WWI, by J. M. Winter

The Guns of August and The Zimmerman Telegram, by Barbara Tuchman

All Quiet on the Western Front, by Erich Maria Remarque

Packard, by Denmann and Wren

Slow Boat on Rum Row, by Miles Fraser. Rum running out of the Fraser River in British Columbia.

The House of all Sorts, *Book of Small* and *Klee Wyck,* all by Emily Carr.

History of the Empress Hotel

Victoria, Then and Now by Emily Disher and Roland Morgan

The Crystal Gardens: West Coast Pleasure Palace. by Berton, et al

Snohomish County: An Illustrated History by David Cameron, Charles LeWarne, Allan May, Jack O'Donnell, Larry O'Donnell, and many others.

This is an outstanding book. For anyone interested in the topic, well worth the purchase price.

FURTHER READING

Three's A Crew , by Kathrene Pinkerton. This can be hard to find, but is just a great cruising yarn written during the 1930's.

Alaska Blues, by Joel Upton. In my opinion, this is the best book on commercial salmon fishing written to date.

Last Call: The Rise and Fall of Prohibition, by Daniel Okrent. An excellent book that gives a national perspective on Prohibition. However, the big time organized crime orientation of Prohibition in Detroit, Chicago, New York or Boston does not really capture the scale and scope fo Prohibition - or bootlegging - on Puget Sound.

For that, read *The Dry Years*, by Norman Clark.

VISIT

The Columbia River Maritime Museum, Astoria, Oregon, www.crmm.org

Center for Wooden Boats, Seattle, Washington and Cama Beach, Camano Island, www.cwb.org

Northwest Maritime Center, Port Townsend, Washington www.nwmaritime.org

Britannia Heritage Shipyard Society, Richmond, BC; www.britannia-hss.ca.

Among other things, as of July, 2010 they were restoring Fleetwood, a 56 foot 1930 rumrunner with twin Liberty engines. Hank would have loved this boat. The entire historic shipyard in Steveston is well worth a visit.

Royal British Columbia Museum, Victoria, British Columbia. www.royalbcmuseum.bc.ca/ . Well worth the trip to Victoria.

Museum of Anthropology, University of British Columbia, Vancouver B.C. www.moa.ubc.ca/

The Museum of History and Industry (MOHAI), Seattle, WA. www.seattlehistory.org

When I was elementary school age, I visited MOHAI with my mother. She pointed out a 'Scale Book', a tally book, printed by Kane & Harcus sometime before Word War II. That one tally book brought history alive for one very young man.

Ross Kane was born in Everett. Members of his family settled in Everett during the early 1900's. He is a graduate of Everett High (Class of 1967) and the University of Washington. He has worked for local governments and social services based in Everett, including four years as an elected official for Snohomish County. His wife, Helen, owned and operated a retail business. Ross did the books and took out the garbage. He is a former board memeber of the Cascade Land Conservancy and marched with the Warm Beach Lawnmower Drill Team.

Made in the USA
Charleston, SC
23 October 2011